Letters of a German American Farmer

A Bur Oak Original

Letters of a German American Farmer

Jürnjakob Swehn Travels to America

By Johannes Gillhoff

Translated by Richard Lorenz August Trost

University of Iowa Press Ψ Iowa City

University of Iowa Press,
Iowa City 52242
Copyright © 2000 by the
University of Iowa Press
All rights reserved
Printed in the United States of America
Design by Richard Hendel
http://www.uiowa.edu/~uipress

Printed on acid-free paper

FRONTISPIECE
Johannes Gillhoff, a sketch by Werner Schinko.
Courtesy of the artist.

Library of Congress
Cataloging-in-Publication Data
Gillhoff, Johannes, 1861–1930.
  [Jürnjakob Swehn, der
  Amerikafahrer. English]
    Letters of a German American
  farmer: Jürnjakob Swehn travels to
  America / by Johannes Gillhoff ;
  translated by Richard Lorenz
  August Trost.
    p.   cm.—(A Bur oak
  original)
  Includes index.
  ISBN 0-87745-719-0 (cloth), ISBN
  0-87745-706-9 (pbk.)
    1. German Americans—
  Fiction.   2. Country life—Iowa—
  Fiction.   I. Title.   II. Series.

PT2613.I63   J8613   2000
833'.912—dc21   99-088016

00 01 02 03 04 C 5 4 3 2 1
01 02 03 04 P 5 4 3 2

CONTENTS

Translator's Introduction   Richard Trost

• •

Johannes Gillhoff, a country schoolteacher in Mecklenburg, Germany, compiled these stories in the early 1900s. His father's collection of letters from former pupils who had immigrated to America served as his source material. Gillhoff wanted to tell the Germans of Germany what was going on among the crowds that left the fatherland for life in the New World. He named his book *Jürnjakob Swehn der Amerikafahrer* (Jürnjakob Swehn Travels to America).

Gillhoff invented the name of the book's hero: Jürnjakob Swehn (Yern-YAcob). No American would identify that name as German. Norwegian? Possibly. A Dane? Also a possibility. Jürnjakob's wife's name is Wieschen (VEEshen), the Low German diminutive for Louise. But there's no doubt that the Swehns were Iowans. Iowa is where they settled, lived, and died. They loved their Iowa. As you read this German book, you will learn to love them and hear yourself talking about the Swehns.

The Grand Duchy of Mecklenburg in the last century sprawled out over north Germany along the Baltic seacoast. Mecklenburg is not a city; it's an area in northeast Germany. In the 1800s crowds of Mecklenburgers were on their way to America. Mecklenburg was a top contributor to the swarms of German immigrants who came to the United States. Some estimate that as many as five million Americans have roots in Mecklenburg. Jürnjakob Swehn was a Mecklenburger, a Low German like the Friesians, the Schleswig-Holsteiners, the Pomeranians, the Westphalen, and the Hanoverians. They are the "Plattdeutsch," the Low Germans. Like so many of his compatriots, Jürnjakob made his voyage across the Atlantic in the 1860s, more than a hundred years ago, and settled in Iowa.

In the 1860s the Civil War was raging in the United States. Some immigrants escaped being drafted into the military in Germany only to be drafted here. But the Mecklenburgers could appreciate a war to eliminate slavery. Of all the German states, Mecklenburg was the last to eliminate serfdom (1820). And then the gentry used those laws to evict many of their erstwhile serfs from their estates into homelessness and poverty. In Fritz Reuter's book *Kein Hüsung* (Homeless) you hear the baron tell the equivalents of Jürnjakob and Wieschen, "If you don't like it, go to America." They did. Between 1853 and 1877, some 90,000 Mecklenburgers immigrated, almost one-sixth of the total population.

Reuter was a nationally known writer in nineteenth-century Germany, a Mecklenburger and a master storyteller who wrote in Low German. His *Kein Hüsung* (my next translation project) lays bare the oppressive social system that dominated everyday life in rural Mecklenburg and motivated the massive immigration. He depicts the tyrannical nobility, the obsequious clergy, and the deadly poverty of the rural working population. The archaic legal system by which the nobility was free to function as judge, jury, and jailor over their farmhands was the muscle of their oppressive habits. That and the nobility's unique authority to permit or deny marriage is the theme of Reuter's book. *Kein Hüsung* opens a window to the widespread sexual abuse, illegitimacy, alcoholism, and violence of the region, which may explain the puritanical ethics of the German immigrant communities in America—and perhaps Jürnjakob's behavior in chapter nine, "All Kinds of Grief and Their Medicines" of Gillhoff's book.

One of the miracles of life in the New World was the emergence of religious faith as the center of individual commitments and the center of the immigrant communities. Since the sixteenth-century Reformation, the church in Mecklenburg was held captive to the state. Martin Luther could hardly have foreseen that instead of being captive to Rome, his evangelical churches would become subject to every petty prince, king, and archduke that presided over the patchwork of independent principalities and powers that made up Germany until their unification in 1871. The grand duke of Mecklenburg was for all intents the pope and bishop of the Lutheran churches in his duchy. Furthermore, in rural Mecklenburg the clergy were creatures of the local nobility. Reuter deals with this conundrum positively in his best-seller *Ut Mine Stromtid* (My Years as the Farm-Boss). His Pastor Behrens is totally the opposite of what so many clergy were. Pastor Behrens is critical of the nobility and sensitive to the needs of the poor; his wife opens their home to bright young women of the parish who have finished elementary school, and she continues their education.

In most rural churches the pastor's financial support derived solely from the local baron, and the local baron had the major voice in who was going to be the pastor and how long the pastor stayed. This resulted in longer vacancies, fewer clergy, and an especially quietistic interpretation of the Christian faith. And, in all of Mecklenburg the churches were Lutheran, except for one Roman Catholic parish and two Reformed congregations, which made it even easier for the grand duke and his underlings to exercise control. Because the rural elementary schools, with some exceptions, were connected to the churches and under the pastor's supervision, they shared in the problems. Mecklenburg needed a St. Vincent de Paul, a saint with compassion for the poor.

Jürnjakob's advantage was that since the parish church was so far from his home, the village schoolteacher enjoyed considerable freedom. In addition to the reading, writing, and 'rithmetic, the teacher also was responsible for religious instruction, and except for sacramental rites, functioned as the village pastor and counselor. Jürnjakob's bonding with this teacher gave him the strong rootage of a personal faith. The teacher was the author Johannes Gillhoff's father.

For the immigrants America meant political freedom, and it also meant freedom from a distant, irrelevant clergy, from enforced church attendance, and from a legally determined tithe to the church. Those Mecklenburger immigrants who stayed with the church in the New World were intent on local control of congregational life, the liberty to choose their pastor, and the liberty to determine the pastor's salary and the pastor's mission. Their American churches were of a conservative confessional faith but with liberal, local, congregational control. Jürnjakob's congregation was a member of the Lutheran Church—Missouri Synod, which today still maintains that tension. The chapters in *Jürnjakob Swehn der Amerikafahrer* about church and pastors fit within this rubric. Amazingly, the hymn numbers cited in the book exactly match the hymn numbers in the Missouri Synod German hymnal, published in 1890.

Another phenomenon of church life in America was the congregational day school. Gillhoff's book shows how education was a primary concern for the Mecklenburgers. In many immigrant Lutheran congregations, the school was organized first, then the congregation. The parish school conserved their homeland's language culture but not their homeland's political culture. Most of the schools were bilingual from the start; the children needed to be able to cope with the new environment. They were hungry for success.

Another advantage Jürnjakob enjoyed was that in Germany his family was not integrated into a nobleman's estate. They lived in a village of small independent farmers. They were a minority in Mecklenburg, but they did exist. Jürnjakob and his brother and his father hired out as day laborers. Their home was on the Timmermann place. (Working for Hannjürn Timmermann, Jürnjakob accumulated the money for his trip to America.) It's possible that Jürnjakob's father left the estate of the neighboring nobility at the time that serfdom was abolished (1820). He chose to work independently. Gillhoff's book tells how the father built the family home on the Timmermann farm. They escaped the degrading servitude of the nobility's farmhands, but they would have had less security in seasons of poor crops and market fluctuations. They were no less poor than the people on the estates, but they did have more personal freedom. And the women of the family would not have been obligated to work in the household of the nobility.

Mecklenburg is a beautiful land: hundreds of lakes, green forests, rolling hills, fish in the streams, sun on the fields, and old churches in quaint little towns. Mecklenburg's people are gentle, genuine, friendly, and caring. Time and history's forward push have worked to cover over the pain of the past, though now there are thirteen years of Nazism and then forty-five years of Marxist-Leninism to cope with. Jürnjakob is a true child of Mecklenburg and more—he is also a real American.

Jürnjakob Swehn was popular reading in Germany, the Germans being especially amazed and amused by the new style of church life among their counterparts in America. The book also became a big hit among Gillhoff's former pupils and their children in America. I heard it read aloud by my Grandmother Krueger back in the 1930s. The book was as worn as the family Bible. Ours was the 1918 edition that carried this aside, "Printed on wood-free paper in the fourth year of the war." Grandmother Krueger liked to comment that in this country you could be a Lutheran without kowtowing to that big shot in Schwerin—or, for that matter, in Washington. Jürnjakob's sarcastic remarks about the man in the White House reflect a similar attitude toward authority. The Mecklenburgers had learned that lesson early, and they had learned it the hard way, through experience. Gillhoff's book is their story; Iowa is where some of them lived it.

Jürnjakob passed through Indiana and Illinois to settle in Iowa. He and his Wieschen were very much a nineteenth-century Iowa phenomenon. They were the settler immigrants who came on the heels of the homesteaders. The Swehn family loved their adopted Iowa homeland.

For many German immigrants and their children, Gillhoff became the commentator on life in the New World. He explained their immigration and blessed their success. They had come to the new land with nothing; they died proud family people who owned their own homes. They were people who owned farms and businesses; they read their Bibles; they were people of faith; they built churches and schools; and finally they sat back to enjoy their success and be a little homesick. Jürnjakob's letters document this process from beginning to end.

One false impression Jürnjakob does give is that, if he doesn't make it in the New World, in Iowa, he would be free to return to his homeland. But if he received written permission to leave Mecklenburg, it contained the stipulation that he was not free to return. The document was called a *Konsens*. Many families have preserved theirs; others have discovered theirs through the process of a genealogical search. In the case of my family, one great-grandfather was smuggled over the border so that the family could leave as an intact unit; he didn't have a *Konsens*. I suppose that he would have been free to return.

Like Jürnjakob's children, my Low German grandmother also was born in a log house, along with her brother and five sisters. Her *Vattings und Muttings* came to the United States in the 1860s and settled in northeastern Indiana. There and in bordering southwest Michigan was an extended community of Mecklenburgers. And, like Jürnjakob, my grandmother's father brought his widowed mother to America. When she died in 1886 at age 91, the lady was the oldest resident of LaPorte County, Indiana. What happened to the elderly left behind by their children's immigration is a gruesome tale of intentional neglect by their erstwhile employers. Some were evicted into homelessness. Many died in public workhouses. Fortunately, some of them were brought to America by their immigrant children.

Jürnjakob Swehn der Amerikafahrer dwells on how family life in America functioned significantly in making a start and being successful in the New World. The working partnership of husband and wife, parents and children, made the farm run. A careful division of duties and of financial responsibilities and rewards contributed early to the immigrant farmwife's independence and freedom in the decision-making process. Children were crucial to the workforce, but the wife as a full partner determined success or failure. My personal experience and pastoral experience among the children and grandchildren of the German immigrants testifies to the farmer's wife as a pioneer of women's equality. As her husband's equal, she shared in the day-to-day workload and was a crucial factor in determining success or failure. Her ability to supplement the cash flow with egg money, baking projects, vegetable sales, etc., kept the ship afloat. Also her budgeting skills, sewing projects, and frugality limited the cash outflow. Years later, the advent of the tractor put her into the driver's seat and substantially increased the acreage the farmer could manage.

Signs of affection in these early marriages were rare but sincere. In chapter 12, "At My Mother's Deathbed," Jürnjakob kisses his mother, and their ensuing conversation about how many times they have been kissed tells the story. Furthermore, his comments about his Wieschen and their conversations show how crucial a successful marriage was in early America. Perhaps they also reflect the reality of marriage in the farm population of that era in Germany, which surely was more political than affectionate, more institutional than intimate, and more a legal contract than a loving commitment.

There has been considerable discussion about chapter 12. Some commentators believe that Gillhoff is describing his own mother's death. Gillhoff's mother was a teacher's wife; the woman in chapter 12 is very much the peasant wife and mother. The emotional glow in the chapter is between two individuals who have never shared their feelings. I cannot conceive that was the situation with Gillhoff and his mother. Johannes Gillhoff never married, and I can imagine he was quite attached to his mother, that he made emotional contact with his mother, embraced her and kissed her on the many occasions when he left home, and particularly when he left Mecklenburg. Furthermore, in my own family, all of the immigrant grandparents were cared for by their children; without exception they died in their children's homes. I would argue that the chapter is telling how it was in America, because that's how it was in America.

Many commentators on the book in Germany and in the United States have speculated about the authenticity of the stories and about the identity of Jürnjakob. After his introduction to the book, Myron Marty, the Ann G. and Sigurd E. Anderson University Professor at Drake University in Des Moines, Iowa, commented, "I would consider the book to be historically plausible."

In recent years, Hartmut Brun of Polz in Mecklenburg has researched the author Johannes Gillhoff. Brun, who has provided the afterword for this translation, sketches the author's life in his *Gillhoff Reader* (Johannes Gillhoff ein Lesebuch, 1988) and tells how *Jürnjakob Swehn der Amerikafahrer* sets a significant memorial to the life and work of a teacher who understood the judgment against life in Germany implicit in the immigrants' departure for the United States of America. As Brun indicates, Gillhoff's book is in part a work of social criticism.

In the first editions of his *Lesebuch*, Hartmut Brun theorizes that Jürnjakob was either a Wiedow or a Jalass from Glaisin in Mecklenburg-

The Lincoln Township (Iowa County) farm home of Carl and Elisabeth Wiedow, thought to be the "original" Jürnjakob and Wieschen. Courtesy the Wiedow family. The home has since been torn down.

Vorpommern. Dr. Eldon Knuth of Encino, California, has also worked on the question and finally demonstrated that the model for Jürnjakob is Carl Wiedow from Glaisin. Wiedow first settled in Clayton County, Iowa, Professor Knuth's birthplace. He then moved to Iowa County. Both counties were home to many Mecklenburger immigrants. This Carl Wiedow and his Wieschen are buried in the cemetery of St. John's Evangelical Lutheran Church near Victor, in Iowa County, Iowa. Beginning in 1988, Knuth compiled a genealogy of the Wiedow family, including Jürnjakob's son who, as the book tells the story, actually did study medicine in Iowa City and did become a physician. According to Professor Knuth's research, 1997 would have been the one hundred and fiftieth anniversary of Jürnjakob's birth.

Udo Baarck of Mecklenburg, working together with Hartmut Brun and others, founded a Gillhoff society which honors the author and has stirred new interest in the book. In collaboration with a sociologist at the University of Berlin, Kai Brauer, they have substantiated Eldon Knuth's research. The gravestones of local cemeteries in Clayton County and Iowa County bear witness to the presence of families named in the book, although the spellings may vary: Timmermanns, Schroeders, Schultzs, Baethkes,

Fruendts, Timms, Jahlas, and Wiedows, . . . but no Swehns. After researching Gillhoff's school records, Baarck and Brun believe these immigrants are probably the original letter writers whose experiences shape the book's stories.

American readers whose parents and grandparents have told similar stories will need to judge the authenticity of Gillhoff's book for themselves. The tales of how it all began for my family support Jürnjakob Swehn's experience. That's why I undertook the translation; it was a way of telling my own story. For this reason I dedicate the translation to the memory of my eight great-grandparents: Mecklenburger immigrants. It's also a way of telling their stories.

The census records of many Midwest counties in the United States witness to the arrival of the Low Germans. There is even a Mecklenburg County in North Carolina, as well as a Charlotte-Mecklenburg school system. They farmed the land, built churches and schools, and contributed a unique band of color to our American rainbow of peoples. Jürnjakob was a mensch.

The Low German spoken by Gillhoff's Jürnjakob is more its own language rather than a dialect. It is the Anglo-Saxon German that went to England in the fourth and fifth centuries A.D. When these Low German immigrants arrived in America and heard English, they couldn't believe that anyone should speak such bad Low German! To their ears, English was a familiar language that somehow wasn't being pronounced correctly. And the true Low Germans like Jürnjakob loved the English language's French vocabulary. Their own language was overrun with French. The Napoleonic Wars had kept them so busy waiting on and paying taxes to the French, that Mecklenburg regarded itself as a colony of the Kaiser of Paris. Listening to the old folks at the card table as a boy, I learned to say, *Dat is mien Plesier*, that's my pleasure. And *De Mamsell hat allens*, that girl has it all.

Language remained a conundrum for these Plattdeutsch immigrants. They finally couldn't speak either good High German or good English. They invented a new *Missingisch* (see afterword). And in the end they had an enormous complex over it all. Somehow, somewhere, someone had interpreted Low German as the bottom rung of the social ladder. Being Low German was synonymous with being low class. In reality, however, Low German is chiefly a geographical designation. In contrast to Martin Luther's Middle-High German, which refers to the dialects of Germany's east-west midsection, Low German is the language of the northern lowlands, of the North Sea and Baltic coasts. It is true Anglo-Saxon German. So the High German for fence, Zaun, in Low German was Taun and in English Town: a place with a fence around it. The High German for table, Tisch, in Low German was Disch and became the English Dish; instead of eating on it, they ate out of it. Schmetterling, High German for butterfly, was Botterfliege for the Low Germans. Bottel is what the Low German says for bottle; in High German it's Flasche.

Martin Luther's translation of the Bible into High German didn't really suit the Low Germans. Their language was just that different. Luther's trusted pastor and colleague on the faculty of the University of Wittenberg, Johann Bugenhagen, made a translation of the Bible into Low German. Bugenhagen could do it; he was a Pomeranian.

In this translation of Johannes Gillhoff's book, I sometimes Germanize to give the reader a taste of Jürnjakob's language, his Missingisch, his mixture of Low German and High German, together with a little English thrown in. His letters to his teacher carry all the signs and sounds of his Low German heritage and his new life in America. It's a simple and straightforward language, crowded with imagery. Gillhoff's introduction to the book is good literary German; it's an obvious contrast to the letters that make up the book's contents.

Some of my German phrases are Low German, some are High German; with few exceptions they are translated by their context. They are intended to tickle the ears of non–German-speaking readers and to resonate for readers who grew up hearing those sounds, especially when as children they were closed out of the adults' conversation. And they reflect Jürnjakob's style, his Missingisch (Renate Herrmann-Winter calls it Kramerlateinsch in her Low German dictionary).

I have also taken the freedom to reinvent some of Jürnjakob's dialogue in my translation. I make it sound like that old-timey farm talk that I grew up with and experienced as a Lutheran pastor in rural Iowa.

The illustrations, with two exceptions, are courtesy of the Gillhoff Society in Glaisin, Mecklenburg-Vorpommern, Germany. They are original drawings by Professor H. E. Linde-Walther. Linde-Walther prepared them for the Steiniger edition of the book. The photograph of Jürnjakob's farmhouse depicts the farm home of Carl Wiedow in Lincoln Township, Iowa County, Iowa; most agree that Wiedow is the original Jürnjakob. The picture is courtesy of the Wiedow family. The picture of the author Johannes Gillhoff is from Brun's Lesebuch and is used with the permission of the artist, Werner Schinko.

My wife, Betty, has transcribed and retranscribed my scribblings on this translation for the past twelve years. Thank you, Betty, for your patient good work.

Jürnjakob's story delights, inspires, and informs. Enjoy it. Maybe somewhere, once upon a time, on your family tree there were branches named Timmermann or Hebenkieker or Jalass or Möller or Wiedow or Dahl or Krüger or Swehn with *vun dummboozle* of a language.

Letters of a German American Farmer

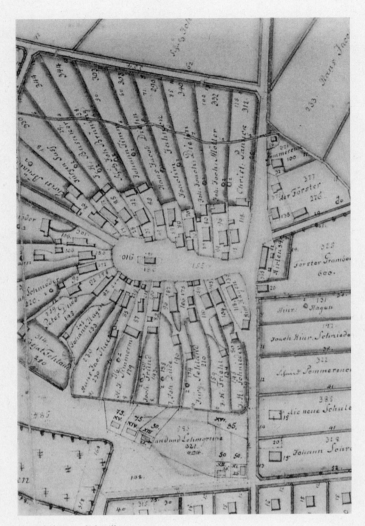

Jürnjakob's Wendish Village.

Author's Preface

. . . .

A quiet rural village lies to the southwest on the Mecklenburger Heath.
The houses follow the Wendish horseshoe pattern with its open side fac-
ing west [translator's note: the Wends were a Teutonic-Slavic tribe pre-
historic to Mecklenburg]. The dark, straw roofs lie low to the ground;
warmly and softly they cover and shelter both the grief and joy of their
farmer families. Just as you come into town, there stands one particular
cottage whose beams and rafters are tired and sagging. This is no dwell-
ing for proud people; it's too humble, and its ceiling is too low. So said
Jürnjakob Swehn, and he should know. He was born and raised in that
cottage, but he didn't stay there for long.

Like so many Mecklenburgers, the longing for a home of his own and
for his own land to farm drove Jürnjakob away from Germany to America.
In the new land life was hard and the immigrants were far away from all
that was familiar, but they kept the connection with their homeland alive.
And at Christmas their letters arrived, addressed to their old teacher's
house. He read them aloud to the families.

Deciphering those letters from America was an art. Mostly they were
sober reports about the business of farming, and about what was going
on among the immigrants' families and friends. Their naive words spoke
loudly and clearly about faithfulness and about their thankfulness for the
teacher of their younger years. He now was the counselor of older souls
in every time of trouble. In the village, no one died without their teacher
at the bedside. The pastor was miles away at Eldena; there was no church
in the village.

The teacher's father and his grandfather had been there before him;
and already he himself had been their teacher fifty-four years. That made
for a strong bond between village and schoolhouse, and that is what kept
those American letters flying into his house.

He also wrote answers to the letters. The villagers came, and because they felt comfortable with him, they spoke in Low German, "*minen Unkel in Amerika en Breiw räwer tau schriwen*, would you write my Uncle in America?" "What shall I write?" "*Ja*, you know that as good as I do." "Good, come back Saturday night and I'll read it to you." Well, on Saturday night there was nothing to add, so the question was, "What's it going to cost me?" "The price is you have to come back." "Well, thank you for that." Which is how things were done.

In those brief, sober reports from the new Americans, reading between the lines you could sense their backbreaking labor. Added to that, the farmer whose hand guided the plow found it a sour piece of work to guide the pen. When the evening's rest came, human energy was so depleted that only the leftovers were there for letter writing.

There was one exception. Among those new Americans there was one who liked to put the alphabet on paper. Let's name him Jürnjakob Swehn; he's the son of the farmhand who lived in the old cottage, there where you came into town. He went the way of his youth, one among the many who went to America. Of the thousands who left, he was quite successful. At first, his letters were sober and brief, like all the others. But when the evening of life came, Jürnjakob began to wake up. He revealed a long pent-up power of imagination.

When the harsh American winter piled up snow along the fences and barns, Jürnjakob took his pen and, pressing so hard that the pen wrote broad, heavy lines, he scribbled page after page. He wrote until spring arrived and the ground began to cry out for the plow's attention.

Usually a bundle of his letters arrived at the schoolhouse on the hill around Eastertime. Our Jürnjakob began to tell his life stories long after his dreams were fulfilled. Like the dreams of Jacob in the Bible, the dreams Jürnjakob dreamed on the sandy soil of the Hornkaten in Mecklenburg had come true. His Iowa farm was already worth the big number, plus all its zeros.

Jürnjakob's letters made sense; there was an internal order in those letters. He had paid attention to his teacher, who said, "When you write *schreib alles hübsch der Reihe nach*, put it all down nicely, one thing after the other."

In spite of their charm I couldn't print the letters as they were. Their repetitions and platitudes needed editing. Some parts had to be lifted out of context and relocated. I eliminated the occasional lack of clarity and also the internal contradictions. But the interruptions in presentations and the unintentional gaps demonstrate how they had come into being out of human life.

With care I have lightened up the shadows and filled in the blanks. I have completed the incomplete of the stories and the business adventures. Immigrants who returned to Germany and letters from other sources provided my material for this. But my conscientious respect for the original letters determined what changes I would make, how I would make them, and what my style would be. In my faithfulness to the original letters, my intent was to be transparently deliberate in setting them forth as the life story of one man: Jürnjakob Swehn, *den Mann and sein Werk*, the man and his accomplishments.

I

Over the Ocean Waves
· ·

My dear friend, my teacher:
Hopefully you are in good health as I am. Once upon a time I listened to all your talks while sitting on my school bench. Now it's your turn to listen to me, as your old student talks his talks. All this talking tells how I came to America and got to be a farmer. I have a house and a barn and acres of land. I have cows. I have food. I have friends. I have the best of neighbors and all those other good things that Martin Luther writes about when he explains "daily bread" in the catechism.

It hasn't been easy. I can still lift a two hundred pound bag of oats, but this scribbling on paper is hard work for my stubby fingers. I can plow a line as straight as a yardstick. But to take my pen and set these letters in straight rows isn't easy for an old man like me. You won't believe this, but I'm a *Grosspa* now. Who can count the years since I last saw your face.

How all this got going, though, is clear to me. I can tell my story as well as the next one. A lot of grass has grown over these old stories and I've mowed a lot of hay since all this happened. As we say here, "dat's all water under de Bridsch," but I say not even water can wash away these memories. You told us that in *der Schul*, which is why I've got it stored in my head. But to get from the head to the pen is a long ways to walk. And man oh man, this pen has a leg thin as paper, and half the time it's kaput. Then the ink makes a blot. Oh man, these pens aren't worth a dumm-boozle. But I'll try now that I've got more time. Already son number two gets more done in the fields than me.

If I don't finish my letter this winter, I'll sit down behind the inkpot again next fall. And when you come to a place you can't read, remember: *Ja wohl*, he's worked hard in his life and there's a whole sack of ABCs he's forgotten how to make. After you think on that, hop over those lines. That's how I do it when my plow bumps onto an old stump.

{5}

My dear friend, I can tell you this. I like writing to you. And a man enjoys doing what he enjoys doing. When you get old, you watch it, so that you don't miss out on any fun. If fun comes strolling by, open up the door right quick to say: "Here's the place. Come in fun, for it is evening and the day is far spent." You don't have to do this when you're young. When you're young, fun jumps over the fence and finds you.

Back in old Mecklenburg, Danckert and Sons in Ludwigslust got me my ticket for America. It was twenty-nine German taler to New York; I bargained and got it for twenty-eight. But it was big money, and my pa was the poorest day laborer in town. I earned most of it working as a hired hand. For three years, I sweat it out by Hannjürn Timmermann, that came to twenty-seven taler, 'cause $3 \times 9 = 27$. See, I took the multiplication tables from Mecklenburg to America. All that money, my hymn book, and one extra jacket went along to America.

These days by you folks a hired hand makes his four hundred mark, ja wohl. He still doesn't have anything in the pockets. By us on the farm in Iowa, a hired hand gets one hundred dollars a month and fodder for his horse. Oh man, you still can't find anyone who wants to do the work. Above all you can't find a girl to milk and work in the house.

I also borrowed five taler from old man Köhn and from Karl Busacker. They didn't even want a signature. That's how I scraped the money together, with a few pennies extra to help out if I got in trouble. Just so the Americans couldn't say, "Here comes another one of these dumb Deutsch-mans, not a red cent to his name."

In the village I made the rounds to say adieu, and make all my good-byes. That went fix and fast. Then it was mother's turn. That went neither fix nor fast. She said, "Now straighten up and make sure you write. I want to know how you're making it. Keep an eye on your shirts and socks, and on your money, so that nothing gets away from you. And don't forget how to pray."

When it was my brother's turn, I said to him, "Take care of her when she gets old. I'll send money so you can buy meat for Sundays and in the winter a woolen shawl for Ma." He said, "Oh man, don't worry about us. First you look out for yourself, that you don't get any water in your boots."

With all that done, I swung my bag on my shoulder and took my pa's old oak *Gundagstock*, his good-day walking stick, in hand. My pa had long since taken his last walk. For that walk you don't need a cane. So I took that old cane in hand and headed for Ludwigslust. Ma stood in the doorway with her hands under the apron and watched me out of sight. It's been thirty-two years since I saw her face.

Behind Hornkaten in the Lieper Hills where the sand is thin, I stood for awhile and looked back. This was the place where you did that: looked back. Old Hannjürn Timmermann always reined in the horses there so's they could catch their breath. He'd just stand there and look back, then say to himself slowly and quietly: "The dear God did a pretty good job of creating this old Mecklenburg." After that he'd jump back on the wagon box and giddyap, way we'd go. That was a man who made few words. If you see his son, say hello for me.

For a few minutes I stood there and looked back. Jürnjakob, I said to myself, you have been by here more than fifty times. But today it's different. How will you make it over there? How many have left here and gone away to foreign parts? The Mecklenburger sand has long since blown over their tracks.

Dear friend, you taught us from the Bible about Jacob and his trip to Haran. Oh man, do you think when I come back I'll have two herds of cows running ahead of me? But not even Jacob had to cross the big pond. So I said to myself, oh man, we'll get back here. Then I started out. That was 1868. I was nineteen years old and on July 20 I would sail out of Hamburg.

With a bag on my back I took off for Hamburg and the Immigrant House. Like everybody else, they're in it for the money. I had to buy a pot of rum from the bartender, ich musste einen Krug voll Rum kaufen. "Otherwise," he says to me, "you'll croak on the way over." That's not what I had in mind, because I was nineteen and I was on my way to America.

People were there. Most of them came on freight wagons. The wagons were piled high with trunks and bags, and up on top sat the people. More than thirty families: whole layers of people. Most of them came from Mecklenburg. Some High Germans and a few from Poland. The Immigrant House was full. We slept in the halls with our trunks and sacks. The Schliesiers sang the Columbus Song:

Columbus was a happy man,
A happy man was he.
He came to New America
From his old Germany
And there he looked for 'taters
'Cause he was hun-ger-rey.

That's all I know. I still don't think it's the real Columbus story. In our schoolbooks it was different. Anyway, they finally stopped singing. The inspector came and wanted to throw them out. Then they quieted down.

Oh man, they were singing again when we got on the boat, but only at first. Then they all sat in their corners and slept. All those weeks they slept through everything.

At coffeetime I got on board an English freighter with my bag and my rumpot. Eleven o'clock that night a police officer came by with a lantern. I showed him my passport. "You're nineteen years old—that's good." The one from Krenzlin showed his passport. "That's good." Schneider from Dömitz had only his baptism certificate: "That's good." Hebenkieker from our village showed his military record: "That's good." But the military record was already five years old. When the police had made the rounds, he smiled at us all and said, "That's how it has to be and it costs everybody two marks." So each one of us came up with two marks. You

know what I think? I think that policeman was no policeman. But that's how the money goes.

In the morning at two o'clock, we steamed down the Elbe River. I slept up on the deck. Down below the oxen were snorting and grunting. In the late afternoon we hit the North Sea and then Holland. I've never seen the likes of this. Dear friend, I can tell you that the North Sea holds one dummboozle lot of water. There's enough to wet down all the sand at Hornkaten. The folks at Bockup can drink of it all they want, and when they're through, the Lüneburger Heide folks are next. And that's as if you spilled one drop out of your big washtub. I said to myself, Jürnjakob, this is all left over from Noah's flood. Just tell me please, what's the use of that much water. You sure could sow a lot of rye on these bottoms.

The North Sea was calm, but oh man, that was only the beginning. In a little while all those whitecaps showed up. That's when our freighter got restless. First he went down and over on one side, then up on the other. Akkrat, like a cow that wants to calve but can't. Along with us was a fine gentleman from Hamburg. Only High German, that's all he would talk, and he had one pretty stovepipe hat on his head. He was so drunk all he could do was hold his head over the side. He spit up and the hat fell in. Away it swam. We laughed. Then he put on a cap like the ones that old Kollmorgen from Grabow sells in his stand at the Martinimarkt in Eldena. I think they cost sixteen schilling.

In the afternoon on that day it got real stormy and the ship went down on its side. I slipped and lay stretched out on the deck. My eyes fell out of my head and my stomach fell out of my belly. They all had a good laugh on me. Oh man, but not for long. We all had to go below and they shut the door. The ship rolled, the oxen bellowed, the women screamed and everybody stuck their heads in the buckets. Some bodies cried out to God. Dat vas like Jonah in his ship. Sometimes I thought about the sand in the Lieper Hills. At least when you stand on it, it doesn't move. And you lie a lot safer in the sand than in the water, besides you can look at the potatoes and rye from the bottom up. In any case it's better than having a ship with eighty-five oxen up your nose. This is probably the end of the world, I said to myself. I'll never have those two cow herds, and old Vater Köhn and Karl Busacker have lost their five taler. They don't even have a signed paper in the desk drawer.

That evening I went up on deck. All night I sat out there since down below I couldn't stand the stink. Up on deck the sky was black as inside a bag, but the air was fresh. That's when I started to feel better. As I came to, I thought about your mother. Once at Christmas she gave me fifteen walnuts—we didn't have any. Another time, in the fall, you gave me a pair of boots. They were too tight for you, and they fit me just right. Those boots held up real good.

After that day there came a second day as bad as the first. The Hamburger with the cap was looking into the water again and away went that cap. Then he put on a nightcap with a tassel. It was blue with white stripes, like Busacker's Grosspa. That's when we docked at Grimsby of England.

The tax man came aboard: "What's that in your pot?" I said, "There's rum in it to keep me alive goin' over the big pond." He said, "One schilling, please." "No, I won't pay it." "You'll pay it or you won't pass Grimsby." "You look now and see." As I said that, I poured it down below my tie line. The others drank the rest. "See you now," I said, "you'll have to let us pass. We don't pay tax on what we've got in our belly." He swore at us mightily and looked grim, but he had to let us pass.

Then we rode to Liverpool on the train, Jungedi, boy oh boy, that moved along. The one from Hamburg with the nightcap stuck his head out of the window and away went that cap. "See here," I said, "why didn't you get that cap a size smaller. Now you're going to get to Liverpool and you'll be bareheaded. What will they say when they see that?"

At Liverpool the one from Dömitz had money and sailed off on a steamship. Me? I had no money and had to wait. A sailboat left every two weeks. In the meantime I learned a few things, moved a few things, and made one and a half taler.

Finally my ship docked. I took one look: this is old and wackelig. I said to myself, if this box full of mold and rot gets to America, it's surely the will of God. Rum will not save me.

Four hundred people were on board, mostly from Ireland. The food stores were given out up on deck: one pound of sugar and one pound of tea. My dear friend, it's the kind of tea I've seen by you but never tasted in my mouth. There was more yet: one pound rice, one pound cornmeal, one pound pickled meat, and a pound of kringel and zwieback. The zwieback was so hard you had to use a hammer to break it in two. Some people did it with their boot heel.

The Irish knew their way around and all brought little bags to use. I didn't know my way around and didn't bring a bag. I just stuck out my hat. Whatever didn't go in went alongside. So I filled my pockets too. Every morning we each got one quart of water. And anybody that pushed in line got one whack over the ears. The Irish knew their way around and stood still. Me, I just stuck up my arm and waved it around. Before I knew it the kitchen boy was out on the deck. And it turned out to be no good for me both ways. First off, he whacked me, and then he sent my hat back empty.

The kitchen stood in the middle of the deck with a door on both sides. At the one door we set our tin pot with rice, cornmeal, tea, or meat. Then we went round to the other door and waited till it came out. If they caught you looking into the kitchen, you got one with a broom handle. That's how we learned the house rules. Dear friend, I can tell you this. Those first days I got some pretty good practice in the house rules. I wasn't used to going hungry.

There was one big iron cooking range in the kitchen, six feet by six feet. On it, four hundred tin pots. They all looked pretty much alike. That's how it is with tin pots, and everybody stole from everybody else's. I ate my pound of meat raw and spit out the biggest worms. Nobody can steal it when it's in your belly. One time I went without for two days and then

came day number three. Somebody stole my pot again, un dat vas dat. In this country honesty won't satisfy a man's hunger. Put this into the catechism: "Thou shall not steal—and I'll be dead before I get to New York." So I took the first pot that came out of the kitchen door and ate up the rice. The empty pot flew over the side of the boat. That's what everybody else was doing. One time I ate the pork of some Polish Jew, because I said to myself: Anyway, it's against his religion. Once in a while he needs my help to be a good Jew. I sure was hungry.

When my pot got warmed up I was happy. In seventeen days it was on the stove three times. Not that it really cooked but it smelled like kitchen and was warm. All in all, the trip lasted seven weeks and two days, but on the 18th day the Lord smiled on me. Dear friend, let me tell you that the head cook had a kitchen boy who got sick. The captain was the doctor and apothecary at the same time. So the captain asked the boy: "What's wrong with you?" He didn't know. The captain said: "Where do you hurt?" He didn't know. The captain took a long look at him. He thought a few minutes—he didn't know either. He thought more and thought harder. Now he knew. The captain said: "I am going to give you number thirteen out of the medicine cabinet." He went to get it. Whoops, number thirteen was all used up. The kitchen boy groaned like the dying. The captain had a sympathetic heart. He said to himself, "My God, I have to help him— he's part of the crew and number thirteen is all gone." So the good captain mixed number six and number seven. That also makes thirteen. What happened then? I'm going to tell you in plain German. The kitchen boy got the run-throughs from here to New York. But the captain was so happy the kitchen boy didn't die that he didn't make him work anymore on the voyage. He just had to stay alive—which is exactly what he did.

There was a French doctor on the ship. His Grosspa had been Napoleon's own physician—his name was Weber. He had one huge head, a coffee-brown overcoat and such a mouth. Now see, I said to myself, if his mouth doesn't bite his ears off by mistake. He ate for three people. He drank for six. He lied for twelve. He said, "The captain poisoned that boy." I said, "Oh shut up, *Halt dein Maul, Franzosendoktor*, you Frenchman of a pillmaker. I wouldn't want you or your grandfather by my bed if I was sick and still wanted to live. The captain is a good man, and if you say one more word about poison, then I'll put you in my handy vise and make beefsteak out of you." At that he shut down his mouth and went off.

The run-throughs of the kitchen boy started off my good fortune. I went to the top cook and said, "Look now, your boy is sick, so you need a new one. How about me jumpin' in?" He looked me all over. Maybe he wanted to see how many taler I'd bring on the scales at the Mecklenburger sale barn. "Can you cook?" "No mensch on earth can make a sparrow lay goose eggs," I answered, "but what you got here for cookin' I learned by watching Ma in the kitchen." He smiled big, and then he said, "Try it once."

That day, for the first time since England, I got plenty to eat. As I stuffed in the last mouthful, I put my spoon away and wiped off my face. A mensch should eat no more than all his power and might can cram down his gullet. I drank water 'til all room in the belly was taken up. The others all had plenty of thirst. This cook was a little fat man and he was fix in his cookin' business. He said, "Go," and I went. He said, "Get over here," and I got over here. He yelled, I jumped. From the wheelman to the cook, from the cook to the wheelman. The wheelman was the boss. One of those times there was a real uproar. It came from the belly. My dear friend, I can tell you, there's plenty in this world and it all comes from the belly. Three Irishmen were screaming for hunger and wanted it out with the cook. The cook sent me to the wheelman. The wheelman figured it out. He said, "We've used up too much of the food stores. For three days I can give out only half of the rations. You'll have to pull up your belts a notch or two." Well, those three men went with their half-rations and their empty stomachs to the captain. Half of Ireland followed them and hollered up a storm. The captain said, "There's plenty on hand. Give 'em to eat, so's they don't go hungry."

That was the good word. Now we cooked up a rice soup — the spoon could stand in it. Dat hat smekt, that tasted good. Everybody got a potful. That ended the racket. They wiped off their faces, looked friendly, and bowed their heads toward us. There was praise and thanksgiving for the rice. Ja wohl. That's how it goes. And we were careful with the salt, and we made sure we didn't burn the soup.

When the top cook saw that he could use me, he also made me boss over the water barrel. We had to pump water out of it, that's how big it was. But there were water thieves among the peoples. Think about that one—that's how scarce water can get in the middle of the big pond. Me, I looked in the other direction when the thieves came. The weather was that hot. After they got their cup half full, I'd look in their direction—I'd never make a big racket. I'd just go after 'em with a stick and make sure they got a couple. This is how the cook did it too—he taught me good. But they got their water and they thanked me with friendly words—it was that hot. We all washed with salt water. You didn't use any soap with that. Which makes no difference, no mensch on board that ship had the habit of using soap.

To keep the kitchen clean was my job, 'cause that ship was a regular pigpen. So much for scratching bugs and lice. One Irishman decided to do the bugs. He had a gray beard and crooked knees. Heinrich Möller made a bet with him. Said Heinrich, "I'll give you all my chew-tobac, if you kill a thousand bugs between here and New York." The Irishman said, "I'll think about it." On the next day he said, "I thought about it—I'll take the bet." He loved a chew-tobac. So from then on, every evening he went hunting. One night I woke up. "How far are you?" "This is the eighty-third," he said and whopped number eighty-three dead with his wooden shoe. In the morning, he wrote on a plank how many he'd killed. No stretching the truth here, he had to show Heinrich Möller the dead corpses. We were a long ways from America, and already he won his chew-tobac. He offered another bet for a thousand, but nobody took him up on it. He was happy. Otherwise, before that he had been sad the whole time because he had no money and no chew-tobac. He had new shoes when he come on board. He showed 'em off to everybody. They were good workmanship. He wanted to trade 'em for chew-tobac, but nobody was interested. And Heinrich Möller wouldn't loan him a bite. Meanwhile he chewed up half of one leather suspender. Afterwards he laughed with his whole face, and he wore the other suspender to America.

My dear friend, I can tell you. The chew-tobac they sold on that ship was worth not one dummboozle. It was nothing but deceit and lies. On the inside there was a piece of hemp with a little tobac wrapped around it.

Let me tell you about the lice on this ship. They were not common lice. Six of those lice could pin down a sheep buck. One day here comes Wilhelm Rump with an ax. "What are you up to?" "Butchering!" "Where do you butcher? *Wo willst du schlachten?*" "You come now and see." I went along. There sat Hebenkieker from our village on the floor and had pinned down one louse. It was a big one and awful to look at. My life long, I haven't seen a beast quite like that. He had captured it along the border between the Irish and the German districts. There's where Rump axed it down. One Irishman spoke up, "That louse belongs to you Deutschmans." Another one said, "That louse is as slow as a German." A third one said, "But it's a good clean race o' people." That's how they kept rubbing us the wrong way with words. I said, "Now listen up, you men of Ireland and pay 'tention to what I'm going to tell you." They said, "What have you got to say?" I made my speech. "All things have a time and place.

But by us in Germany live only little common lice—they run around in good linen nightshirts. But you can't find a beast like this one between the Alps and the North Sea. She even wears a red saddle on her back. You just don't find that by us. That louse belongs to your district and carries your passport. I can see it's Irish since you all wear blue underpants, whose color isn't worth a dummboozle because it comes right off. That means you all got blue legs, and you got blue hind ends when you get up in the morning. This louse looks like it belongs to you, because her legs and her hind end are blue. There's overpopulation in those underpants of yours so she's immigrating. That's how she landed on our border."

At this place in my speech I stopped. All of Ireland rose up against me. So I put on my longest legs and you should have seen me get out of there.

Now then my wife, Wieschen, interrupted and said, "Don't be writing such things to your teacher, it's not right." I said, "Wieschen, I promised to write it all as it really was. Which means the louse stories also belong to the story." Dear friend, I can tell you it was no worse than God's plagues upon Pharaoh, and all that's in the Bible. Oh man, we are not stretching the truth. "Wieschen, the chapter on the Irish louse has to be."

There was a girl on board the ship from Breslau or thereabouts. She said to me, "I am twenty-eight years old and have a good background. You come with me, and we'll go to Baltimore." But she was one nest of lice, and I said, "You're not good enough backgrounded to suit me. You've been on this boat as long as I have, and I've not seen you comb your hair one time." She said, "When we get to the land, I'll comb my hair. There's no reason for it out here." I said, "Oh lady, don't bother yourself for me, *meinet wegen sollte sie sich man keine Umstände machen.*" After this the French doctor was with her quite a bit. You'd run into them in all the corners of the ship.

On one of those days I saw the first officer on his knees in prayer. I said to myself, now there's a pious man. Jürnjakob, look up to him. So I walked on my toes when I went by him. When he quit his prayers, he stabbed a sailor in the leg with his sword because the poor mensch didn't get into the sail as fix and quick as he wanted. The words he used to do that are not written in the Bible. Dear friend, I can tell you that. So I said to myself, So that's what it means to be holy in the new country. Once that sailor got up into the sails, the officer went back on his knees and out came more prayers. I made a long way around him and looked at him real good from the side, and I said to myself, first pray, then stab, then pray again. How do you make that rhyme together? Dear Lord, don't let me meet this kind in the dark without a good oak walking stick. If there had been a pastor around I would have asked him. But as for me, I'll stay with my own faith and have no more fear or respect for that first officer. And that's the last time I walked on my toes when he was praying.

Meanwhile, this ship kept moving 'cross the pond: no signs, no wheel ruts, and no train tracks. The blue of the water just didn't stop, and finally we were all waterlogged and miserable from the wetness. So many got sick I couldn't count them. We began to make talk that America didn't even exist. One said, "You just see now this isn't going right and before you know it we'll be over the edge of the earth." But I knew better. No mensch will ever fall over the edge, no matter how far he travels. At the most he'll travel into the earth. That will be our final and last journey.

We were all stiff from sitting and laying around. Nobody could really work anything out of his bones. Too bad there was no cord of wood to cut or acre of rye to mow. So I said to the captain, "This is a sad part of the world. I don't want to live here." He laughed at that and then kept puffing on what was left of his cigar. He looked out over the water and looked very serious. But there was nothing to see, just water. He did it just as if he could see where he was going, and he swerved neither to the right nor to the left. This kind of man can teach you how to live your life—that is, if you want to make something out of yourself.

Finally, here comes America. That made us all happy, *da waren alle froh*. Me too, since the cook gave me a dollar and said, "You did your job real good." So at that I washed me up and threw my mattress with all its living creatures overboard. Everybody else followed suit—it was like a big party. We were all together joyful to get rid of the lice boxes. Then our French doctor was put in to check in one of those dark corners of the ship. The first officer even used his foot on him. Whether or not our first officer got down on his knees afterwards and prayed is beyond me. I can't put it in writing.

As we got closer and closer to America, the captain got us all together and made a long speech. He was a good man, so we listened with all our might, which didn't do us much good 'cause we of the Germans didn't understand a word. Then he got mad and began to let us have it. Still, nobody understood him. At this he really boiled over and finally chased us all back to where we came from. Still nobody understood him, and even today I don't know what he wanted to say.

When we arrived at the docks all of us had to stand up and be counted, and none of us knew why. The only one missing was our French doctor. Finally, he came sneaking along behind us. He ducked way down and crawled under the skirts of the girl from Silesia, the one with the lice. She didn't say a word. The ship's crew looked all over for him and cursed him a hundred times, all for nothing. When the officers and crew disappeared, he appeared and ran off. She after him. He stopped on a street corner to catch his breath. After that they went off together. I'd sure like to know what was going on there, which goes to show you what a dummkopf this Mecklenburger was.

Now we all stood on the land that doesn't move back and forth. It felt good. I counted my money: two taler and four schillings. This plus one dollar from the cook. So I said to myself, You are on the way to your first million. If you can get all the way to the second, you'll make it good. You'll buy the whole country and everything in it.

My dear teacher, you taught us in school that the sun comes up here in America when in Mecklenburg it goes down. My dearest teacher, let me tell you how much you deceived us. The sun comes up here in the morning and goes down in the evening the same as by you folks. On my first day here I gave that my special 'tention. With the moon, it too works out to be the same as by you. All during the trip I said to myself, it's real good that the earth is round. That works out real well. Otherwise, the sun and the moon couldn't move around the way they need to, and we couldn't have made this trip to America quite so slick. All that has a good, solid basis and was well thought out, just how it needed to be. God has quite a good head to think with.

My dear teacher, I have to tell you there is one thing I don't understand. On that trip from England to America, for seven weeks and two days the sun came up in the morning and went down in the evening the way it's supposed to. That works here just like it does back home. But when we got to this place, all the clocks were set back six hours. My dear friend, please explain to me what this is all about. I wonder where those six hours disappeared to. Maybe they're down there in the deep with all those mattresses.

This isn't a letter, this is a package. I've been working on it for three months. "Nu, you look fix und find a way 'tween dose Owls und Krows." For the next letter, I've already ordered two pounds of paper from Chicago. Oh man, but I still got lots to do.

2

The Longest Month
. . . .

In New York they showed me the Immigrant House. I went into the main hall and threw my bag under a bench. Before too long here comes a Frenchman. He spoke German. He looked us over, one after the other. When his eyes got as far as me, he asked if I wanted to work by him for one month. "What do you pay a month?" I asked. "Twelve dollars." "Ja, then I'll do it if you live on the way to Chicago, because that's where I live." He really lived over a hundred miles north from there, but I was such a dummkopf with the American directions. In the evening we went upriver by boat. I asked, "Why don't you hire a farmhand out of your own village?" "We don't live in villages — everybody here lives alone on their own farm." "So," I said, "like the small farms in Mecklenburg." He laughed. No one likes to be laughed at, especially not by your new boss.

Now it was time for bed. He asked me, "Have you got enough money to sleep in a bunk here on the boat?" "No." So he found himself a bunk, and I took my sack along down to the boiler room. It was starting to get cold. After a while they said something — I just sat in the corner and pretended I was asleep. They said something again and pointed upstairs. I didn't make a move. So they finally ignored me. I sat there in the corner all night and actually did sleep. Ja wohl, these Americans are friendly people.

That morning we landed in Hudson. Along came a handsome buggy. A man was sitting in it, looking up and looking well dressed. I took off my cap and made a low bow: *"Dat ist ja wohl der Grossherzog,* the Grand Duke of America." "No," said the Frenchman. "We've got no grand duke here." So I put my cap on and said to myself, so what is a country with no grand duke?" Then we rode 18 miles on the train. That cost 53 cents. It put a big hole in the bottom of my first million. At the station his daughter was waiting with a horse and wagon. She was a girl who was good to look at, all primped up and pretty. But the horse was a mess and the wagon a real rattletrap. We headed homeward. My sack rode along, and I wobbled on behind. A sack like that is much better off than its lord and master.

Then the good part began. At last I got something to eat. I said to myself, Goliath the giant couldn't eat more salt pork, bread, potatoes with the jackets on, and gravy than I did. At the end I was full and as I laid my knife down, I said to myself, oh man, oh man but now America begins to look better. My Frenchman said, "I see by your prayers that you're not a Catholic." "No, I'm a Lutheran." "Ja," he said to me, "we have the cream and you Lutherans have the skim milk." "Ja," said I, "and then comes the big black cat and licks up the cream." My Frenchman's eyes got real big.

One day he asked, "What books you got in that sack?" "Oh," said I, "a whole row: Bible, hymnal, catechism, and Stark's prayerbook. With books like that a mensch can go a long ways." Every once in a while he paged around in Stark, and when he'd give it back to me, he'd say: "That is a good book."

Another day I was supposed to milk the cow and couldn't. By us in Mecklenburg, women milk the cows. The beast soon figured out that I didn't know teat from tail. The cow looked at me with total disgust and slapped me in the ears with her tail. At that moment she also kicked out, and I and the bucket flew into the manure. From then on the Frenchman milked the cow: with him that went one, two, three. Again, later, I was supposed to yoke the oxen and plow. I went to get 'em off the pasture. When they saw me coming, they took off, I after them. They went further, faster. I said to myself, America is absolutely crazy. Even the oxen got nerve in this country. So he, the Frenchman, yoked 'em up. I said, "No lines for these oxen?" "No," he said. "You drive 'em with words and with a stick." And this they call the New World. Man alive, I think Columbus made a mistake. The oxen pulled the plow on a chain. That was something I was familiar with. He took 'em around the field once — I followed behind. He told me the words I was to say. You got to remember those beasts don't understand Deutsch. Words like that I never heard before in my whole life.

Then he drove with his daughter to town, and I was the king of the plow and oxen. It went pretty good for a field full of stumps. By the time I was on the second round, I had forgotten all the Frenchman's words and was talking Low German with the oxen. But when I said *Heih!* they stood still and cocked their ears, and when I said *Hoit*, they stood even stiller. When I said *Kem* and *Tud*, they took off like lightning — I held the plow. They ran like crazy — I held the plow. They ran into the bush — I held the plow. There in the thicket patch, I looked 'round and said to myself, O the God of my Fatherland, what's happening to your children in America? This is worse than the Turks in Constantinople. Then I took a breath and laid it on those critters with a stick until I ran 'em out of the thickets. But I got 'em good. After that the field plowed better. But it looked a sight, and man oh man, I was glad nobody from our village was around. Otherwise no farmer in Mecklenburg would hire me as a fieldhand, and especially not Hannjürn Timmermann.

On the next day I was told to cut wood, hardwood naturally. My Frenchman said: "An American cuts at least four cords a day and stacks it. If you can do two, I'll be satisfied." But that turned sour for me too. Then he put me out to mow his buckwheat, which the Americans do with a long-handled sickle. Now I had heard of long-handled sickles, but I'd never seen one and had never used one. I said, "I'll mow with a scythe and do twice as much as you can with a sickle." Off we went. I first with the scythe and after me came two beanpole Americans with sickles — one, two, three and they were right at my heels. They stood there and laughed. I mowed some further and sweat a regular storm. I mowed with might and main. They were right behind me again. I was their prisoner. They mowed in a circle 'round me. Then I fell behind them. I said to myself, the cuckoo can have this country, and then I looked at the blisters on my hands. Only there's no cuckoo in America. But man oh man, the scythes in this country are a problem. They are cast metal and can't be sharpened with a hammer. If you try it, they'll break. You have to sharpen them with a stone. They only cost three marks in German money, but that's all they're worth. A good scythe made by a German blacksmith is hard to find and costs seven to eight marks.

That turned into one of the longest months in my life, but finally I got hold of its short end. Only, man oh man, soon I had to let loose of it. My Frenchman wanted to give me and my sack a ride to town. It was fifteen miles according to the English system. But I wanted to stay another week and help thresh the buckwheat. He offered to pay me, but then I began to have second thoughts. He offered to let me have all the meat I could eat. That was a brand new idea for my life. That was a language no mensch had ever talked to me. That was a deal. I stayed, I threshed, I ate. When the week was over, he gave me seven dollars for the whole time and said, "That'll do for a greenhorn like you." And he didn't even drive me to town. But his daughter had a heart of mercy — she gave me a real loaf of bread and a piece of lean bacon.

With all of that I got myself up and going and started on my way. The bacon tasted good, and when it was gone I stopped at a farm. It belonged to a man from Schwabenland. I threshed for him for four days, one dollar and twenty-five cents per day. But an Englishman who slept alongside me that last night stole the five dollars. He even prayed like a Christian before he went to bed and before he got up. Again I was broke. I looked for another farm. "Do you want to thresh?" I said yes and stayed — and again made six dollars. I left there and went on. After that I got robbed twice and was also fooled out of some money. It seemed to me that every crook in America heard that I had arrived and was laying in wait for me. It was like the territory between Jerusalem and Jericho, only without a Good Samaritan. That's not how it is in the old country. In Mecklenburg we don't have these robbers, crooks, and smooth talkers.

I left there and moved right along. I came to a hill. That hill was dressed up like Putt Hill in our village. Even had a pond on top. Only this hill was higher. Up on the top I stood still. I saw myself from the inside and I saw myself from the outside, from bottom to top. And look, I stood there and had nothing but a jacket, a walking stick, and my God. I owned nothing but the bones under my skin and the sack on my shoulder. Then and there I drew a line under the first month. I thought about what had happened and then I said to myself, Jürnjakob, you have been a dummkopf. You have to learn to be careful. You have to pay 'tention in this land. Otherwise you will never get further than one calf's tail with your idea of two herds of cows, and a calf's tail will look mighty funny going in and out of them big barns you're going to build. You're also going to have to learn to do your work like the Americans do. Old Mecklenburg is too slow and steady. You figured that out mowing buckwheat. Plowing and cutting wood was just so-so. You've got the muscles, but oxen have muscles too. You have to get a different schooling to work in America. Jürnjakob, you have to put your brain to work, otherwise nothing is ever going to come of you. Otherwise in a year's time you'll be back in old Mecklenburg, but this time like a freak in a circus show. The kids will point their fingers at you, "Look at 'im, dat's der Jürnjakob. He was too dumb for the Americans, so they sent him back to us in Mecklenburg."

Those were sobering thoughts. So I looked into the four winds. But that wasn't me that looked, it was the old Jürnjakob. I thought about my Grosspa. Grosspa came to a corner in his life and didn't know which way to turn. He threw his hat up in the air and said: "Wherever the wind takes it, let the wind take me." To listen to Grosspa, that was a funny story. But it was not a funny story for me in America. Here you don't dare go according to some breeze or follow Grosspa's old hat. So I threw my sack with the bacon in it on my shoulder, took Pa's oak walking stick in my hand and down the hill I went. From that day forward no one stole a thing from me or smooth-talked me out of anything. I went straight to New York and never turned around once. I looked steady forwards.

A hilltop like that is real good in a lifetime, even if it doesn't last very long. A mensch thinks clearer on a hill. All kinds of people have stood on hilltops. I know one who liked to climb a hill when he wanted to be alone and talk to God. My dear teacher, you introduced him to us.

A mensch can talk to himself better on top of a hill. A mensch can drop his sack or whatever else he's luggin' around a lot easier on top of a hill. A mensch can also look back and forth, and up and down into his life. I looked back and forth, and up and down on my first month in the new land. I also looked up and ahead, and thought about how I have to live my life in order to move ahead. After all that, I climbed down and came back to where the people are. God doesn't give us hills so that a mensch stands on a hilltop forever.

When I got to New York, I was back where I started. I still had one dollar. But the others from our village had just got off their boat, and I saw them all with their names: Schröder, Schuldt, Timmermann, Düde, Sass, Wiedow, Völss, and Brüning. All together we took the train to Iowa — Heine Schröder lent me the money. I rented myself out there in Iowa for one year at two hundred and ten dollars. So far, that was my best move. Schröders had a daughter, Wieschen. So I stayed there for one year and then went on to a neighbor's farm for six months. After I got through that year and a half, I counted my money. It came to three hundred and fifty dollars. I went to Wieschen. It was Sunday afternoon. She was sittin' on the porch, busy with her knitting needles. I set myself on the bench and began to be polite. We talked weather and we talked crops. After that, I said: "Wieschen, wieviel Geld hast du zusammen? Wieschen, how many dollars you got together?" She went to fetch her old leather purse, the one from home. She had a good two hundred dollars. I laid my three hundred and fifty next to her two hundred and said: "Wieschen, I know a little farm over by Springfield. It's got only two cows and twelve pigs — but for a beginning, that's plenty. I want to run it, that means rent it, if you'll come along." She folded her hands and looked straight ahead, almost forever. Then she run her hands over her apron once or twice. After she did that, she said "Ja" and gave me one of those hands. Good Lord, I said to myself, now look at me — I got myself a wife. From that day on I was one happy mensch.

Coming into the land, one dummkopf is as green as the other. What do you think? How smart was I about America? I was as smart as a hired man's pig — one stinks as bad as the other. If stupidity hurts, then in the New York harbor you would hear nothing but wailing and mourning from morning to night. But you soon learn your lesson. In this country you get set on your bottom quicker than in the old country. And when your behind gets set down a few times, you get real careful and learn to run on two legs. If you can't do that, save your money for something besides a ticket to America — don't show your backside to Deutschland. In Deutschland the dear God still protects the Dummkopfs. Over there, "the mensch is 'dem heavenly Father in 'dem heavenly hands." That's not so in America. For most of these folks money is God. Oh, I could tell funny stories about these Deutsche dummkopfs who've come over here, but I don't want to make believe I'm better than they are. If anything, I'd be telling stories about Jürnjakob Swehn.

Now my inkpot fell on the floor, and I sopped up these last few words from down there to up here. Then Berti, my daughter, put more ink in the pot. She did it with a teaspoon, and she said, "That's what happens when you got such a mensch for a father." Ja wohl, those are the girls we got in America, *so sind die Gören hierzulande.*

3

My Own Farm

• •

Six months ago you asked if Jürnjakob had ever been homesick. No, not once. Oh, maybe just a little bit when I first got here. I don't really know how being homesick gets going, but as far as I'm concerned it never got going with me. Old people who come over here never get used to the place. That's because they've come over too late or because there's no strength in their bones. During the day while they're busy with work, everything goes pretty good. But evenings, sitting around, or if there's bad weather, they start to complain. *Dann sacken sie zusammen und lassen den Kopf hängen.* They fall in a heap and let their heads hang low. They put their hands between their knees and think about old Mecklenburg and are full of misery. To cheer them up is nigh impossible. "To everything there is a season," says Solomon in the Bible and reckons up a pile of everythings, even gathering stones and scattering stones. But old Solomon forgot about going to America. It wasn't the style in his day.

There's nothing here for old people, and there's absolutely nothing here for people with no get up and go. The air bites too hard in America. Here, you have to have iron in your blood. Here you may not hang your harp on a weeping willow, if you have a harp. Here it's not as gemütlich as it is back home. Here nobody has time for anybody. Even the smoke in the chimney doesn't take its time the way it does in Mecklenburg. By you in the old country, the smoke crawls around and sneaks out under the door, through a window, into a crack. Slowly it rises in the chimney and then looks around and says, "Let's snake along the street for a ways." In America, the smoke goes up, up, and away, and takes no time to say goodbye to anybody.

No, I'm at home here now. Around here almost everybody talks Low German and comes from the old country. I came across the pond when I was young. I married here. I raised a good family. I have built here. I have planted here, and here I have harvested. My sweat lies all over these acres, and sweat does its job here just like by you.

On second thought, that's not the case. Ach by me, sweat has got me vun dummboozled more than by you in the old country. In my village I was born a hired man, and I would have stayed one all my life. Even if I had my own house, I still wouldn't have had any land, and my kids would all be maids and hired men.

We have had to hustle here and work hard, much harder than in the old country. That is the God's truth. For all of that, I made something of myself. That is also the God's truth. Here I made myself free. Here I stand with my own two feet on my own ground and am nobody's slave. *Das Freisein ist schon ein par Eimer Schweiss wert.* To be free is worth whole buckets of sweat.

My pa got paid four schilling a day. Only at harvesttime did he get more. The wind blew through the walls of his hired-man house. Here I've built a good house with eight rooms and all that goes with it. Back home we had four windowpanes, and one was cracked as long as I can remember. Here we have many walls and they're all tight to the weather and all stand fast. The windows are big, they're new, and they work with weights — they don't swing out the way they do by you in Mecklenburg. Our windowpanes here are twenty-four inches by twenty-six inches, and on the south side of the house we have a big window three feet by five feet. It's all one glass with little colored glass panes set in around it. The trim on the doorways and windows is something I did myself. The carpenter wanted sixty dollars to do it and that was too steep for me. Everybody here has a big porch — we got one too.

Then we rebuilt and remodeled the house. I did it, and I did as much and as well as I wanted to. When it was finished, I had the whole house papered. That cost thirty dollars, the labor cost twenty. Outside and inside, the remodeling cost fifteen hundred dollars, without figuring my work. I had a few scars to show for all my labor. I didn't always hit the nail on its head, and when I thumped my finger the blood jumped out and ran down my arm. Wieschen said, "So, *dat hast du nu dorvon*, there you have it now, from it all. I been thinkin' you'd do that." Ja wohl, that's the womenfolk. But she still wrapped that poor finger up for me, and on the next day I was back at it with hammer in hand.

No deal, I won't trade this for that old thatch-roofed house in Mecklenburg. I didn't own as much as a cow's tail over there. One time, when I was round eight years old, old Düffert's ma gave me a pig's tail. Mensch, but the pig was already cut off. Anyway, you can't make a silk scarf out of a pig's tail. No, I can forget about that. Ja wohl, I don't need to pout about the old days gone by.

Now I have ten horses, eighty cows, one team of oxen, and about one hundred and twenty pigs. Before we had fewer pigs. But these past few years crops have been good, so I have more. Chickens number up to six hundred, give or take. You don't count chickens over here.

But this winter, I want to tell you about my livestock. If you're a real farmer, you'll do what real farmers do here or in Mecklenburg. First, they talk livestock. Next, they talk livestock. Finally, they tell you what they forgot to tell you about the livestock and go on from there. First, let's talk about pigs.

In America, pigs have a curly tail and talk in Low German so I can understand them: "oink, oink." Otherwise, over here, everything's different. You don't raise pigs in a shed or in a narrow stall. That's what the Germans did when they first came over here. You did it the way you learned it back home. But this land has different customs when it comes to raising pigs, so we had to change our ways. Pigs in America run free and gets lots of sunshine. Pigs love the light — that's why they're so much like us human beings. That's why they're so healthy here, and we read in your newspapers that American pigs have trichinosis. We have to laugh, 'cause look, in your newspapers we're always reading that farms and markets are quarantined because of redrun in the pigs.

On my three hundred and twenty acres I can raise fodder for all my cows, because that's how the land lays. There's also plenty pasture for the pigs, almost forty acres. They go in and out from the barnyard. Around those forty acres there is a fence post every eight feet. Where the post goes into the ground there are two six-inch boards and above the boards three lines of barbwire. For pigs, we figure three or four months on pasture. Before long, them pigs weigh in at a hundred pounds, and with ten pigs per acre it comes to forty dollars an acre. Here though, pigs go for less than by you. We're getting four dollars a hundred pounds, so it takes a hundred pigs for it to amount to something. If you put in corn and get fifty bushel the acre, that comes to twenty cents on a bushel. There's a difference that fills your pocket. Your money bag says, "Man oh man, I like this land."

When the corn is ready, we go at it like this: we shovel it all into a pile and set it on fire. When it's burned good, the pigs come on to the pile and eat from the edges on what has already cooled off. Ja wohl, these American pigs like that. Then they go for water. February 2nd I went to Chicago with eighty pigs. They brought six hundred and eighty-five dollars. After

New Year's, I'll go again. It's only too bad I can't get 'em to a market in Deutschland, then I'd see some real money.

Oxen are next on the plan, 'cause we got all that hay. At Christmastime I shipped twenty head to Chicago. They brought in some over eight hundred dollars. For us that's a good price. Right now milk cows are cheap — one good cow costs fifteen to twenty-three dollars.

This year I picked over three thousand bushels of corn. I sold four hundred at thirty-five cents a bushel. For us that's a good price. And we fed our cows quite a bit of that corn. We cut it green and pack it airtight in the silo. It keeps real good. Them cows give more milk with that green corn fodder than with clover hay.

Otherwise, when we work with cows it goes like this: we chase 'em out on the pasture, but no cowboys in sight. They come back in on their own. In winter they stay in by the barns. When the grass greens up, they go so far out you can't see 'em, but when it's time to milk they come back home. The milk drives 'em in. In wintertime it's 4:30 in the afternoon, and in summer it's when the clock strikes seven. Our clock stopped. No calamity. We waited 'til the cows came in. So we set the clock according to the cows. Next time I went to town I compared our time with the town clock. You know what? Ours was right, *siehe sie ging richtig.*

This year so far, we've sold thirty-six calves. They were the ones we already had at harvesttime. They took their milk from their mothers. Saved us all that milking. They did it for a few months, then we weaned 'em and put 'em on oats. They brought in five hundred and ninety dollars. By you they would have been worth twice that price. Selling calves is no party for me, but why should a mensch make money for the butter factories? One of them Cream Barons and Butter Kings came to visit, ja wohl, in a car. He was a real Yankee. People like that want to buy our cream. His story was, "I'll buy all your cream. I'll buy all the cream you can produce in one year because you live out here so far from town. You won't have a worry in the world." I said, "Ja wohl, that's real good of you. You should pickle that one idea for when times get bad." He said, "I'll pay you a good price." I said, "For all of me you can pay to butter the road, and I'll give you that much for nothing." He took off in his automobile. He never showed up again. That kind is out shopping for a Low German dummkopf. He'll need to get up earlier in the morning to fool me, and he's making no impression on me with that new car.

Mit dem Mist, ist das hier so, dass er nicht so geehrt wird als bei euch. Manure has no honor in America like the honor it has in Germany. In Germany every forkful is lifted with due respect, and children pick it up off the street and take it home. In America your ground is virgin forest, and in the beginning you don't need manure. In the beginning the ground is rambunctious — it produces nothing but silage. After a few years he quiets down. Then you got good ground. Then he produces grain like you people in Germany have never seen. Finally, with time he gets tired, then you got to come with manure. My neighbor lets manure lie round all over his place. There was manure by the buildings and manure behind the fences. I says to him, "Let me haul your manure off. I'll do it for nothing. I'll do it because I'm a good neighbor." So he said ja wohl, and I hauled it off. Over a hundred loads. My acres licked their chops. But the next year he called it quits with good neighboring in the manure business. He hauled it onto his own fields. He smartened up.

This winter I want to write you a few words about eggs. Here they cost more than by you in Deutschland. Today in America they cost one mark eighty pfennig the dozen. That comes 'cause they all go to New York. There they sit around until the Egg Barons get the best price in the stores. They push the price down for us. Trouble is, we can't push the hens down so they quit layin'. We eat eggs until we're all crowin' and cluckin'. Finally, the heavens and the earth look like the insides of an eggshell with the yolk as the sun.

Two years ago, we couldn't stand to look at an egg. It was misery. It was like one of Pharaoh's ten plagues. That was when feeder pigs were

cheap, too. We figured we'd give one free pig for every dozen eggs. Nothing doin', we couldn't manage that either. And the sows were havin' pigs by the dozen. I mean they produced like frogs and pollywogs. There was an oink in every corner. "What do you do now?" I says to Wieschen. "Do you remember what old Hannjürn Timmermann said to me when they had such a plague in the old country?" She says, "So what did he say?" "He said his grandma lived through torture like that and told him she fed the pigs to the chickens. And his grandma was a real Christian lady.

"You are vun dummboozled dummkopf, Jürnjakob." Wieschen said. "You are a worst of all dummkopf. *Heil und deil bist du unklauk.* How can you believe such old superstitions. What are we coming to if chickens eat the pigs? God's order is that chickens eat rye and corn and bread and 'taters. It's against God's order for chickens to eat pigs." "Ho ho, Wieschen," I said. "You don't remember how in Pharaoh's dream seven lean cows ate seven fat cows? And that stands in the Bible, and that is not against God's order." "Ach," said Wieschen, "mensch, that was a dream." Then I looked at her in a friendly way, held her hand, and talked nice to her until she finally agreed with me. So we butchered those little pigs, cooked 'em and fed 'em to the chickens. We had one problem solved.

What happened next? The chickens began to lay eggs so fast we couldn't gather 'em. One egg after the other. It was pure misery, and I couldn't stand it a minute longer. I wanted to turn into stone. I sat there frozen with my hands in my lap, Wieschen too. She scolded, "Now we've made us into clowns for the whole neighborhood." When she says that, you know she's mad. I said, "Wieschen, that's not the way. Now I have a plan." "Don't tell me, another plan? You going to bring more grief to this house?" "Wieschen," I said, "in earnest, this is a plan. Don't make fun of this. Just you listen and pay 'tention. Do you want to eat more eggs?" "No." "Do you want to eat more pancakes?" "Don't talk a word about pancakes." "Good, then we've agreed and unity makes strength. Now I tell you something. We're rid of those baby pigs, so now if we feed these eggs to the calves, we'll be rid of all them eggs. Our misery will come to an end, you watch and see. We'll all be happy."

"Jürnjakob, you are one dummkopf of a Deutschman. And if you get another idea like that, make sure you don't tell me. First you feed pigs to the chickens. Now you want to butcher the calves and feed them to the pigs, so that them pigs hurry up and have more pigs that we can feed to the chickens. I'd say, that's a round-trip from one end of the farm to the other. Next you'll be frying chicken to fatten up the cows. Dat is a business. Dat is a business."

With that said, Wieschen fell into her rocking chair. But in a minute she was up and out of the house. I looked at her going out the door and said to myself, what that woman said about a round-trip is not a lie. We've got a merry-go-round here on this farm — it's the merry-go-round of God's big wide world. With that I stuck a dozen fresh eggs in my overalls and went to visit the calves. Oh boy, oh boy, they licked their chops. When Wieschen saw that, she was no longer unhappy. She filled her apron with eggs and helped me. So we fed eggs to the calves until they could hardly beller. They had big smiles on their faces, and that little bull calf stamped his feet for joy.

My dear friend, I can tell you them calves got fat and shiny like a rooster with ten hens and all the corn he could eat. If another plague like this pig and egg plague ever comes over this land again, we'll do another round-trip through the farm. But please don't tell this story in Mecklenburg or they'll laugh me to scorn, from the first of those Deutschmans to the last.

In those first years after we bought the farm, eggs were cheap. We were happy to get eight cents a dozen. It was in those years that the story of our rooster began to unfold. We called him the Governor.

On the edges of the farm there was brush and forest, and in the brush all kinds of chicken-eating varmints. Our chickens wandered over the fields and into the brush. When they returned home they were always fewer in number than when they left home. We didn't have that many chickens in those days, so we still counted them. I said to Wieschen, "It's not workin'. We got to do something," Wieschen said to me, "Ja, you do something, only what?" Said I, "You pay 'tention. I'm buying a glock, a little bell. This bell, I will hang around the neck of that big black rooster, because he's the Governor. Then all them chicken-eating creatures will take a trip. The hens will all know where their lord and master is, and when there's trouble they'll get movin'." Wieschen said, "Jürnjakob, du bist nicht klug, you're not all that smart! What will people say?" I said, "There's no taxes paid on what the people say. Besides that, it's all the same to me." "But that rooster will go crazy." "Just wait," I said, "just wait." She still mumbled this and that, but she smiled. That's a good sign from Wieschen.

So His Honor the rooster got his bell. Then I got scared. He ran round the place like a crazy one, but the more he rampaged, the more the bell klingelt. He picked at the bell, didn't help. He rolled on his back and trampled his feet in the air, didn't help. He looked pretty funny, and I said to myself, ja, just so he doesn't do a suicide and jump in the horse trough. At first the hens ran in all directions when he came round with his tingel tangel. They ran into all the corners and out onto the fields. They flapped their wings and squawked for fear whenever he came round with that bell on his neck.

I said to Wieschen, "You don't see much love or loyalty 'mong those chickens either. You hope it's better with people." She said, "You look here, you hang a bell around your neck and run 'round here like a spook, then we'll see." So there I got it. But life is at least halfways habit. In the end it all worked out, and it looked almost as if that big black rooster wore that bell with pride. His hens got used to it, and it really helped against all those chicken-eating varmints.

It was about this time that one day a German-Russian woman came by who was on the way to visit her son. She heard the tingel tangel of that rooster's bell and saw him struttin' round in all his pride and glory. For a while she stood there and, without saying a word, she looked him over, up one side and down the other. After that, she said, "What is this that I see with my eyes and hear with my ears? I have lived sixty years. I have traveled from Russia to America. I have never seen the likes of this. Did your czar order that roosters in America wear bells?"

Now I explained to her the whole story and how it came to be. She listened with her ears, but her head couldn't understand. She shook it real good and said, "How can this be? America is one crazy place. When I write to my relatives at home that the roosters in America wear bells and walk round like governors, they will say 'The old woman is now cuckoo in the head.' Ach, my dear God, I sometimes wish I had stayed in Russia." But then I said to her, "Don't have any regrets that you got out of the old country. The Kaiser of Russia wouldn't buy anybody a rooster or a hen after his wolves ate up their chickens. And as far as that bell goes, just don't worry. We human beings like to hear music. So why not the chickens? We are all created by one God. And, they lay more eggs by that bell music. Pay 'tention, when you get to your son's place, you hang a bell on his rooster's neck and you will praise and give thanks to the Lord for Old Jürnjakob. Besides, you don't have to write such stuff to your relatives in Russia."

At that she got gemütlich and said, "*Ja, es ist hier vieles anders als im Russland.* This is real different from Russia, and I've had to change many ways. The worst has been with my teeth. When I was getting ready to leave the old country, the tooth doctor from Jekaterinsolaw came out to us and said, 'If you want to get into America, you have to have all your teeth. Otherwise they'll send you back. The czar of America is real strict about teeth.' I said, 'Is that really true?' He said, 'Ja, that is for sure. The czar of America has proclaimed seven teeth laws, and I can see by your mouth that you won't be legal. So you're not going to get in.' I said, 'What can I do about that?' He answered, 'The czar of America wrote me a letter. He said that he will only admit people from Russia who get a set of false teeth before they leave the old country. He does this only because he is very merciful.' 'Is that really true?' 'Ja, that is for sure. The American ambassador in Odessa also wrote me a letter about this.' 'But I'm traveling through Germany.' 'That makes no difference. First of all, they won't examine you 'til you get to New York.' So he pulled all my teeth and fixed me up with a set of new false teeth. It cost me a bundle of money. So I came through New York real good and have already seen much of this country. But this rooster of yours tops it all."

She looked that rooster over one more time. He stood on the fence and crowed and waved his head in all directions. When she finished the cup of coffee Wieschen had cooked for her, she traveled on. But as she walked off the place, she looked around two or three times. She looked at the governor of the hens, and then she looked at us, and then she shook her head.

Last year, our oats reached shoulder height. We held our heads high like you do when your crop looks good. Then started Pharaoh's plagues. First it was the rust. Then it was rain. After that our oats laid on its back and held its legs up to heaven. That lasted longer than we wanted. The rain lasted even longer. Finally, them oats looked as if they had been danced on, and that's how they stayed. I have said again and again, the good weather we used to have will never come again 'cause the world is getting more evil all the time. So finally we started to mow. They weren't worth the string to tie 'em in bundles. Lots of farmers round here put a match to their fields and burned 'em off. On forty acres I used up sixty pounds of string and at that I could only get the machine to tie half of 'em.

A wet summer can't be hung out on the clothesline to dry, and that hurts. Still it rained another four weeks — stuff grew like crazy. That summer we didn't even bother to bring the crop in. I drove the wagon onto the pasture and dumped them oats bundles in rows. The cows and oxen shook their heads and complained about this awful mess. Still, they started to work on it and by the first of October they had chewed up the last bundle and stamped the straw into the ground. Ja, that's how it comes and goes sometimes, and we didn't hold our heads high anymore, 'specially when we remembered them oats. That is what you call *Ordnung* in German — a mensch gets it in the neck every once in a while. Otherwise he wants to set his behind on the throne of God and be king of the hill.

4

Life in the New World

• •

The worst thing in this country is trying to hire help for the fields or for the house. *Die sind schwer zu bekommen*, they are hard to find — and it's even harder to keep them. That's particularly true of hiring a woman. To begin with, when we came to America Wieschen got three dollars a week working on a farm. Nowadays we pay four to five dollars. And then they only want to do the easy stuff. For the hard work you have to get a man. In town, wages are still higher. A cook gets seven dollars a week, and if she has to do other things, she gets eight. In our village in the old country, that's what a woman earned for a whole year's work. And for that she worked hard from morning till night. As we got started with this farm, Wieschen and I did everything. Them were the hard years. Some days Wieschen and I were at it until 11 o'clock at night, binding wheat and oats. You better believe we'd never worked that hard in our lives. But we stayed healthy. The farm was only a little one, and we were renters. Now we have a big farm, and we own it — and we still work hard.

Today everything gets done by machine. We put on the elevator what a man's arm or what his shoulder carried in the old days. That's how you do it in this country. And that goes for everything from mowing to storing it in the barn. We sow with a machine, and naturally we thresh with a machine. That means we don't hire anybody. They stay out East. There they get by with eight hours a day. Out here in the West, on the farm, no one wants to hire on. Harvest is the worst. Nowadays they get four or five dollars a day and all the meat they can eat. But it's hard work and you have to stay with it. You work from sunup to sundown, and at harvesttime here in Iowa the sun gets out of bed real early. Them days we save on water. Nobody washes or gets a bath. Nobody combs his hair. There's so much chaff in the air your face looks like my Wieschen's pincushion or like the back of a hedgehog. So you get this thick dirt coat on your face. That protects you from everything.

Ja wohl, that is a real thick coating of dirt. And believe me, if you wipe off the sweat with the back of your hand, it doesn't do anything for your natural God-given beauty. Man oh man, I'm just glad no picture painter came around to do us and then send you the results. It would scare you out of your wits. You would say, "For sure, they are not people. *Das ist eine Horde schwarzer Teufel, und sie kommen eben frisch aufgewichst aus der Hölle.* That's a tribe of devils, all waxed up and fresh from hell." When the worst of the work is over, we go back to soap and water. You'd never believe how much soap we use on a farm like this. With that much soap the president could give the White House such a scrubbing you could see it all the way to Mecklenburg.

At harvesttime, students come looking for work, even professors' and pastors' sons. There you see another difference between America and Deutschland. They come from college. They are on vacation. They all go out to the farms. Now they don't work the hours that we do, but when they're done, they have anywhere from ninety to a hundred dollars in the pocket. In winter, when it's all books and classes, they put that money to good use. Sweat makes nobody a dummkopf. People and the land look different on a farm than they do in the books. That book paper gets in the way of your really being able to see, *da ist das Papier den Augen im Wege.*

Working like this together with us in the fields is altogether different from like a pastor's evening visit. So he comes some evening with his black suit on and such polite conversation, "My dear brother Swehn, how are things going for you?" This way they learn how much sweat a loaf of bread costs. At first it's a sour experience for them, and they complain to high heaven. In the evening they can't sleep because they're too tired. Once in a while they fall in a pile. Then Wieschen has to play doctor. After they get a layer of dirt on their skin they work better, and finally they really do work.

Other students go from house to house during the vacation. They come with books and pictures. It's easier work but the income isn't for sure. But I know one who turned that into a regular art. He knew how to get you to buy books. He ran off at the mouth like the water off the wheel in a mill race. He made lots of money. One summer's vacation he made four hundred dollars.

In America we only use the scythe for small jobs. Our scythes don't hold an edge like yours. Once in a while we'll order a scythe "Made in

Germany." That is one hammered out by hand. We Americans can't do that as good as your Deutschmans. But man alive, on our farms we can't do it with a scythe. Where in the world would we get all the arms to swing 'em?

With girls to help out in the house, we've tried everything. But nothing much has come of it, and it's been no fun. First off we hired two from Poland. No go, so we tried Americans. I took off for Chicago to see what I could find. I looked up Wilhelm Sass to see if he could help.

For a few days I looked things over and I looked over the people. I went home without hiring anybody. Now I didn't relish coming home alone, because I had promised Wieschen I would find her some help. At first she scolded pretty bad, and I listened to her real good 'cause it's best if you let your woman talk herself out. When she quieted down, I said: "Wieschen pay 'tention to me. In Chicago there are whole regiments of women on the streets. But I'm 'fraid to talk to 'em. They walk around in high-class white dresses. Hey, they aren't headed for a cowstall. Nein, sie wollen ins Theater, no, they're going to the theater. Ja wohl, you would make big eyes at this. And if you want to talk to 'em with their white dresses and gold watches, just tell me, and boy oh boy I'll write to Wilhelm Sass today." Wieschen wasn't interested for me to write. She said, "No, it's better that you don't bring one home. Noooo." She said, "But now talk some more about what you saw in the city."

"Oh, my dear Wieschen! I saw a whole mountain of stuff and still more. I saw babies, lying in little carriages and being taken for a ride. I thought they were 'bout a year old. They wore gold rings and bracelets, and with all such junk like that they were decorated from one hand to the other. My dear Wieschen, how will you ever be able to explain that your children have learned to walk and are all grown up now and have never worn a gold bracelet? You have sinned against your children." Wieschen said to that, "Jürnjakob, get off'n that pulpit and just tell what you saw." "Ja, even street cleaners and men unloading the coal wagons were wearing big, thick gold rings."

"So, nun hab' ich davon genug gehört." "Now I've heard enough," she said and took out another stocking to be darned. "Rings, bracelets, white shoes, white dresses, gold watches that don't work. Too bad that old Martin Luther never got to see that," said Wieschen. "Why is that too bad?" "He would have had to work all that into the catechism. You know, when he tells what 'daily bread' means in the Lord's Prayer." "Wieschen," said I, "once again, you know best." "Well now," she said, "get going and tell me more of Chicago. Or is this the end of your diary?" "Not by a darn side," I said. "I saw so much in Chicago, you could darn a mountain of stockings before I finished telling it. One thing I have to tell is the chewing business." Wieschen said, "Well, you didn't have to go to Chicago to see all that. That's something you can see right here on the farm. Just eat your bread and butter standing in front of the mirror." "Wieschen, pay 'tention and let me talk. That Chicago chewing was different and had nothing to do with eating. In Chicago everybody chews, and it's not even lunchtime. Mensch oh mensch, the old ones chew tobacco and the young ones chew gum. They chew in school and they chew in church. And to top it off, they spit. In all of old Mecklenburg no one can spit like those Chicago people.

"Now let me tell you. I rode the streetcar. Up front stands the one who steers. He spits out the front at almost every corner. He stops and then he spits. On the back end stands the conductor. He spits out the back way. He only spits while we're moving. When we stop the conductor is busy, so he's got no time for it then. Mensch oh mensch, that's how they take turns. So then you walk down the center of the car and people are sitting on both sides. They all open their mouths to move the gum from one side to the other. Then they chew: Open, close, open, close. Wieschen, you know when I watched all of that, do you know what I said to myself?" She said, "Nooo, that I don't know. You tell me."

I said, "I thought about the farm I worked on back in the old country." "Now what made you think of that?" "Ja, when I walked down the middle of the streetcar, that was like Hannjürn Timmermann's barn. Only the streetcar wasn't so wide. His cow stalls stood on both sides so they could watch us and we could watch them: chew, chew, chew. First on one side, then on the other. Open, close, open, close. Ja akkrat so was that in Chicago."

"Ja wohl," said Wieschen, "we're happy you're home. Now sit down and drink a cup of coffee. Your mouth gets dry from all that talk." "Ja wohl," I said, "let's do it. Only you have a cup too, because then it tastes better to me. Those last few stockings to mend can wait 'til tomorrow."

We enjoy our farm, and we're happy to be away from the city. And you've heard the story now of all that I experienced in Chicago as I was lookin' for a girl to work in the house, dat heff ick all's in Chicago belewt. . . ."

Wieschen sat in her rocking chair and watched the world go by. In this country rocking chairs and womenfolk go together. There has to be one in every house. Wieschen has learned that lesson here very well.

5

The American Farmer
· ·

In America people like us get old and tired. I'm beginning to get a real
gray beard, and my grinders don't grind the way they used to. They wobble
all over the place and then fall out. I've been having quite a time eating the
crust. But I can still read without glasses, and I don't have to stretch out
my arms to hold a book. Writing goes pretty fast with me too. Only thing
is, it does take a little longer with the work. For years I have pushed these
old bones hard, and only in winter has there been any time to think. Now,
somebody's at the door, *Es klingelt*. Wieschen is already out of the rocking
chair — now she's not old and tired. Me, I'm putting the pen to rest. I'll
write some more soon. It's our neighbor at the door. *Ick weit all, wat hei
will*, I already know what he wants. I should cut off the horns on his calves.

In America the farmer has to do everything and be everything: carpenter, cabinetmaker, blacksmith, bricklayer, even a shoemaker. I set up some
workshops here on the place. Even got a machine to drill holes in steel
and iron, with all kinds of nuts and bolts. Otherwise a body has to be in
town every other day, the only thing that leads to is more money out of the
pocket. We make everything we need. As far as it goes, we try to stay away
from town.

We've even drilled a well here, two hundred and fifty feet deep, and we
set a windmill on it that pumps water. At first this was more than I could
think. I said to myself: Oh man oh man, how will this work? A windmill
that mills water? But in this country you learn these tricks quicker than in
the old country. We are quick and we are *fix*. And when we say *fix* in German we mean we got the get up and go.

A big farm like mine needs all kinds of machinery to keep it going
in a forward direction: cornpicker, haymower, hayrake for two horses,
and a hayloader. You see that on the picture I'm sending. Heinrich, my

son, made it when he was here with his picture apparatus. We have one disc with plates, and then we have a regular disc. We have a plow, a cultivator to work the corn, and a cornplanter. Of course, we also have machines to unload hay and to upload manure. And, we're getting a new cornplanter. The salesman didn't have one but ordered it for us. Now when I say corn, what I mean is maize. I'm not talking about you Deutschmans and your rye.

Oh man oh man, but we sure got no wooden hayrakes here, the kind you use by hand. Anything in the fields that you can't pick up with a pitchfork or with the horse-drawn rake doesn't get picked up. That's a difference between Deutschland and America. Over there you have to rake together every little stray blade or stem of hay. That's because you Deutschmans live all crowded in on them little acres. When we get as crowded as you are, we'll start to use a handheld rake too. Really, it's always too bad when even one blade of grass gets wasted. God's blessing rests on each and every one. But we haven't got the manpower, and we haven't got the time. So, it gets left behind in the field.

My dear friend, I can tell you with that hand-raking in the fields, it's just like when the old folks get to thinking about the life they've lived. As long as a mensch is young, it's one thing. *Da macht er lange Schritte*, he takes big steps. He goes ahead. What gets left behind doesn't worry him. He's got no time for it. But when he's old, in his thoughts he walks though his life one or two or even three times. He picks up one thing here and another thing there. It's the kind of work he can really do and think about, and he can think through what he's done with his life.

Look, old friend, when a mensch has lived a long time, he likes to take his rake and glean in the memory fields. Usually he doesn't find much more than bits and pieces — isn't much more there. He can't begin all over with plowing, sowing, and harvesting. Now and then, though, he finds a few ears of corn that got left behind, forgotten. These he gathers up. When he gets into those high years, he loves every minute of remembering.

My farm has three hundred and twenty acres. Here you call that a big farm. The middle-size runs about eighty to one hundred and sixty. A middle-sized farm of one hundred and sixty acres belongs to me too — I set that next to the big one. But I've got a few houses on that one and I rent it all out. If your place is over three hundred and twenty acres you usually rent some out. Usually, a farm here runs about one hundred and sixty acres, because in the beginning the government granted that to the homesteaders. The government divided the land into quarter mile sections and surrounded each section with a road. So you have four farms of one hundred and sixty acres on each section. A little farm comes to eighty acres. You know what an acre is? One acre equals one hundred and sixty Mecklenburger quadratruten. You know what a morgen is, that's one hundred ruten. So a morgen is three-quarters of an acre. Now you know how big an acre is. A big farm here in Iowa comes to fifty thousand ruten. That's two Mecklenburg farms, which is what our village has.

My dear friend, you see how it all came true for a kid off the sandy land of Hornkaten in Mecklenburg who dreamed of having two herds of cows as he moved out into foreign parts. Now we have plenty of everything, plenty land and plenty livestock. And it all cost plenty sweat.

Whether a man keeps more cows or hogs in this country depends on his ground and how much help he's got. That's where I got a good deal. My ground works for both cows and hogs. A man does have to be careful here not to plant too much corn. Corn makes for good pigs, but corn also makes good ground poor. On a big place like mine you've got to think of everything. I can't make a plan and do pigs this year and next year go for milk cows. Once you got a plan, it takes years for it to grow up and ripen out. Raising animals and breeding them, buying and selling them goes on for years.

On a farm you've got to stay with a certain order of things 'cause until your plan is worked out, prices in the market already can change seven times, and you can wind up workin' for nothing. This happened to me, and year after year I threw my dollars to the cows and pigs. Then I said to myself: Our dear God hasn't given us a head to hang between our knees, and we don't have arms just to cover our sides. That goes against God's order for the world and is no way to get ahead. We have to hold our heads high and look out for ourselves and put our arms to work. Jürnjakob, when your plow bumps into a stump or a stone, throw it over, or go around it. Then you'll plow another straight furrow.

With good and friendly words like that I talk to myself and get on with the work. Times get better too. Just don't let your head droop and hang between your knees. At that rate, you'll lose everything. In this country that's ten times more true than by you in the old country.

Der Boden ist hier jetzt auch schon teuer. These days farmland has gotten plenty expensive. One acre costs anywhere from one hundred to one hundred and fifty dollars. If your place is any good and you're close to the railroad, an acre will go for two hundred dollars. Twenty-five years ago, the price was fifty to seventy dollars, and fifty years ago when Iowa was all government land, the ground was sold plenty cheap. Some farmers paid three to ten dollars an acre. Whoever had his pockets full of gold in those days is in these days a powerful man. That is to say if he did his business right. But you can count on five fingers the ones who had their pockets full and you don't have to start over again by your thumb. The rest of us started with nothing and worked our way up. We didn't have any gold, just two strong arms, and that's worth somethin' too.

6

Our German Neighbors

· ·

Hans Wickboldt lives six miles south of here, and himself owns a little farm of eighty acres. His brother, "Fatty" Wickboldt, the one who always slept in school and never paid 'tention to anything, woke up here in America. He sold his place in Iowa for one hundred fifty dollars an acre and bought another place in South Dakota for fifty dollars an acre. One hundred and twenty acres of this new ground were broke in. The rest of it still lies there the same way our dear God created it. That's cheap. Just so the land agents didn't humbug him. Cheap land has become suspect. Man oh man, but you have to keep your eyes open. Whoever wants to farm should stay in Iowa. That's what I think. In Iowa there's plenty of everything: plenty water, plenty hay, plenty corn, plenty potatoes, and plenty opportunity.

Johann Schröder lives eight miles east of here. Four years ago he went to Dakota. What he got was three bad harvests, one after the other. He had it up to his chin. He came back. At first, he had giant Dakota raisins in his sack and talked big about Dakota. Now he's been converted. Now he says, "Just shut up about Dakota or I'll get real mad." But life has its odd ways. If a man has an itch, he's got to scratch it.

Karl Schneider lives the same distance north of us. He bought three hundred and twenty acres for twelve thousand dollars. Now that's a good buy, even though some broken ground came with it. He's in debt for five thousand dollars, but he's made improvements and has brought the debt down quite a little. His wife has been sickly, though — that held him back. He's got debts and he's got worries — and there's a big difference between the two. The debts get thin and the worries get fat because his wife probably isn't going to get better. She's a Mecklenburger from Hohen Woos.

My brother-in-law sold his place and is renting three hundred and twenty acres up north. But his ground is wet. It's also colder there. He doesn't really feel good and wants to come back here. He's even got money on interest — that means in the bank. Round here you can't rent anything anymore. And it's not too different by him. Anything that lies above the 100° latitude and to the west, lies beyond the rain line. A man needs to keep his nose away from that. Otherwise he'll get to looking pretty grim.

You asked me about Jochen Jalass and how he's doing. That's a story with a happy beginning and a sad ending. Four summers ago, three big guys with beards appeared on our doorstep, one even had a gray beard. They stood there all broad and wide, and then they said, "We want to visit you, and then we want to see where land can be had. Tell us, do you know who we are? *Kennst du uns noch?*" I walked round 'em. I looked at 'em from before and behind, but there was nothing that I recognized. So I said, "In my eyes, you aren't exactly the traders out of the story of Joseph and his brothers. You've just come to see where there's land available to farm. You are Mecklenburgers and you're from the gray counties, so round Eldena. I can hear that in your Deutsch. Otherwise, I don't know who you are. So tell me, where do you come from?" Then they said who they were, and that they were all out of our village. The one with the gray beard was Jochen Jalass, the blond was Fritz Schult, and the one with the brown hair was his brother. They all said hello from you and from my brother and from all the other ones there at home. They stayed a whole week with us.

We four old friends and childhood comrades were happy as larks. It's more fun being together with old friends than alone with old memories. They all came over here on free tickets. One cousin brings over the other. One brother brings over the other, until your whole relation is in America. Jochen Jalass got his ticket from his older brother.

When Jochen arrived here, his brother lay sick and didn't even know him. They hadn't seen each other for forty-seven years. Jochen started school the Easter that his brother left for America. On his sickbed, he couldn't believe that the man with the gray beard was his little brother. It took forever to persuade him. Finally he figured it all out and then cried his heart out. He patted him on the cheek as if he were still that little six year old. And the other one sat on his bed and told him all the stories about what was going on at home.

Our Jochen story has a sad ending. After his brother got better, the two of them were going to town to trade flour for corn. A man from old Krenzlin in Mecklenburg was also along. They were on a cart that runs on the railroad tracks. That's something we've got here: carts that run on the tracks. But a train sneaked up on them. The other two pressed themselves thin against the wire fence along the tracks. They yelled at Jochen to press on the fence. But Jochen wanted to throw the cart off the tracks, so the train wouldn't derail. The train threw the cart off the tracks and Jochen underneath it. He only lived a few minutes. He was a mensch you could rely on. He was really a hard worker. It was too bad for him. Es ist Schade um ihn. We were all sad.

You're probably saying to yourself, What are they doing building a cart that rides on rails? My dear friend, I can tell you that in things like this you soon figure out what side of the ocean you're on. If in Germany a farm cart would travel the rails and a train would run over it, every detail would be inspected to see whose fault it was. When something like this happens in the old country, everybody calls for the government to protect a person. Over here, it's a different story. There are no gates at the railway crossings in Iowa and when somebody gets run over, people say, "What's he doing on them tracks when there's a train coming? He should know better." Government in this country doesn't worry much about a person. In this country, people have to look out for themselves. When by you folks there's a railway accident you read in the newspaper: two dead, five wounded. Then the article goes on to tell their names, where they were from, and who they are. At the end they tell about the trainload and the cars. Here it's the other way round. Here the papers write first about the damaged goods and then at the end: sixteen dead and eight wounded. Railroads here are mostly private companies. They build pretty flimsy. There are some sections of rail lines that have a real bad reputation because there are so many accidents on 'em.

You asked me about Org Warnholz. In school we called him "Heben-kieker," Head-in-the-Clouds. Only the shah of Persia would know where old Hebenkieker has landed. I've never heard from him. His daughter lives here in the neighborhood. She never says anything about her father. She's in bad shape. She had one guy who sat in her rocking chair for a week, and let her look after 'im. He came to this country when he was twelve years old and still doesn't have twelve dollars to his name. She gave him the glove. In Iowa that's a saying. It means she showed him the door. Sie hat ihn laufenlassen.

My dear friend, today I'm going to tell you a parable. It's snowing out-doors, so I have the time. This will show you how with little money the first ones who came to America from our village could buy themselves a place, a farm. Those were the Dubbe brothers. The one of 'em didn't like it in Minnesota. So he moved to Wisconsin. He did real well there. Then he wrote to his relatives. I read that letter when I was just a kid. The letter carried the date February 18, 1851. Dubbe had bought two little farms, each was forty acres — together they cost him eight hundred and fifty dollars. Nowadays, that's just a little bit more than a big tip. The one place came with four oxen, two cows, fourteen hogs and fifty chickens, together with all kinds of stuff for the house and the barn. All that and eighty bushels of corn and two hundred bushels of potatoes. The two places lay next to each other. So he made 'em into one farm. Add to all of that, good buildings, level land, and heavy soil that in good years made forty bushels of corn per acre and in so-so years, twenty-five. And all of that for eight hundred and fifty dollars. Just think of it! Nowadays a farm like that of eighty acres with all the stuff you need to get started costs four thousand dollars. And that's what people bid — or, I mean to say, pay. According to old Dubbe's letter, in America they ate no black bread only wheat bread. Our whole village shook their heads over this. People said: "Sounds like the promised land." Dubbe wrote that there was also plenty honey or whatever you take for sweetening. Dubbe had so many sugar maples on that place, he didn't even count the trees. He drew off the sap and thickened it for sugar or syrup. Every year he had six hundred pounds of sugar and twenty cans of syrup. He put a piece of sugar in the envelope. It made the rounds in the village. I never did get to see it. By the time it got to me, it was all licked up.

Dubbe also made syrup out of pumpkins. Last fall he hauled ten wagonloads of pumpkins home. There weren't that many pumpkins grown in the whole district of Grabow in Mecklenburg. Quite a few fruit trees came along with that farm and a piece of woods with oak, beech, cedar, and some trees he didn't even recognize. When he wrote to me he hadn't started yet to fatten his hogs. Round the middle of February he worked on that. He paid out a whole five dollars in one year's time; that came out of his pocket. Beyond that he owed nobody anything, and nobody could demand he pay 'em one red cent. Not even the president. Only thing was, at the time wages were real high. So when Dubbe wanted a wagon built, himself he furnished the wood and cut it all to size and fit. But the wagonmaker still charged him forty-six dollars.

Otherwise that was like listening to a great song of praise. All that for eight hundred and fifty dollars. Just think of it! When our folks in the village heard of that white bread, sugar, and syrup, of that cheap ground and hardly any expense, they all shook their heads and said: "How can it be that there's that kind of country in our world, and we haven't heard about it until today?" In fact some of those Mecklenburgers put on their shoes and socks and left for America. The first ones were Dubbe's brother and sister-in-law. He sent them free tickets, and even old Willführ got things together and left. He was eighty years old. He's the one who said: "Once in my life I want to eat my fill of white bread." Only thing was, he died on his way across the big water. *Bloss, er ist unterwegs auf dem grossen Wasser gestorben.*

But old man Jauert warned the people: "What will I do with my white bread if I can't spread thick butter on it? Look, Dubbe has a real farm but he's only got two cows. That doesn't fit us. In Mecklenburg every farmer butchers at least one cow in the fall. With only two cows in America, you'd only have one left. Nooo, I'll stay with my black bread so I can spread it thick with butter. With eats like that, a body gets real strong. And believe me, I don't intend to plug up my belly with that old sticky syrup. Then those hogs runnin' round outside in February — that's 'gainst God's order for the world. Anybody knows that come fall, a real pig belongs in the barn and eats from the oats bin. Only that way do you get some decent bacon. But running round outside gives you a real mushy old bacon. That's not meant for my belly. And as far as I'm concerned, there's plenty work right here. Me, I stay put." Which is what he did, and he converted quite a few. They agreed and stayed in Mecklenburg. The real big immigration came later. That's when I left, and I have no regrets.

But by the time I got to the promised land a farm cost me a lot more than it cost Dubbe. Just think, eighty acres for eight hundred and fifty dollars. Put that in your pipe and smoke it.

At this my wife, Wieschen, interrupted my scribbling, "Jürnjakob, all you're doin' is writing about the farm and about money. Now why not tell him about the kids." I said, "Wieschen, if I'm writin' about business, there's reason for that. But if you want me to write about the kids, there's reason for that too." We've raised a good family. So now I'm going to give you the word about our kids.

7

As the Children Grow Up
. . . .

My oldest boy studied in Iowa City. He wanted to be a doctor, a real people-doctor. At first Wieschen couldn't bring herself to like it. She wanted him to be a pastor. Every mother loves to see her son in the pulpit. But he had no hankering to preach. And he got his way. It cost us plenty money, but he made good progress. He's got a good head, and he knows how to work. In his study room in Iowa City it was high style to look at people from the inside out. I says to him, "How do you do that? You sure can't put a hole in the belly and look in?" "No," says he, "we cut 'em open." Says I, "So that they can catch their breath?" "No, we do that so we know for sure exactly what a person is like on the inside." He made it clear why all this is good for people; 'cause today some are healthy, and tomorrow they're sick. Well I guess it has to be that way, but I says to him, "You do what you want in your school, but you stay out of my belly when I get sick. You've got nothing to see in there. That's one thing you need to promise me." At first he couldn't bring himself to like that. He says, "It could be, Father, that you get sick on the inside and an operation is the only way a doctor can help." I says, "That's in the hands of God, my child. And then you're not going to be my doctor. You'll have to get somebody else who knows his stuff. It doesn't feel good to me to think that you're poking around inside me when I'm your father." Well, finally he did make me that promise.

Course, he's my oldest boy, and since I have the time there's more to tell. Last winter while he was at college, he coveted worldly things against both the ninth and tenth commandments. He had it in mind to have a gold watch, a gold ring with a big stone, a gold tiepin, and all such things as that. That's nothing real bad, but the idea of it all bothered me. It doesn't fit into our family. So one day I walked with him out onto the fields

a mile or two and tutored him a lesson. It helped. Now, how did I do it?
Wie ich das gemacht habe?

My lesson went like this: "These days I've been daydreaming about my old village in Mecklenburg and our house there. For sure I'm gettin' old, and I do think about those things anymore. So now I want to tell all that to you so that you can imagine what it looked like and what that life was all about. It's good for a mensch to know where he comes from.

"Your German grosspa and grossma and I and my brother lived in a thatched-roof house. It had a low ceiling, but in our village it was the longest house. Inside there were two rooms: a little bedroom and then a big room for the kitchen and for sitting. If you're tall you'd have to keep your head down so's not to bump it on the rafters. That was no house for proud people. But if you stumbled into any of the potholes in the floor, then you could hold your head high. That's just how it was. The floor was

made of clay that we dug outside the village on the Püttberg. Oh man, it's just that a clay floor always breaks down and you get potholes. But on Sunday Ma would spread a new layer of white sand over it. So for one day a week things looked pretty decent.

"Things were real comfortable for storing potatoes. We didn't have to go down to the cellar or even to the pantry. All winter we kept 'em under the bed in the sitting room, so's they didn't freeze. Now that bed was even big enough to hide a fair-sized piggy, or just one medium sized. That way we had somebody to wake us up in the morning with a grunt or a squeal. Saved us from buying a clock.

"The walls of this house were made of lathe, covered outside and inside with clay. Straw was mixed into the clay. That way it held up better. In spring we could smell the lilacs through those walls and the sunshine came through, so we didn't have to open the door to let in a warm breeze. That's about how comfortable we were. The heat stove was made of good old bricks and was faced with clay from the Püttberg. The stove was a wonderful green. You could ask every potter in all Mecklenburg and not a one could tell you where that green was from, and the President himself doesn't know it. That was my Pa's secret. He had mixed cow manure in with the clay — that's how the stove got that beautiful green color . . . *darum sah der Ofen so schön grün aus.*

"We got our beds, trunk, table, and chairs free of charge. Pa made 'em. The wooden trunk had a separate little box on the left side, as the style was. In that compartment lay our money sock, as the style was. But we could all sleep comfortably because the money sock had no money in it. A little mirror hung on one wall. The silver backing was gone in several places, but we could see ourselves pretty nice in that mirror when we wanted to. There was also a Christ on the cross hanging on the wall and a Saint Genevieve. They had neither glass nor frame. They were nailed right on the wall, so's they couldn't fall down. As long as I can remember they were there, always.

"When it was time to gather wood, we and Ma would push our wheelbarrow to the other side of the fir trees behind Roden Söcken and pick up dry wood. That was one hour to get there and one hour to get back, and it was fun. Once in a while we'd see a squirrel in the trees. But Ma had to push until we got big enough to take over. She often had to set the thing down and catch her breath.

"Pa got paid four schillings for a day's work. At harvest there was work. Threshing would start already at three o'clock in the morning. For us boys threshing was a regular holiday. Sometimes we'd go up to the farmer's in the afternoon and play in the straw stack. Sometimes his wife would give us bread and butter. See, that's all it took to make us happy.

"This was what life was like until our Pa died. He had no strength in his lungs. He caught cold at harvest that year. From there it went into pneumonia. On his last day he said to Ma, 'This is not good — the harvest isn't in, but my time is up. Busacker will give you the boards, he promised me that. And old man Köhn will make the coffin without charging you. And our teacher will have the children sing *Christus, der ist mein Leben*, Christ Jesus Is My Life. Our teacher promised me that, *das hat er mir auch versprochen.*'

"Then Pa folded his hands and died. While Köhn's father nailed the coffin closed, I held the nails for him and felt very important. We were all just little kids. But after this Ma often had red eyes from crying.

"So, my son, now you know where we come from. And I don't need to tell you where you're going. Until you get there — where you're going — the main thing is that you be a real mensch who understands what he's doing. And when you get to that point here in America, then you need to travel to Germany, where there are some really good doctors. You will study there for a year and then come back here. Over there you'll have to stop at our village and see that old thatched-roof house for yourself and let that picture sink into your head and into your heart. You'll have to use your photograph maker to take a picture for me — just so it doesn't make that ol' house cave in. This picture I will hang in the front room. But this needs to be a good picture and that means you've got to know your stuff or you're not going to get a decent picture. In the next few days you've got to buy a good photograph maker and start right now to practice taking pictures. That old one you've got is good for nothing. People get scared when they see us in those pictures. That last picture you made of me and your mother, I have to say that's against the fourth commandment. But as for the rest of this, what we're talking about, that jewelry and all that others, just get that out of your head. In our family we don't need that."

He looked at me with a kind of a dead stare and didn't say a word. He did shake my hand. Then we headed for home. The boy did study in Germany for a year and stayed by you three days. He was in the village a week. The picture I asked for he brought me, and it is a joy in my old days. He even brought a picture of you in the school. And a picture of the stork on the roof of Brüning's house. Just think of it, the boy had never seen a stork 'cause you don't find them here. Can you believe that? But still, he had his own way, and about a year later he got himself a gold ring. But it was a simple one and completely smooth. I gave in and went along with that.

Of my second boy, I'm not telling much. He can write to you himself. His head is too hard for learning. In place of that the dear God has given him strong bones so that all his life he'll be able to take care of himself. He has grown and grown, and as he grows more he gets more bigger. His shoulders are powerful and broad and his legs are such that in a few steps he's already measured an acre. Oh man, but it's a good thing we built new when we did. He doesn't fit into little rooms. But wherever he joins in, everybody has a good time. You see, he has a very happy spirit. That's just the way he's made. And he knows farming from the bottom up. For farming his head is all doors and windows. Already he can stick me in a gunny sack. Ja, *den haben wir auch gut gereest*. Ja, we raised him up good.

Wieschen and my daughter Berti are baking today. That means stay away. That's also how to do it when they're washing clothes. I go into the kitchen, I say to Wieschen as I'm walking through, "Wieschen, we have to build again. This kitchen needs to be ten feet longer." "How come?" she says and looks at me as vun dummboozled mensch. Even Berti looked at me strangely. "Ja," I said, "this kitchen is too short for the bread — its head sticks in the oven and its hind end is in the yard. That's not even healthy for bread." Then she begins to scold and Berti chimes in, and now she's scolding again because I told her I would write that to you. So Berti says to her mother, "What a dummboozled mensch! Right Mamma? I need to twist his beard again — he's getting too smart in the mouth." My dear friend, I can tell you, those people who button right over left belong to a totally different nation.

This stove and oven in our kitchen are made of rolled steel. You can bake bread in that oven in thirty minutes and cook on the stove at the same time. This stove has six lids and under the oven is a space for drying fruit. Only this year we got no fruit. This stove cost me sixty-six dollars and that's without reckoning my labor. In America we have no big round brick ovens, topped off with clay, like the one under the plum trees in Köhn's backyard. I do think about old man Köhn every once in a while. After he stuck the bread in the oven, he would sit on that rock on front of it and fold his hands. It seemed to me that he was praying for a good batch of bread. I never saw his breadbaking fail. He was the kind of neighbor Luther writes about in the fourth petition of the Lord's Prayer: "Daily bread means everything that is required for daily life. . . ." Ja wohl.

My dear friend, last month my pen ran out of breath, but now we're ready to go to work. I really like to write. Especially in winter, it feels good to work on these letters.

8

A Little Farm and a Log House

• •

Things are real good by us these days. But the getting going has taken several years. What I wanted to do was put my feet under my own table. That's why I came over here: I had the feet — it's the table that was missing. Where to put that table was also missing. But my captivity in Egypt ended in freedom. My wife, Wieschen, had the same ideas I did. First of all, we wanted a little place so as to spy out the land and look it over from the inside out. Then we moved, and we moved again. All that took five years [translator's note: it's 1874 Jürnjakob Swehn time, and he's twenty-five years old]. I got real well acquainted with this land. Then I took hold, but slowly and cautiously. I am a Mecklenburger. We're not built for speed. I started off with a little farm, not too dry and not too wet. It was in the woods and miles away from the nearest neighbor. At that time you could still find cheap land.

The first thing we did was build a log house, *wir bauten uns ein Blockhaus*. There was plenty wood. I picked out the trees and cut 'em down. I trimmed and squared the tree trunks. At each of the four corners of the house I set up four huge logs — they could hold up during a storm. The others got laid up on the sides, that's how you get four walls. I plugged the cracks with clay. Then I smeared plaster over that, inside and out. That made it look better and made it hold up better. I also built a shed for the livestock.

Upstairs in the log house I built an attic room, and downstairs I dug out a cellar. The house had two rooms, just like old Mecklenburg — one for living, that was also the kitchen, and one room for sleeping, with two beds in it. I made the clothes cupboard myself. The cupboard was peculiar — he didn't want to close. Only when I pushed on his belly with my knee would he work the way he was supposed to. And then he'd squeal like a pig. As long as that cupboard lived, he squealed. I also made a chair and table. Each one got just the right number of legs. But they wobbled, and that's not proper. Man oh man, the windows were small, only two panes each. In the corner stood a little iron stove. It behaved itself real good in the summertime, but in winter it quietly made its own stink. Man oh man, but you can't please everybody. There are no tile stoves in America. In America everybody has a stove made out of iron.

When the house was finished I rejoiced. Now there was a beginning, and it was mostly the work of my own hands. The neighbors only helped lay up the walls. Building a log house doesn't take much time. It's the getting ready to build that takes the time. Laying up the walls usually takes only one or two days.

So I rejoiced. But every once in a while I found my Wieschen in a corner or outdoors twisting her apron strings. And as I cozied up to her in a friendly fashion, you'll never guess what she said. "If only the front room were as nice as the pigpen at your teacher's place in Mecklenburg."

Ho ho, I said to myself. This won't work. Jürnjakob, you get busy and cozy up to her so she gets a different faith. Otherwise you two will be in trouble right from the start and unhappiness will move along with you into this house, and then neither God nor mensch will be able to help. When the children are here, this will take care of itself. But till then you got to be her prophet so that she's not always twisting those apron strings.

So I took my Wieschen by the hand and went with her, once around the house, and then we went into the house. I pretended we were seeing it for the first time, and I had to show her everything and tell her all about it. "Nu, you look at dis all, Wieschen, and see how fine it is. And it's all good wood, und lauter gesundes Holz. The dear God grew these trees just for us and we didn't even know it till we got here. The trees didn't know it either, and the president didn't know it, and no mensch knew it, only the dear God. This is the same kind of log house Abraham built for Sarah. And Joseph the carpenter built akkrat such kind of houses. And even Joseph didn't have any better wood than ours.

"You look at them four tree trunks holding up the corners! You can have faith in them. They point in the same four directions we learned about in school. Nu, look you there around the corner: you can see down the meadow, over to Bäukenburg. That's the direction to our old Mecklenburg, and when you look that-away you can fold your hands and feel a peace. And over that-away, over that hill, the president of this land has his house, so when you look that-away you make a nice curtsy and I'll bow. Won't cost us a red cent.

"And now windows. Two of them. Old Noah had only one on the ark.

Now the sun looks in at that east window every morning and says, 'Hello! Get up! Go to work! I'm already out of bed.' In the west window, the sun peeks in when it's evening and says, 'You there! What's going on? Now's time to hit the hay. Tomorrow's another day. Sufficient unto the day is the evil thereof.'

"Then there are all those cracks in the walls. That's not all bad. Them cracks serve a purpose." Says Wieschen, "Tell me what they are good for?" And by now she's not twisting on her apron string. "Ja," I say, "dere's vere the fresh air comes in and the smoke goes out. That works better than those newfangled chimneys those townfolk have figured out. Ach, and Wieschen at night, when we're in bed and outside it's moonshine, all we do is turn our heads to see it. We don't got to get up and run to the windows like the rich ones do."

But Wieschen says, "What about when it rains?" My theory there is, let it rain. That works like real, genuine shampoo for the hair. And it's free. That makes hair grow good. Rain is also good for the land, but now I know she's got me. She's quick to say, "Ja, for the land it's good, *für das Land ist es gut aber nicht für die Betten*, but it's not good for the beds." So she has the last laugh and enjoys it. And I'm glad, 'cause laughing is better than crying. Laughing makes the eyes shine and polishes the heart.

So now it's my turn to talk. "Wieschen, you are a hundred times right. But now we're going to take that big tarp, pull it up over the bed and sleep deep. A roof like ours is just right and much better than if I would take my hat off and say 'Roof's done!' Nein, Wieschen, that houses in America also have roofs and are hollow on the inside is one dummboozled gut idea for America. And, it's a really good custom. *Das ist eine gute Sitte.*

"One step further. We're not done with this by a darn side. Here on the south wall is a hole. When our neighbors drive by we can stick out our hand and wave 'How goes it?' And when I'm in the field and somebody comes by, you don't even have to open the door. That helps, too, when tramps come along. You can size 'em up through that knothole."

My dear friend, I can tell you that that hole in the south wall did its duty for many years. If one of that other kind came along, we said hello through the wall, and we also said have a good trip. And if I was outside and Wieschen was inside, and I needed something, she'd pass it on out through the hole. But in winter we stuffed it with rags. One time I was in the field and she forgot to latch the door. And now a peddler stood there with his wares. But she didn't want to buy anything. Then he looked with disgust at our log house and said, "Oh man, you can see, this is where the *Powerlieschen* dances." She hauled off and gave him one or two with the broom handle between his shoulder blades. She had words for it too: "Man oh man, you can also see here how the poor women swats flies." That one moved along without a blessing and without doing any business.

My sermon on our house kept right on going. "My Wieschen, if you think that we have a one-room log house, you've missed it. 'Cause we have here three rooms and a kitchen." She looked at me bug-eyed and gave all the walls and me a good once-over. "What I say is true. Now pay 'tention." So I gets a piece of chalk and make two lines down the floor, crisscross. "Finished! Now there are three rooms and a kitchen. We just saved the money of putting up walls. Walls only get in the way when it's dark and you bumps your head on 'em. This one here is the sitting room. That's where we'll have that calendar with the pretty pictures — the one that storeman in town promised me. Let me say this, Wieschen, even the president doesn't have more days on his calendar than we do."

"Ja," said Wieschen, and she laughed. "It's a fine sitting room and there's where we'll put the visitors. They can sit under the calendar. Schön! And next door here is my room. This way everybody has their own saloon, and when we've got something for all of us to discuss there's no wall in the way." At that she even nodded yes and started to get excited, "Naturally, here is my kitchen, 'cause here is the stove. And next door here is the dining room, 'cause most half of the table is in there." "Oh, Wieschen, I agree. And when we want to take a little walk after dinner — it's good for what ails you — we've got the bush park in front of the door. Tell me now, how does this compare with the grand duke's palace garden in Ludwigslust? Dat is man an old tail-end of a stück. Ne, mit den Tusch ich noch lang nicht. I'm not trading places with that one."

Seehste, look at that, that's how she got another mind and left off with her sadness. Which was a goodness. A new beginning with no end of work, and then a sad heart, twisting on the apron strings don't go together. But I have to say, after the children arrived, they saw to it that she stayed happy. She didn't have time to be sad. That helped, 'cause by then I was mostly out in the fields. That's when I noticed how it goes when you know who and what you're working for and what keeps that chimney smoking. Then's when your ax bites in those trees but good and your scythe moves forward through grass and grain. From then on things moved ahead and things got better.

When I got the house done, I turned my ax on the brush. I was a real lumberjack. And that ax ate the woods. I made a mountain of firewood. For years we didn't have to worry about what to burn.

Now the house was clear, and I had pushed the woods back. I did that year after year. If I could, I grubbed out the stumps. If they sat too *fest*, I let 'em be. So then I planted and sowed around the big stumps. That was a picture. But you'll never believe the crops. Stalks on the corn like sewer pipes.

Later I dynamited them big stumps. That's the quick way. And I got me a team of horses. In the beginning that was plenty. There were no roads. Wherever you could get your wagon through, that was the road. That's how we regulated traffic. We did it ourselves. But tipping over was a part of it, and it happened to everybody. In those first years, I tipped over in the wagon more than anybody in our village did in twenty years. I was getting real good at it. Real roads came years later. Now it's all right. The roads are even straight. At first they were dummboozled crooked.

There's not much to say about the work. You can't put sweat into pen and ink. And sweat and work go together. Day in and day out it was the same. There's nothing to say about that. But as the years went on I turned the bush into fields and pasture. I pushed the woods further and further back. It was really thinned out. That made the ground worth more money.

My dear friend, I have heard it said that you have fewer blizzards when more ground gets plowed up. Is there anything to that? Somehow I can't figure it out. Luckily, we haven't had too many. But when they come you can thank God that they don't turn your house into a pancake.

While we were still in the log house we had a blizzard here. We stretched a rope from the house to the barn to find our way. We couldn't see our own barn, it was snowing that hard. Without that rope we would have lost our way and been killed. That blizzard even broke down one of those thick cornerposts on the house. Luckily, he [the blizzard] moved on. But wherever he went, we didn't have to mow that next year. He even took his toll in the woods. That next year we built us a stone house. Wieschen lost her faith in cornerposts. Me too.

Sundays I don't work. My father held to that and my mother too. Wieschen and I hold to that. One day a week the mensch needs to have peace and quiet, also the livestock. Besides, it's against the third commandment to work on Sunday. For most farmers in America, Sunday is a sleep day. When we don't go to church or don't go visitin' we sleep. In those first years we often couldn't travel far, 'cause it was too much for the horses. Five miles one way and five miles back on those roads was a long pull. So we slept, and we slept.

You don't need to think though that we were totally alone and godforsaken, like natives in the bush. We had plenty excitement. Once we lost a cow. She got out and by us that's different then by you. We don't just go out and find a cow and bring her home. No, it's more like Saul when his father's asses got out and got lost. I was a whole day underway before I found her. There she was in a clearing in the bush and grazing as if by us there was a famine. That she took off on a hike was not the worst thing. I could understand that — even a cow likes to see some different scenery. But that she grazed so on those old sour weeds when at home she got good fodder went against my grain. So I give her a few good thumps with my stick and then we headed home. Wieschen was happy to see us. This was her best milk cow.

Now here comes a different story. I drove to market with some pigs. We were still living in the log house. I was sitting up on the wagon seat, while down in the box them pigs were goin' wild. I talked to 'em friendly like — didn't do any good. I hollered at 'em in Plattdeutsch and American: "You quiet down." But the beasts paid no 'tention either to my Plattdeutsch or to my American. All to once, that biggest pig jumped and I and the wagon seat flew off and down we went. As I was picking myself up, here come those seven pigs. They scattered in all four winds. The hams took wings and off they flew. Even pigs like to see some new scenery. I after 'em in a pork-chop gallop. That was a job. I sweat it out, but I finally got 'em all back in the wagonbox. One big fellow broke his leg, 'cause he made such a revolution. That leg cost me some money.

My brother-in-law had such a time too, but by him it was different. He hitched up his horse, and he took a calf to town in a big box. Calf was quiet and my brother-in-law was quiet on his seat. The two of them went their way, didn't think bad of each other, and daydreamed along. Brownie pulling the wagon said nothing, the calf in the box said nothing, and the one in the middle said nothing. You know Heinrich as well as I do. It was a pretty warm day and he shut his eyes a little. That wagon jumped up and down, creaked and squeaked, then the back end come loose and the box slid off. Heinrich kept on going. He got to town and pulled up by the butcher. The butcher comes out, "Nu, vat gives here?" Says Heinrich, "A calf," and points with his buggy whip to the back end of the wagon. Heinrich is a Mecklenburger, he doesn't talk much. Says the butcher, "A calf? Ver you got him? In the White House?" Finally Heinrich turns around and — well, that face I would like to have seen. I collect faces like that. So he drove back, and there was the calf in this box. He was lying down, waitin' on Heinrich. Calves don't like to walk far. He was waitin' for a ride.

Now comes something different. Dat ist der Stinkkatze. We call it here a skunk. You don't have them. But don't let that bother you, 'cause that stink is a once-in-a-lifetime experience. Our dear God did us no favor here. The skunk is about as big as our cat, but his tail is longer. Those beasts smell awful and on rainy days they like to come up to the house. This is when a man learns that once in a while we could do without a nose.

One morning the children were sticking their noses in the air. I gave it no never mind. My question was, "Why so highfalutin' mit your schnute this morning?" I opened the window a little 'cause they pointed that way with their noses. But I never got a window closed faster than that. It wasn't that they were so highfalutin', it was the skunk smell in their noses. And the beast was already up and away. Once, of an evening, we had opened up the whole house after a rainstorm. All at once, like a cloud, it came in at the doors and windows. It was the stinkkatze. We closed everything up, quick. But it was already in, and it stays around until you have your fill of it.

One time the second boy shot one at a distance. Then he tied a long string on its legs and dragged it away. He tried to be careful because he didn't want to get it on his clothes. But we did have to bury his shoes and socks for a few days. My dear friend, you won't want to believe this, but you'll have to. There are people here who actually hunt this animal. When they get one, they cook out the fat and eat it. Their story is that this is the best of all cold remedies. Well, that takes a whole wagonload of faith and a strong stomach. No, if you would get a whole year's stink together in our old village and drain it into a bottle, that would be like incense compared with vun stinkkatze. Ja, well, my dear friend, in Chicago there are society ladies who wear a fur muff and collar of a stinkkatze in the winter. They say, that animal has been stinked out. I asked Wieschen about this. She said, "Ja, such a skunk fur is fine. I'd like to wear some." So I said to her, "I'm not having any stinking in this house. Get yourself a nice lambskin and hang it around your neck, that'll keep you warm." At that she made a mouth like a sugar scoop and said, "Vattings, our dear God also made the stinkkatze." So I said, "You're right, but it's still no masterpiece. And if you start with creation, I can tell you this: Eve wore only a fig leaf." She walked out of the room at that one. My dear friend, you won't believe me this one but you'll have to. That is a wholly different nation that hangs fur around the neck. And to make sense out of that, you'll have to make the nose stop its smelling.

9

All Kinds of Grief and Their Medicines

• •

Now comes an altogether different story. My dear friend, I want to tell you how I converted a mensch from drinking too much. His name was Smith — he was my neighbor for years. Here in our neighborhood we've got quite a few like him. He was highfalutin' to us and acted as if it was all grace when he stopped by. But see, even in a shirt this kind is naked. When they come home from the saloon, you see 'em layin' in the ditches. A year ago I counted six in one night.

My Smith understood three of the arts and sciences: stick up your nose, lazy around, and get drunk. That's why his place looked so awful. With that drinking, he got started in the morning and carried on all day. During the day he was a quiet drinker, evenings he began to talk. At that his third word was, "I was born a Christian, I was baptized a Christian, and I was confirmed a Christian." He had that down pat. But I heard it so often that I said to myself, Man oh man, just wait, you just meet me in the dark, and I'll teach you some confirmation. It was his wife who I was sorry for, and it was for her that I converted him. It went like so.

I had to go to town, and as I drove the horses down the street I see my Smith sittin' in the saloon, and at that it was a time when he needed to be at home. Whoever around here runs to the tavern all the time doesn't get much respect. As I noticed him sittin' there, the horses pulled up. I got down from the wagon and went in. I got a schooner of beer from the barkeeper. The others were already at the pure word of God, which means they were drinking whiskey. Smith sort of looked over at me and said, "Hey neighbor, come on over. I'm going to treat you." I said, "You don't need to treat me. I can treat myself. In an hour I'm coming by here. You be ready and come along. You wife is waitin' on you. *Versteh?*" He got a little edgy. He looked me over. He looked over his whiskey brothers. The old Adam in him was sittin' on the fence, dat means he limped on both legs. His drink friends said to him, "Don't pay no 'tention to that Deutsch-man. He ain't got no business ordering you around." So he started to buck and talked about being a free man and that he was born a Christian. I said, "I be back in an hour," and I left. An hour later I was there. His schnapps buddies were all gone, and he had run out of money for treats. So I took him by the arm and dragged him out to the wagon.

After I packed him in, I gave the horses the go-ahead, and then I said, "You still got a bottle in your pocket. So I'm tellin' you, from now on you don't drink a drop more, as long as you be on my wagon, *versteh?*" After we were a ways out of town, we drove into the bush. It was dark. I acted like I was asleep. But I had a little crack open in one eye. He looked at me, then he looked into the bush, then once more he looked at me. I was asleep except for one little crack. Then my Smith reached into his coat pocket and pulled out the bottle. He put it up to his mouth. Then's when lightning struck, and it wasn't from a bad parent. The bottle flew into the bush. I said nothing. He said nothing. The horses just kept on going. Now he started to think and to talk. First he sort of grumped around, then he got louder. Then he got mad, "Who do you think you are? You got no rights over me. I'm not gonna take anything from you. This is a free country. And it's not brotherly, and it's not Christian to knock that bottle out of my hand. I paid for that whiskey with good money. I been born a Christian."

After he got that far, he got no farther. I said whoa and pulled up. I said, "Ja and you been Christian-baptized and now I'm gonna Christian-confirm you. At that I laid him over a sack of grain and gave him some

confirmation with the handle of my buggy whip. I cut that handle off an oak tree about a year ago. You could trust it and with gemütlichkeit I got the business over with.

With that takin' care of I set him up on the sack, and off we went. So I said, "That business is over with. All right. You say this is a free country, so I used my freedom. I'll answer for it before God and the president. And also I'm going to keep an eye on you now, and if you hit that bottle again you're gonna' get it. You can bet on that. That's our secret agreement. I'm not doing this for you. Don't imagine that. It's for your wife. And it's so that your farm doesn't go to the dogs. If you hadn't let that whiskey take over your brains, you'd be sayin' to yourself, 'This whiskey bottle is nothing for me and this bottle is going to bring me into the grave.' So Sundays when we visit the graves and yours is there, somebody will say, 'Ja, dat is der Smith. Seven years he said to the bottle, I'm a-gonna git you, and in the eighth year the bottle got him. Ja, as a baby he sucked on a milk bottle, that didn't last very long. Then he began sucking on a whiskey bottle. That lasted until he got bottled. Now let's look at another grave.' On Sundays that's the funeral sermon about you and your bottle. *Das sind sonntags so die Grabreden über den Text von deiner Buddelei.*"

He choked up a little and wiped his eyes. I don't know if that was 'cause of my buggy whip or my sermon. So I kept on talkin', "Let that drinkin' be, straighten up, and I'll bring over a few loads of hay to help you out. To hold that hay down I can throw a sack of oats on top. Wieschen will have a ham and some sausages for you. That's better for the digestion than whiskey." Nu, man oh man, I giddyaped them horses.

He still lived neighbor to us for a few years. I kept a close eye on him and he knew it. But I have to say, until he sold his place and moved away, he behaved real good, and toward the last his farm looked quite a bit better. See, I converted him. People are all different. Some are converted by God's word and prayer, others by sickness and grief, and the third bunch by somebody's good example. But them last ones are converted by a stick and that's the sort that he belonged to.

It happens that you can booze more than you have the thirst for. It can also happen that you can let it be. You don't have to booze. The mensch doesn't need to drink so much that he runs over. Here's where I and those wild women agree. They want to dry up this country. But with the way they want to get rid of this boozing, no, I don't agree, *ne, damit bin ich nicht einverstanden.* A while back a dozen of them women got together here. They wanted to dry up our town and make a Temperance Town out of it. But they couldn't do it, 'cause they ran into the Unrighteous One.

He was Krüger the saloonkeeper. They begged him for the sake of heaven and earth to close his tavern. They paraded in front of his house. They prayed for him and they sang for him. Nothing helped. Then they threatened him with all the fires of hell. Finally, he said, "Na, if nothing helps, I'll have to do it. I don't want to sit in hell. But if I do you this favor, you have to do one for me. Only one little bitty one, will you do that?" "Ja," they said, "we will gladly do that." "Schön," he said, "Good, now pull up your skirts and show me your bloomer bottoms." They all ran off and never showed up again. Nein, Iowa will never be made into a temperance paradise like Kansas. There are too many Deutschmans here. I'm not one for drinking a lot, but I am one for drinking a little. But when I see a mensch drink water by the gallon, one glass after the other, just from lookin' at it I get frogs in the belly.

In this country we've had good health most all the time. For that we can not thank God enough. If Wieschen or I fall over out here in the bush, I hate to think what would happen to us. It's just too far to go for a doctor. Out here, nature has to help itself. When nature gets feeble, you pull up on the reins and get her to trot.

Ten years ago I had to go to the doctor. And I didn't want to. To me doctors smell like the graves in a churchyard. Na, my punishment for thinking like this is that my oldest boy is a doctor.

My problem was that I was all stopped up *hartleibigkeit*. That's usually not me. Home remedies weren't helping. So the doctor gave me his remedy. He said, "You take this — this will help." It didn't. I went back again, he said, "*Hast du laufen gemusst?* Did you have to go?" "No, it didn't work. Your medicine is too weak." "What! Too weak? *Und du hast nicht laufen gemusst?* Aren't you ashamed of yourself? That was enough to make a buffalo go. Na, you wait. I'll get you to go." So he gave me still more, and this time it worked. And how it worked. It cost me a dollar and a half. Na, the medicine man also has to make a living. Otherwise they don't see much of us farmers.

Now you know how some folks do it. They save all the leftover medicines and then they use them, sometimes a year later. Sometimes they mix 'em up and use 'em on altogether different sicknesses.

Johann Klüss had a horse with a bad leg. It didn't get better, and it didn't get better. The horse doctor gave him something to rub on it. It helped. Months later old Johann had it in his foot. And what did the mensch do? He rubbed it on his own foot. He claimed that stuff really did the trick.

But the best one was our neighbor Smith. The one I *verconfermiert*. He got some medicine for his wife. She had gout in the foot. She was supposed to rub it in. Well, two years later Smith had the flu. He took his wife's medicine. He said, "That was really 'spensive." Na, that was a Smith. As long as that kind is warm inside their fur, they never smarten up.

Just once I did a power cure. We were in trouble, and thank God everything turned out all right. My oldest boy was six. He got the diphtheria. We thought it was a sore throat, and we guessed that it would soon let up. And when we figured out what it was, it was too late. I harnessed up and went to get the doctor. He came back alongside of me. He examined the boy. He hunched up his shoulders, and he said, "There's no more that can be done. You got me too late. I'll leave some medicine. You can try it, but probably it won't help." Off he went.

It was nighttime, and I stood at the window and stared into the darkness. I prayed. Wieschen cried. The boy gurgled. He couldn't get any air. He got blue in the face. Then I had an idea. I thought, the doctor has given up on him. So, I can try something desperate. It can't do any more harm than's already been done. I poured a coffee cup full of kerosene and got him to gargle on that. He did it for quite a while. Then he started to spit up. It was all black. He got his breath and his face turned normal; it wasn't blue. Man oh man, but his throat was raw for a long time. That kerosene ate it up. But it also ate up what was suffocating him. Then I looked out the window again and had a few words with the Lord. Wieschen cried for a bit. All to once, I said, "Wieschen, I can't go to bed. *Ick denk man*, I'll look after the cows. You sit in that rocking chair and close your eyes. *Der Junge schläft*, the boy is asleep."

My dear friend, I can tell you that over here there are some strange cures. Three winters ago I visited with Mecklenburgers in Michigan. Their boy also studied to be a doctor. But he's a bend-and-break doctor. So far he's only worked on two people. Folks haven't got faith in him.

He bends and breaks people, and they're supposed to get better. He bends and breaks them on their living bodies. One hour costs two dollars. When we were boys we did it to each other for nothing. But I wanted to try it — I said it's a headache. So he started to bend me and break me. It felt good. But only in the beginning. All to once he got me where the ribs are short. That's when I jumped up and ran off. It tickled. He lost out on his two dollars. But his boy was playing on the porch. I gave him a nickel and said, "*Dor köp di 'ne Kauh för*. Now go buy yourself a cow." Wieschen sent his wife a ham in the mail.

Indian Stories and Letters from the Children
· ·

So, now my pipe is on fire and makes everything smell like tobacco smoke. Wieschen gives me a scolding 'cause *de ol witten Gledinen*, them old white curtains are gettin' yellow. "Wieschen," says I, "you don't know one color from the other. How come dat old black smoke from my brown pipe colors white curtains yellow?" And she says, "Jürnjakob," says she, "how come that a farmer's black cow with red socks eats green grass and gives white milk and yellow butter?" *Und in de Käk*, and in the kitchen there's laughter. That's my daughter, and she says, "How is that possible, Vadding, that the brightest lightning comes out of the darkest clouds?"

So, I had it. When you get into it with the womenfolk, you're in trouble. That's a whole different nationality that wears its hair long.

Last winter, your grandchildren wrote to me and wanted some Indian stories. Well, I can't do it, because I don't live around them, and I don't know them. I have the newspaper and an almanac. I have a Bible, a hymnal, and a catechism. I know my way around in them because they are God's Word. That's how come I know about the Cretans, the Arabians, and other characters. I also know the Parthians and the Medes, the Elamites, the Cappadocians, and the tail ends of Libya by Cyrene and folks like that. Ones, you hardly can pronounce their names. But in the Book of the Acts I haven't read anything about Indians.

Then those kids want to know if I have seen any Indians around here? No, not a one. We just don't have any as neighbors. They've all been pushed back and westward. Around here it's nothing but Low Germans, just like to home. Maybe a few High Germans and some English. When the four Dubbe Brothers moved to Minnesota, there were quite a few red men up there. They talked a whole different language. But they all got along good together.

Now two years ago I saw some of the red folks. I was visitin' Heinrich Fründt in Minnesota. You know him. He's the one whose Pa dumped over a load of your hay. And then the second time around, he got it in the barn but it all leaned over to one side, against the wall. It's his son.

Heinrich's youngest boy studies for pastor and has been pastoring some in a little town not far from his pa's farm. Some Indians lived near there — I saw 'em. Man oh man, their reservation is about seven miles away. Of feathers and tomahawks and scalps and stuff like that, we didn't see a thing. They act pretty sensibly, just like other folks. You can't fool them either — you can't make 'em out to be like *Eulenspiegel*. Only difference is, they're red and we're white.

I don't even know if they're good on horseback. At the World's Fair in Chicago they were in a big parade. But those Indians were really whites. They painted themselves red and dressed up like Indians. One of them was a Mecklenburger from Teterow. He was a Lehmbecker. You knew he was a white, and he was an eulenspiegel. I don't approve of that. He had four scalps with him that his barber had made.

The real genuine Indians came from their camps to town on pony carts. Ponies are ponies and can't be used for hard fieldwork. Usually they run loose in the bush. When you need 'em for work you have to catch 'em. Afterwards you just turn 'em loose again. In winter you stall 'em. And in winter they grow a real furry coat.

Indians have one main problem. That is drunkenness. I am no prohibitionist or temperance preacher, but I can't say I approve of drunkenness. One evening when I was coming home from the pastor's, some Indians were lying drunk in the ditch. That's how much whiskey they consume. Then I stopped the horses and looked at 'em, one after the other, and said, "Und sometime you'll all want to be angels! Na, our dear God will not be pleased when boozers like you come before him. All I can say is, maybe St. Peter will have a time bouncing you out." But they paid me no 'tention. They just stupor along.

It's only a few miles to their reservation, but they still like to beg for a place to sleep. No one wants to take them into their house. One showed up at the pastor's house, full of booze, just as pastor was fixin' to leave. His wife got a real shock. But when she was finished with the Indian, she managed to get him out of the house and lock the door. Folks say that they have a habit of taking things that don't belong to them. Their idea of property is a whole lot different from ours. Akkrat, so it is with some white folks too.

One of those Indians found a horseshoe that accidently was still nailed to a horse's hoof. But you can't believe everything you hear. Some people turn and run when an angleworm crosses their path.

That they have fallen into bad habits is because of drunkenness, and the whites bear the guilt for that. The whites have driven that booze devil into their bones. Now it's verboten. But they still do it. They do it like this: a peddler shows up at the Indian's with a big pack on his back. He's got colored ribbons, needles, chains, glass beads, and so'n Funzelkram, all kinds of junk. But his big pack comes off his back and inside it's hollow and full of brandy.

One guy came to their reservation with a merry-go-round and did a good business. But towards evening they were all staggering around. You'd think that going round and round made 'em dizzy, düsig. But then it came out that their düsigness had other reasons. That was namely brandy. That merry-go-round guy had brandy inside the horses and pigs and lions of the carousel. Under the tail and under the pigs' bellies were faucets. Even the wooden floor was hollow and full of brandy. They finally caught up with him and threw him in jail. They chopped his merry-go-round into firewood. And that's how it should be. The whites have nothing to brag about, neither to God nor to their neighbors. They should be bringing Christ to those Indians and getting 'em acquainted with work. Instead they give them the worst whiskey, it's rotgut. They should be helping 'em up, instead they are ruining 'em. The white man has corrupted the red man. The whites have poisoned 'em.

Nein, das ist doch nicht richtig, no, that's not the whole story. The reds are in trouble because they don't work. The land belongs to them that work. That's true all over the world, and it's also true here in the States. America will only succeed because of work, and the red man doesn't work. Here, in the last few years, some have built really nice little houses. But they don't keep 'em fixed up and cleaned up. And they're no good on the farm.

Missionaries are busy at work to convert them to Christ. Our pastors say that then they'll learn how to work. They want to undo the sins of the schnapps. I believe they're too late. I believe that before the red man converts to Christianity and to work, he'll be dead and gone.

All the rest of the Indian stories you'll get from Berti and from your grandsons. Because I promised Berti a trip, I took her along with me. She stayed at Fründts over Christmas.

My dear friend, this time it's Berti who's going to make a letter swim over the great water pond. It's letter number one. I'm going to glue him up tight so that no water gets in. If he drownds, please write me about it.

Dearest friend,
This summer I went with Father to Muscatine. There my eyes saw a real steamboat. In fact, I took a ride on it. That was schön. If I have the time, I'm going to travel to Germany and visit you. You are my father's best friend and also my best friend. But our Pastor Fründt's wife is another really best friend.

Our new teacher is married. His wife is also really nice. She is teaching me how to crochet.

In school we're getting a Christmas tree. Also at church. I have already been confirmed.

Father lies on the sofa and smokes until our white curtains are all yellow. Mother sits in the rocking chair and scolds. But he just laughs it all off. That's because it doesn't make work for him — he doesn't wash the curtains. But I still love my papa.

I have learned to ride. I learned two years ago. I often rode with the pastor's wife to see the Indians in their camps. I and Papa visited the Fründts. If one of your grandsons has time, he can come over and visit us. I want to look him over. Please, tell him from me, and don't forget. What's his name? We can ride out together. Father says that he doesn't have to bring his own horse along.

Father says I'm supposed to write you about the red man. I said, "Yes, Papa." So, on the first day when I went to town and got me a pencil two real Indians rode by. Their children don't come to the German school. They only go to the government schools. There's nothing wrong or bad about Indians. It's just that Father complains about them because they don't work.

The little Indian girls are very shy and duck down and scatter like baby chicks. We had over a hundred this summer — chicks that is. But the Indian boys like to play ball and hit good. In school they are very friendly. Also in church.

But they don't want to be converted. So the pastor is really after them. His wife helps out in the Indian mission. She can't count up many converts either.

One Sunday Pastor was away. So Hans rang the bell. Hans is the brother of the pastor's wife. Hans has blue eyes and brown hair. He's studying to be a pastor. When he finished ringing the bell, he played the organ. But see, I pumped the wind and Pastor's wife preached the sermon.

First off, she told a Bible story. You know that story. It's the one about the storm, where the little boat was covered by the waves and Jesus just kept on sleeping. Then she explained the story and they listened up. When that was over, Hans played and I pumped up the wind. He sure can play. He also wants to study music. He's going to give me lessons. That will be wonderful.

That Sunday there were no converts again. Which is really too bad. Now I can't write you why this is happening. Father says it's because they're lazy. But Mama says, "Be patient, it'll come." The way God's Word works is the way Father works. When the farmer plants, he can't harvest on the next day. That's the way it is. I can understand that.

Now comes something new. That's our cat. First she jumps up on a chair, then onto the table. Now she takes her paw and pats me on the cheek. That really tickles. I walk slowly through the room. She walks alongside of me like a dog, back and forth. Cats do not like to run — it's their nature. Her name is Little Pussy. But Papa says her name is Miess. She is black and white. Now I'm going to chase her away.

The Indian women wear their hair loose, and they wear no hat. For their dresses they need twelve to fourteen yards. They wear a loose jacket and a long wrap-around. On Christmas I was at their celebration. The synod gave them twenty-five dollars. The farmers gave them something for the stomach and to keep warm. Pastor's wife bought a whole bolt of cotton. Hans brought it from the store. I went with him. I said, "Let me carry it for a while." He said, "No, that's not proper for young ladies." He meant me. Well, so then, man oh man, do it.

The pastor had to help cut and sew. She sat next to him and explained how he should do that. It didn't go according to our styles today, because every skirt had five panels so that you can wear it when you ride horseback. Then we sewed bands on the skirt, six plus. My most honored teacher, you can imagine how long it took to do this.

Evenings, my little kitty gets lively. Father sits and smokes and writes. mother and I knit and darn and mend. The kitty sits on the table like the president and watches our hands. She doesn't like it when our fingers move so fast. She gets up real quietlike. She moves closer. She takes her paw and taps on my knitting needles and on Father's pen. She crinkles up her face. She wants to say, "Oh dear people, don't be in such a hurry. You can't keep this up forever. Calm down. It will all get done in its own time, according to Solomon, as Father says." After this, she goes back to her place. Then Father puts down his pen and we put down our needles and we all have a good laugh. That's our break time from work, because you can't work and laugh at the same time. A really good arrangement. But kitty stays real quiet and doesn't laugh. When she's quiet like that, Father says an unruly child can take a lesson from her. He means me. He's always picking on me.

The cotton for the skirt was dark blue with white polka dots. That's why we put red bands on the skirt, the waistcoat, and the sleeves. That way it looked real friendly and not dull. I folded it all up and that was the story of their Christmas clothes. Dear friend, I can tell you that they also got shoes, stockings, hair ribbons, and handkerchiefs. Hans said that three years ago they tied the handkerchiefs around their necks. Now they use them for their noses. Also, they have big kerchiefs that they tie around themselves when it gets cold on the reservation. What presents did you give the girls in your school this Christmas?

Their boys get pants, shirts, handkerchiefs, scarves, and combs, also nuts and candy. But they don't say thank you. It's their custom from old times that they never say thank you. But I could see it in their eyes that they liked their presents. Their eyes got real big. And they looked at us friendlylike.

They are polite. Much more polite than the Germans and the English. Some of them even bow their heads. They do it in church and also on the road. Hans says, "Some Germans could take a lesson from that." They always call out: "How do?" That means, how do you do? *Wie geht es ihnen?* But they don't say this as a question. It's more like a greeting. It's like when we say, *Guten tag.* One time we met one in the woods. He spoke to us in French, and Hans said his French had a really good accent.

It's really the truth though that they are often tipsy. Father is right when he says that. So in the evening I don't walk those paths that lead to their camps. The other girls also don't walk there, because too many of them are lying in the bushes.

When I'm outside my kitty always walks next to me. She acts as if she's a dog. Father says, "It's a mistake that she was born a cat." He says, "She needs a name like Stromer." He says, "That's what the Mecklenburgers call their dogs."

When I'm visiting neighbors she comes along, and Sundays she likes to go to church. So I have to chase her back home. Once she did come along. The other kids thought that was funny. She stood behind me. She said, "Meow." She said it right during church. I was ashamed down deep in the the gray ground, *in die graü Grund.* That's one of Father's Mecklenburg sayings. The church elders chased her out. Afterwards I got one of Papa's scoldings. I promised that it wouldn't happen again. So we made up, and it never did happen again. But I was ashamed of myself for a whole week.

I'm starting to play the organ. I'm taking lessons from our teacher. Our organ is in the parlor. Father says, evenings he wants to hear the songs he sang when he was in your class.

Now look, Father made that inkblot. He presses too hard on the pen point. It squirts and then breaks all the time. His fist is heavy and used to pushing the plow.

Papa is a favorite person, but he only shaves on Sunday morning. So during the week his cheeks are scratchy, and on Saturday his chin is a forest. Papa has such broad shoulders, the whole family can hide behind them. The inside of his hands is like tree bark, and they scratch when I touch them. He is a happy person and moves real good. When he gets going, I have to run to keep up. But in his right eye he has a rust spot. It's a streak that runs southwest. Father said he wanted to pass that on to me, but there was a mistake and both of my eyes are totally rusted up. Hans says my eyes are gold-brown. I say that is *Quatsch,* which means nonsense. But I like to hear Hans talk about my eyes. Sometimes they are even blue. Write me about this. I need to know why. Please don't forget.

When Papa sits still and reads, I sneak up behind him. Then I pull his beard. Then he reaches out to get me. Then I get scared. Then I jump back. Then we both have a good laugh. Then he makes a serious face and says, "Girl, do you know the fourth commandment? *Dirn, kennst du das vierte Gebot?* Is that your Sunday afternoon fun, to pull your old father around by his beard?"

Papa loves to hear me sing your songs, but he sure doesn't think much of bird songs. Once when I was saying nice things about the nightingale, he says, "Ja, when one of them nightingales weighs around eighteen pounds at Thanksgiving and sings like a turkey, I could get interested." Father belongs to the tribe of Israelites that like to eat and don't like to go hungry. Last Sunday we ate chicken the way black people cook it. Mother and I cut the chickens up. I dipped the pieces in cornmeal, and Cora dropped one piece after the other into a pan of hot fat. The fat and the cornmeal give the chicken a thick crust and keep in the juice. Mother says the black people's recipe sure beats the German one. Papa wipes off his mouth and says, "The people who make a recipe that good are not among the least of God's nations."

Cora is my oldest brother's wife. He looks after lots of sick people. She's here to visit with her little Charly. Father carries Charly around on his arm. They both like that. Yesterday Papa carried him around in the parlor. Then he stood real still. He took his pocket watch out of the left pocket and stuck it in the right pocket. After that he shook his finger at Charly and said, "My little chicken! Don't you get into my vest pocket the way you did on Sunday. My watch stopped!" Father is very particular about his watch. Evenings, he hangs it on a hook, but then he can't see it very well from where he's sitting. Cora hangs her watch on another hook — he can see her watch real good. But when he wants to see what time it is, he won't look at Cora's watch. Nein, he turns himself all the way round till he can see his own watch. Cora says, "Papa, why do you insist on doing that?" Father says, "My child I don't want to wear out your watch!" And he looks at her, real serious like. Ja, that's my Papa.

That's also how I know him. If I don't understand something that's in the newspaper, then I ask him about it. Once people were complaining about our railroad. They didn't like the way the last car on a train rattles and jerks. It was even in the papers. I said, "Papa, what can we do about that? — to keep the last car from rattling and jerking? Is there a cure?" Ja, he said, "I know a cure. Ich weiss ein Mittel. They should unhook the last car, then it wouldn't rattle and jerk around." What do you say to that? Ja, that's my Papa.

Last winter he had to drink a cup of linseed tea every evening, because he had a very bad cold. He didn't want to do this. And I kept an eye on him. This was how he did it: (1) He walked around it several times. (2) I put my handkerchief over my mouth to keep from laughing. (3) He made a face like three days of bad weather. (4) I put my handkerchief over my mouth. (5) He drank the tea and shook with the chills. (6) I broke loose — I couldn't keep from laughing. (7) He grabbed me by my braids and praised the tea. He said, "You should drink a cup of tea like this every evening — it would do you good." (8) I said, "Nein, Vater, when I see you drinking tea, it's better than a whole bottle of medicine."

Often Father says, "A mensch needs order in his life. When things get funny, a mensch needs to laugh, when things get serious, a mensch needs to get serious." For us, that happens at evening devotions. That's when Papa takes care of everything that got left behind during the day.

Last week, old man Reusch visited, and mother wanted to cook an applesauce. But while I and Cora were peeling the apples, we ate too many. mother scolded, she said it's not right to do that when we have so few apples. But we had a good laugh over it. That evening Father opened the Bible and said, "Tonight we're going to read Proverbs, chapter twenty-eight. He read and he read. Then he said, now comes verse twenty-four. That is a verse that children and young people often don't take to heart. Now this is a word of the Lord they need to note so that they can live according to it. Then he read the twenty-fourth verse: "Whosoever takes from his Father or mother and says it is not a sin, he is a son of perdition."

Ja, said Mother, die schönen Äpfel, those beautiful apples this afternoon. Papa didn't say a word, but he read verse twenty-four a second time, slowly. I and Cora turned red, clear behind the ears, as Father reprimanded us out of God's Word. Then he read further on in Solomon. When he finished the chapter, he looked at us, one after the other. Then he asked me: "In what chapter do you find that verse?" I couldn't even remember it. He asked Cora. She didn't know it either. He said to old man Reusch, "This forenoon you said I had raised a fine family. But when I ask the young ones about the Bible, they don't say a word." mother said, "Na, they're still young." Then Papa looked at mother, "Do you know which chapter we just read?" She said, "Ja, give me the Bible and I'll read it for you."

Papa said, "Between a clover field and a cornfield there's a real narrow line, and also between worldly things and holy things. But God gives the mensch eyes and understanding so that he can see that line." He said it all quietly and peacefully. All three of us were quieted and ashamed. Today, I'm no longer ashamed, but I'll also never forget Proverbs twenty-eight, verse twenty-four.

Praise the Lord! This letter is done. I have been working on it for seven weeks. So I'm really pleased. Are you pleased to hear from me? You have to write me soon.

Greetings from Berti, your dearest friend.

Nu, Bertis Bruder schreibt einen Brief. Now Berti's brother writes a letter. Honored friend!

Now it's my turn to send a letter over the water of waters. Wie geht is dir? How goes it with you? I'm doing good. Honored friend, I have heard that where you live everybody speaks German. Therefore I want to write you in German. But I do better in English. Father has to help when I do German. All summer long I went to German school and learned from a map of the world, three feet by four feet. You live on the tiger's back, because on the map, Germany looks like a tiger. But I can't see your house. Father says that's because it's behind the Bäukenberg.

We have three different reading books: the first, the second, and the third. I'm in the third book. In German school we really learn the catechism. We also learn hymns. It's hard. Some don't get it, that's also hard. Then there's the paddle. Some get that. Some kids are just plain lazy. But we have thick clothes on, so it doesn't come through. First of all, we have more than one undershirt on. Then a sweater. Then overalls. Then a jacket. But over that I wear a heavy coat. In school I take the coat off. How is anybody going to get through all of that? And sometimes it's just a woman. Only in the summer does she get through.

Father always gets through. But he makes me take stuff off. I say, "Father, this is embarrassing." He says, "That's no problem, I've got time." When he's through I feel bad. I say to myself, Is this a life? I answer myself, It's pure sauerkraut! Afterwards, we get along better.

When the mud is bad the girls stay home. Yours too? I like that. If we get there too late in the morning, *das geht*, that's all right. This winter I went to German school again. Next summer I'm English. In school it's only my tongue that's English, in my shirt I'm German — that's what Father says.

When I was little I wanted to be a millionaire. Father says, "That's a good job." I already own two dollars. I said, "Father, what's the pay when I get my first million?" He said, "When you make your first million, you'll get counted in the next census."

Lieber Freund, ich kann dir sagen. I tell you I like to eat. Father says, "That's what you get for being a Mecklenburger."

We eat our lunch at school. Home is too far away. We take our lunch pail along — once upon a time my lunch pail was a syrup can. The cover is a frying pan. We lay them on the stove at school with our sandwiches and sausage and bacon in them. The stove is flat on top. Na, there's where they get broken in. But our teacher, she has a good nose and complains about the smell. Father says that's because the stove stinks. I say it's because she has a German nose.

We also take mother's canned fruit to school. At noon we have an hour's time to eat and play. That's not enough. When I get to be president I'm going to make new laws so that lunch lasts two hours. We play hunter and the deer, also teeter-totter. That's a good ride. We also play prisoner. But then we run off from the policeman. He just stands there with a long face.

In the winter we jump from the fence headfirst, *kopfüber*, into the snow. Another thing we do is drill through the snowdrifts with our heads. One boy got stuck. We pulled him out by his feet.

The girls also have games. They play little Mary sat on a rock, run through, run through, over the golden bridge, *Fuchs du hast die Gans gestohlen* — fox you stole the goose — and on and on. But they are just girls.

We also play games during school, only the teacher better not catch you. If she does, you'll be sorry. Sometimes we drop matches on the floor and rub them with our shoe soles. That really stinks. Then she sees it — she sees it with her nose. That was the end of that game.

Last fall we made music with goose feathers. But she saw that with her ears. And that was that.

Honored friend, all good things end too soon, especially if they're fun. When I get to be president, there's going to be a different *Schulordnung*, order in school. And the teacher will have to give us our goose feathers back.

Once there was a day when we had to make up and write sentences. A girl wrote, "A chicken reaches with both feet until it stands on the earth." We had a good laugh over that. Father also laughed about that. Another girl wrote, "In March the rabbits lay eggs, and they hatch in August." We had another good laugh. There are many rabbits around here. Father wants to wish them all to Siberia. *Aber see! Ich fange sie in der Falle.* I catch them with a trap.

Last summer I did the corn by myself. We also bought a hayloader. It takes a swath eight feet wide and is hitched up to a wagon. I drive the horses. Father's in the middle and makes that hay fly. Sometimes he falls on his back. Then I whoa the horses. After that, we go home with a hurrah. We unload in five minutes. The door on the gable of the barn is seven by ten feet. But sometimes the forkful is so big it won't go through.

Last summer we hauled in eighty loads. The barn doors move on wheels and get pushed back. When we empty the wagon we load it with manure and take it out on the field. We do the manure like this: a cable runs through all the stalls up to the door. A bucket hangs on the cable by little wheels. With a lever I drop the bucket and fill it with manure. Then I push the lever and the bucket goes up. I give it a push and it runs on the cable up to the door, then the cable goes down and runs outside the barn. There the bucket tips over and dumps the manure in a wagon. We have a big farm with all kinds of stalls. So we also have lots of cables and wagons. It's a regular cable railroad in the barn. Na, well, that's how we work with our manure, 'cause we're practical people.

Mowing is something I'm good at. At first I did poorly. The scythe wobbled back and forth, and Father watched. He finally said, "You're like Joab. First the sword eats this one, then that one." And he shook his head. But anymore the scythe doesn't do much. The machine does the mowing.

John Williams is a year older than I am and a foot taller. *Aber see! Ich schmeisse ihn runter.* I wrestle him down. Then he kicks around with his legs in the air. Then he *schimpft*, "Dammed Germans!" and tries to boot me. Once he really got me. So I grabbed him by the back legs and dragged him through the wheat stubble. I said, "I'll drag you to Chicago if you kick me one more time." He just meowed around. He's got legs like our black sheep buck. But mine are thick and tough. Father says, "You did good, throwing him down."

Half of the pigs in Iowa are dead from cholera. We haven't lost any. Our pigs really cleaned up on the apples last year. We had lots of apples. This year the frost came too early. Our apples froze hanging on the tree. One neighbor lost three thousand bushels. We ordered three barrels of apples from Michigan. Each barrel holds four bushels. A bushel of apples costs a dollar sixty-five cents and the freight for a barrel was a dollar forty-seven. It took ten days for them to get here. But they arrived in good condition.

Our house has a telephone. So do our neighbors. Our telephone can talk Plattdeutsch — Low German. Father bought a piano. Honored friend, do you know what a piano is? In Springfield they wanted four hundred and fifty dollars for a piano. Father bought it in Chicago. It's the very same piano and cost three hundred seventy-five dollars with freight. I'm supposed to learn how to play it. I'm also supposed to learn how to play the organ. That is very hard. The organ cost eighty-five dollars. Ploughing with the machine, sowing, and mowing are things I like to do better than to pound around on them white and black keys. Wrestling with John, that's also something I like to do.

I have a BB gun, but I haven't hit a rabbit yet. There's too much room behind the rabbit and in front of the rabbit. I'm much better at hitting chickens — they're not so quick. When I get one, mother scolds me and then she cooks it.

Ich bin dein Freund, I am your friend. Hans

At the Chicago World's Fair

· ·

It's been quite a while since I last wrote you, and now for several weeks snow covers the land. So I'm sitting in a warm kitchen and writing this letter with my own hands. I aim to tell you about my trip to the Chicago World's Fair. To tell it will take longer than to see it. Na, the snow will probably hang around until I'm finished. The drifts are so bad you can't even see the fence. Now the trip was already quite a while ago, but I still remember everything I saw and heard.

Old Schuldt came to me. He said, "Do you want to come along to see the World's Fair? Völss is coming too." My question was, "What do you want there?" "To see something and to get taught something." "That's going to cost quite a bit of money." "We'll fill our pockets before we go." "Going to be a big crowd there?" "When we arrive there'll be three more." "Are we taking the wives?" "No, let him who loves his wife leave her home. Otherwise after we've seen it all, there's nobody to tell it to." Now that made sense to me.

My buyer in Springfield got married. He wanted to go on a honeymoon, but he didn't really have enough in the bank to do it. So he left his wife home and went on the honeymoon alone. It was cheaper that way. Afterwards, he had all kinds of stories to tell his young wife. Whether or not she was happy about that, he didn't say. Neither did she.

After I thought it over, I left my wife to home. I pulled on my best World's Fair boots and went along. About nine the train was ready to leave Springfield, but it was a full house and we needed to hitch up another team to the wagon. Then off we chugged. At seven o'clock the next day we were in Chicago. *Jungedi, die Menschen*. By golly, lots of people. We went to a hotel — one dollar for board and room. They even gave us a lunch to stick in our pockets. By the time we got to the fair, we had sat on it so hard we couldn't bring ourselves to eat it.

We had to walk a mile to get to the lake, and then ride three miles on the streetcar. It cost ten cents. Then I left 'em all behind. They were too slow. Völss said, "Don't get in trouble." I just got going. Whatever int'rested me, that's where I stopped to stare. What didn't int'rest me, I left behind.

A little kid started to cry. I looked around. It was a girl about three years old. She was lyin' on the floor. I helped her up, I thought: this is stupid, a little girl in all this confusion. What is she going to get out of this? Then her mother got there. She screamed at me, "You knocked my child over. Can't you big drink of water watch where you're going?" I got out of there in a hurry.

I walked into the German House. There were the apostles in life size watching quietly as the people went by. I hurried to see them, I had eyes for nothing but the apostles. Some sixteen feet before the apostles, there was a step down. My foot caught and *bums* I went down, nose first. Man oh Man, I hit hard. I layed at the apostles' feet. All eyes were on me, and they laughed. But the apostles didn't laugh. Not even Judas. They just looked on quietly and earnestly. *Sie kuckten ganz ernsthaft weiter.*

The next day we went out again, and I heard somebody start cussing. He knew what he was doing. I thought I'll listen in. He's using some really new words. So I shut up, that way I could keep an eye on him. But Schuldt said, "He's cussing you. You knocked over all his bananas." I didn't notice. Anyway, we hurried up out of there, and I said to myself, Jürnjakob, you need to look where you're going and what you're doing or you're going to get in trouble. So I took hold, and then we went into the California Building. They were selling orange wine. It looked pretty good. Schuldt said, "I'm up for three glassses." Völss said, "Me too." I said, "And me too." Each one of us downed three glasses. Schuldt licked his chops and nodded yes. So did Völss. So did I. All of a sudden Schuldt looked to heaven and said, "My stomach *geht auf Touren,* is churning up a storm." Völss said, "Mine too." I said, "Mine too." "I think it's that orange wine," said Schuldt. "So do I," said Völss. "So do I," said L. We got going and had to go.

There stood a Yankee, six feet tall with a stovepipe hat. He looked us over good. "Walk in, gentlemen. Walk in. Only five cents." Those were his exact words. But I can't give you an exact picture of his face. That was worth another ten cents. And there was a big curtain over the door. I think this long lanky American did a pretty good business that summer.

There was a lot to see at the World's Fair. Even the Salvation Army came on with weeping and wailing, with singing and praying. They marched up with flags and hallelujahs. First they stood still, then they stomped around, beat their chests, lifted their eyes to heaven, and made quite a spectacle. It was all intended to get us to repent. According to them, Chicago and its World's Fair was Sodom and Gomorrah. And if fire and brimstone didn't come down on it, they were the ones to be thanked. They put on quite a show, and people listened to them the same way they listened to the guy who was peddling cotton. Then they moved on.

America is not much for going into your closet for prayer and then pulling the door to. Another group that wanted to convert the heathen was the Mormons. We were the heathen, but we weren't about to convert to the Mormons. What would Wieschen say to that!

On one corner a preacher stood on a box and declared a new religion. His aim was to improve the world and make it healthy. After he finished, his helper came with a collection plate. But at this the crowd left. We thought we'd take in that sermon on improvement and good health. You can always use some of that, if it doesn't cost too much. We pushed ourselves up front. And who's standing there? Krischan Hasenpot. He comes from Mecklenburg, around Grabow. Krischan lives in our neighborhood.

There are all different kinds of people. Some are like so and some are like Krischan Hasenpot. My dear friend, I can tell you he doesn't have his head on right. Usually he's quiet. Once in a while, though, he gets going with God knows what for ideas. He's no dummkopf. There he stood. He was right up front, and the preacher on the box was working on him. First he talked about being nervous, how you get that way, what it feeels like, and that this is the sickness above all sicknesses. "And this is the sickness you've got," he said to Krischan, "I see it in your eyes. Behold, the Whiskey Devil has got into you and brought along his six brothers. They have made themselves at home in you and are running your life. You must quit drinking and turn to a sober life. Repent! Repent, so that the devils depart from you! Otherwise, you'll be dead in a year's time."

That's how they crowded Krischan Hansenpot and pounded on him. At first he listened thoughtfully. But in his life Krischan never drank a drop and when the man on the box preached the seven devils, of boozing and that death was a-comin', old Krischan shook his head and said, "*Dat is en scharpen Tobak, säd de Düwel*, that is one strong tobacco, said the Devil, when the hunter gave him some twelve gauge of shot in the face." This preacher didn't know any Grabower Plattdeutsch, so he bored into him even harder, "It's because of you that the Lord has sent us here today, my brother and me." Krischan looked at him earnestly and said in Low German, "Birds of the feather, said the Devil, get together and he walked off with a lawyer." "From afar we have come to you," said the preacher, "to bring you the love of the Lord Jesus." Said Krischan, "Schmart people like each other, said the fox, as he ran off with the goose." The preacher and his brother began to schmier it on thick — praise, friendly words. They thought Krischan was going to repent and be converted. They put their arms around him. But he wiggled free. They lifted their eyes to heaven and praised the Lord. Then they mopped the sweat off their brows, and Krischan said, "When people start singing, then you can take your seat, said the Devil, and sat down into a swarm of bees."

After that the two of them began to pull little bottles out of a crate.

They showed them to the crowd and called out: "The world's salvation! The world's salvation! This recipe comes from the Holy Land. Three thousand years ago an angel brought it from heaven. Then it was passed on to the Indians. They hid it like it was the greatest treasure. But the spirit said to me: fast, pray, go, seek, find, learn, heal! Therefore I'm here and here it is for all of you. The world's salvation. The Virginia Wonderwater." At that Krischan stretched out his neck and said, "Simple but schön, said the Devil and painted his tail green." "In these past few years this has healed peoples of all nations from one ocean to the other, even in France and Peru. I sent it to missionaries in Africa, and the Empress of China ordered it for her son. It's only a little bottle, but what it brings is the salvation of the world." Krischan answered, "Something is better than nothing, said the Devil, and stuck his tail in the tar bucket." "Five to ten drops of this medicine in a tablespoon taken with water, will drive out the Whiskey Devil and all his demons. This Virginia Wonderwater is the best remedy for dizziness and constipation. Rub it in the eyes of the blind and they will see. From Mexico an officer wrote me. He had lost a leg in battle. So he rubbed this medicine into his wound and lo, it helped. Look all of you, here is the letter with his original signature. This is the universal salvation of the world! The Virginia Wonderwater! Today, only one dollar the bottle! One bottle for one dollar."

Then they came at us with a bottle and a collection plate. Nobody bought anything. So they began to storm at us. Still nobody bought anything. So then Krischan Hasenpot said, "These eel fish are really thin this year, said the Devil, and he had an angleworm in his hand."

So we went back to the Deutsche Haus. There we had to give ten cents for a glass of beer. Other places only wanted five cents. This made me angry. Then I wanted to smoke a cigar. What did it cost? Twenty-five cents. Then really I got angry. I said, "The Germans are worse than the Yankees." "Oh," the bartender said and laughed, "don't scold so. You're a German yourself." I got over it, but I didn't buy a cigar.

Next we came to another show. The Yankee was preaching out front, "Welcome! Welcome. For only ten cents you can see the whole world!" That's cheap, I said to myself, we'll have to go in there. But all it amounted to was a couple pictures on the wall. That's all there was to see. I said, "There's nothing here. This guy is making fools out of us. But over there, behind that red curtain is probably where you see the world." So we lifted that curtain, and when we did, just that fast we were outside again. There was the world. As an extra, there was a pile of junk in the corner. We had

a good laugh and came to the Persian House. The man standing in front
said, "Here the King of Persia lies in a casket, embalmed. Only twenty-
five cents." My answer to him was, "You can give me your whole King of
Persia, in vinegar or salt brine. He's not worth a nickel. It would be best if
you'd give the old man some peace since he's already over the hill, he was
a king." In the Egyptian House we saw the Pharaoh out of the Bible for
only twenty-five cents. Man oh man, he sure had changed. I didn't recognize him. Na, he soaked in the Red Sea for quite a while. Then he came to
Chicago and that's no small thing.

So then we tried the Turkish House. A real Turkish girl was there who
could talk German and English. She was selling silk handkerchiefs. I
looked at a few, thinking of Wieschen. She said, "You are the only person
at this fair who can buy this scarf for two dollars and fifty cents. Everybody
else pays five dollars, but you must not tell it around. I thanked her in a
friendly way and explained that I couldn't expect that of her. Then I asked
where she was from. She said, "I am from Damascus, the oldest city on
earth." "Ho ho," I said, "there are houses in our village from the Thirty
Years War, and in Grabow some houses are older than that. But tell me,
where is Damascus?" She sort of looked into the four winds and said, "It
lies over there!" But she pointed to the northwest.

"That's just what I thought," I said. "You don't know your way around
here." Then she got *patzig*, saucy, and said, "*Was weisst du von Damaskus*,
what do you know about Damascus?" "Oh, I know Damascus good. There
is a street there named Straight [translator's note: see Acts 9:11]. But you
probably don't live there." "No," she thought, "that must be on the other
side of the city." "Ja, that must be where it is. But you should look into
that and rent a place there when you're back home. Look it up in the
Bible." She looked at me like a cow at the new gate. I walked off. Afterwards I bought some scarves for Wieschen in the city.

That evening when we got out of the streetcar and walked along the
street, we ran into quite a crowd. I saw a top hat come rolling across the
street. The people trampled it, and I said to myself, somebody lost his hat
and that's too bad. It was even a new hat. Behind us, somebody started to
cuss. Now he was an expert. He must have gotten shoved by somebody in
the crowd. Maybe it's his hat. Schuldt said, "That guy is cussing you. He
thinks you stepped on his hat." I sure didn't know anything about that.

At the end we were sick and tired of exhibitions. So we headed home.
The train left at one in the afternoon. We stood on the platform. It was
three feet off the ground, twenty feet across and really long. People had

crowded it full. I said to Völss, "Go quick, there around the corner to the butcher *und hole Wurst*, and get some sausage. Then at least we won't die from hunger. But ten minutes is all we have." Five minutes went by. The sausage boy was still not back. So I said to Schuldt, "I'll quick look around the corner to see if he's coming. I ran off. He still didn't have the sausage — the butcher shop was packed. When he and I got back, the train was gone. Schuldt was unhappy, "You fooled around too long with your sausage — the train went right past your nose." Völss got worked up because Schuldt wanted to be righteous and make the other one unrighteous. Said Völss, "That train didn't have to pass by your nose." "What do you mean?" "All you had to do was turn around and that train would have passed your *Achtersteven*, your big behind,"

The two of them argued around until the next train pulled in. We left with that one. My dear friend, I tell you that's how it is in this life. When folks leave they are one heart and one soul. When they get back everybody's picking on everybody else.

The sausage helped settle us down. It was a good sausage, and I got busy and talked 'em into making peace. Then they started to go after me. Schuldt said, "You just shut up. It was high time for us to get out of Chicago. It's a wonder you didn't get us thrown into jail. First you upturned half the World's Fair, and then you bumped over a police so that he fell into the street. There he lay — as long as he was — it was raining and his hat rolled into the street. It didn't hurt him any. He got himself up, and even laughed. I helped him straighten up, and he said, 'That's what I get for being so stumbly.'" I must have poked him with my elbow and down he flew. It's a possiblility, and probably that's how it happened.

Now *weisst du von allem Bescheid*, you know what really happened, and I tell you this: no ten horses will ever get me to another World's Fair. It costs too much money. Your hide is all they leave you. If over there in Schwerin [capital of Mecklenburg] you have a World's Fair and you decide to go, first you'll not only have to sell a calf — you'll have to sell the cow. Otherwise your money won't reach.

And there are crowds of people, a whole mob of them. But they don't behave like the crowd at the St. Martin's Day market in Eldena [November 11]. And then to top it off, I created plenty disturbance. I need open country where little children, police, banana bunches, and top hats don't get in my way. I belong on the farm. I have to be able to stretch out my legs and arms.

It's your turn now to write to me. And I hope you've been waiting for some time on a letter from me. You may not forget us. I've been looking in my postbox 118. So far there's been nothing there but things from sales people. I said to myself, Jürnjakob, you have gotten excited for nothing, and I left the post office downhearted. There was no letter from you.

Here in our neighborhood we often talk of you. In fact one night I dreamed about you. You came to visit and everything here seemed strange to you, even the cows and the pigs. You said, "Jürnjakob, I pictured your farm altogether different than it is. But I can tell that you've been diligent, and I love that. I'm looking forward to coming back." You looked me over real friendly and out the door you went.

Then I woke up, and that morning I drove into town. I thought, today there'll be something in my postbox because I saw you in my dream. But when I checked, it was empty again. So I went home and admitted that dreams don't amount to much. The world is getting more evil every day. But I tell you, you may not forget us. 'Cause we don't forget you. And if you come to visit, you will be pleasantly surprised. But when you come, come for the whole summer. Then you can visit all your old school kids who live around here. That will be a pleasure for us all.

Some Sundays *mennigmal*, we all sit together. The children are off by themselves. But we old-timers talk about you, about the village, and about old times in Mecklenburg. You can help us get things straight when you come visit. 'Cause you were there for all those old times. Man oh man, you will be surprised to see that those school kids all have grey hair.

Sometimes I say to myself, how does that happen? Once upon a time I was a little boy sitting on a school bench. Now all of a sudden, I'm an old man with a grey beard and am talking about the Chicago World's Fair. How is that possible?

I believe that if I were back in Germany, then I'd be a little boy again, and I'd be your pupil. In this country, though, time gets away from me. And I have to hurry to catch up. And I've hurried, but now anymore I can't catch up. I have to stop too often to catch my breath and hold my head in my hands. And by that I get further behind.

Weisst du, do you know what happiness is? I'm happy that the sun still has the calendar harnessed up. Otherwise time here in America would be altogether different than by you.

Weisst du, do you know what I'd like to ask? I want to ask if you have a grey beard like your old school kids here?

Weisst du, what Wieschen and I often say? Too bad our children couldn't have gone to school by you. Then I'd say to Wieschen, "That doesn't work.

The girls would get their socks wet going all that way to school in Mecklenburg. All the time, they'd be late getting there, and have to sit time after class."

Now I 'spect it's time for you to milk cows, and I have to look after my own. Dear friend, I tell you Wieschen liked the scarves I bought her in Chicago. But she hasn't worn them. Not once. And she hasn't asked much about the World's Fair. That made me wonder. I saw so much in Chicago, I even learned quite a bit. But I still haven't figured out my Wieschen. When it comes to her, I've got lots to learn.

12

At My Mother's Deathbed

• •

Dear friend and teacher! Today I'm only going to write a few words, but in the coming weeks I'll finish the letter. My heart is heavy. Last Wednesday, the twelfth of April, *ich habe meine Mutter begraben,* I buried my mother. I greet you in her name. And she wanted to thank you for all your generosity to her. See, this is what I want to write you and tell you.

Mother lived to be seventy-two years, six months, and five days. Of that long life, she was by me almost six years. When I sent her the ticket to come to America, she was happy to make the trip. We hadn't seen each other for over thirty years. And she had grown old and wasn't getting around very well.

But like most of the older ones who come over here, she couldn't shake off her homesickness. She had it just like old man Fehlandt. He had it good here by his kids, but something was missing. As big and as rich as America is, America couldn't give him what America didn't have: his old home. Old trees don't transplant well. After a while they look sickly and then give up the ghost.

Mother never did feel at home here. Whatever we saw in her eyes, we did for her. We all but carried her in our arms. She never heard an unkindly word. But the land was a stranger to her. The house was strange, and the farm too big for her to grasp. Our little ones were all big and didn't need to be carried around. There were no goslings or baby chicks to look after. The old folks like to do that. And to mend and darn socks all day is no fun for anybody. She couldn't just sit still with her hands in her lap — she wasn't made like that. She never once sat in a rocking chair. She said, "In my old days, I'm not going to learn how to drive a rocking chair. Daytimes there's a real chair to sit in, and at night there's a real bed to sleep in. I'm not having anything to do with this thing that's not a bed and not a chair — it won't even stand still." Now she's dead, and last Wednesday we took her to the cemetery.

She wasn't sick for long. In the spring we had a sharp wind, and she got it in the chest. I called the doctor in secret, because she didn't want me to. He talked real friendly to her. But he said to me that she's not going to get better. He prescribed some drops, but she didn't want to take them. Slowly her appetite went down, and she got really weak. Her fingers were so thin, just skin and bones.

At the end, I sat a lot by her bed and held her hand. We had good words for each other. Those weeks I started to think things over for the first time since I've been in this country. By my old mother's bedside, all that hard work and all that worry fell off my shoulders like a stranger's coat. Again, I was my mother's *grosser Junge*, her big boy. She said to me, "You're too hard at it. Don't work so hard. Take your time. Take time to come to yourself. Thinking is good for a mensch — you aren't only on this earth to work. You've used all your scythes and threshed all your grain. At the end, the last harvest comes soon enough. You don't have to chase after it."

That's how she talked to me. And her life was nothing but work and worry. So I paid 'tention to her, and took it up in my heart and thought about my life. Look at that, I said to myself, mother is right. A mother is always right when she talks to her children. Because she wants the best for them, and she will find it too.

Mostly we talked about the old country. She said that for the old ones in the village who couldn't get to church anymore, you'd get them together in the school on Saturday evenings and read a sermon from Harms or Scheven. Then she told about the Christmas doings that you put together for the children and the old folks. They'd start to get excited about it already in September. Then she said that for the old ones in the village, life in winter without your Christmas and without those sermons was like an old ragged jacket.

Also, she began to talk about her childhood. I knew nothing about that. You know how it is with people, when they get old and the legs don't want to go forward, the thoughts commence to go backward. Once she said to me, "When I think back on the old times and then I think about today, it's like I go from one room into the other. It's only dark in the doorway. And you get through that pretty good."

See, that's what the old woman had to say. I listened. It was awesome. I patted her hand and said, "*Mudding*, Ma, what you just said, that could be in the Psalms." It was getting dark outside, and Wieschen was busy in the yard. Ma whispered to me like she was ashamed, "Jürnjakob," she said, "you can give me a kiss. It's been a while since anybody kissed me. In this life, I've only been kissed three times: once when I married your pa, Jürnjochen, then, when you where born, and a third time, when Jürnjochen died. Now I want to finish up and follow your pa. So you can give me one for the journey." But I said, "Mudding, for me it's been the same as for you. And I can tell that I am your son. We both have things to catch up on."

So I leaned over her, real easy, and gave her a good kiss. She patted me on the cheek as if I was her *kleiner Junge*, her little boy. Then she laid herself back in bed and was very peaceful. I went outside to look after the cattle and was so alive in my heart. I said to myself, Jürnjakob, there lays an old woman and she's your mother and she's going to die. You never really got to know her. See here, now that she's dying you're finding out who she is.

This day ended and then came another. It was her last day. It was a Saturday. She ate and drank like a little bird. When the work was over and *es schummerte*, it was evening, I sat by her bed and held her hand. Her pulse ran like a racehorse. I sat there for the longest time. It was a ceremony — it was like church when there's Holy Communion and both candles are lighted. Those were my thoughts when I looked into her eyes. She had just

regular blue eyes, but this evening there was a glow from them as I've never seen in this world. But now I saw it with my own soul.

Wieschen lit the lamp and was friendly to mother. She gave her a little something to drink — her lips were all dry. Then Wieschen said to me, "So, Jürnjakob, now read from the Bible."

I read about Lazarus. And when I finished Ma said, "There's a psalm I'd like to hear. I can't remember how it starts but it has to do with sowing and harvesting." "Mudding," I said, "I know what you're talking about, it's one hundred twenty-six. When the lord — "

"Do you hear me, Mudding? 'Like those who dream.'" "I hear you my son." And I read the whole Psalm, right up to the end. "With joy, Mudding . . . and 'they bring in their sheaves.'" "But I don't have any sheaves to bring." "Ja, Mudding, when the end comes, we're all naked and empty handed."

She was quiet for a while. Then she said, "Get out the hymnal and read: *Christus, der is mein Leben*, Christ Jesus, He Is My Life." So I read that one. She folded her hands and said the words along with me. She said, "When your Father died, the teacher had the children sing that hymn. Now read for me: *Wenn ich einmal soll scheiden*, When Once I Shall Depart This Earth." I read both verses.

Then Wieschen gave her something more to drink. She nodded to Wieschen and squeezed her hand. She even ate a cookie, and when I offered, she ate another half. As she finished it, I was so happy I said, "Oh, Mudding, *wat is dat schön*, how beautiful that you ate something. You'll see, when it warms up you'll feel better." She smoothed over the bedsheet with her hand, looked at me and said, "Get better? Don't even think it. *Du muss bloss noch beten*. Just you pray that it won't go on too much longer." My dear friend, after she said that I felt a shiver run through my soul, 'cause I'd just been so happy that she ate a little.

Again she smoothed over the sheet, and her soul was tired to death. Me, I thought about her life — it was nothing but trouble and work. Then she folded her hands again, looked at me, and her eyes got big and deep. Already something was there that hadn't been there before. I can't find the words to tell about it. You could look into her eyes like into a bottomless sea. I put my hand on hers lightly, and we waited. But we didn't wait long. She said, "I want to be in Heaven, *mir wird die Zeit lang*, it's taking too long." My dearest friend, I'll remember this until I die. Just the way she put it, it should be in the hymnal. Then again, she folded her hands under my hand and that's how she prayed our old children's prayer: "*Hilf Gott, allzeit*, Oh God, help now and always, and ready me your child, to be with you in joy and *Seligkeit*, all blessedness. Amen."

After that amen, she turned her head a little to the left, as if somebody was coming. And somebody came. I didn't see Him with my eyes, and I didn't hear Him with my ears. He took her by the hand, and her soul walked away with Him. Just like I said, you go from one room into another. She went home, the way a tired child falls asleep when it gets to be evening. And she's no longer in a strange land.

I opened the window, so's her soul could leave. It was a dark night and a hard wind rustled through the trees. The lamp wanted to go out — it had burned a long time.

My mother was the wife of a common laborer. But when I think on how she died, there is something fine and still and beautiful in my heart. Something that wasn't there before. I can't put it into words. But when I'm out in the field in the midst of plowing, I stand still for a minute and listen to myself. I hear it in me, *was meine alte Mutter*, what my old mother said at the end. I hear it real plain as she said it, tired and quiet. Ja, that's how it is, I hear my mother's voice in myself. And then it's a real Holy Day. It's like the curtain to the Holy of Holies lifts up, and you can see a little bit into the beyond. Then I give the horses a giddyap, and we go back to plowing. But I just can't get over the wonder of it all.

I was still just a little kid. On Pentecost morning I slept in — I wasn't supposed to do that. It makes you the Pentecost fool. All of a sudden I woke up. I felt something soft on my face. It was my mother — she stood there and tickled my face with a lilac. She did it real quietly and looked at me with so much love. See, that's the first memory I have of my mother.

13

Churches and Pastors in America
· ·

I'm sending you a picture of our new church. We finished building a year
ago. Doesn't it look good? But we have a debt on it of almost two thousand
five hundred dollars. Crops have been good this year, so we hope to pay it
off before Christmas. We don't dare wait any longer. Otherwise the good
Lord will think: These are strange people here in the bush. They build me
a new house, and now they sit there and sing, "Now thank we all our God
with hearts and hands and voices," and they've got a debt of two thousand
five hundred dollars on it.

The building looks a little bare up there on the hill. But the grounds
will have to wait a year. For the time being, a beautiful church with bad-
looking grounds is better than an ugly church with nice-looking grounds.
But I'll say to you, an old coat with a new apron doesn't suit me.

This church has a real tower. When I see it on Sunday mornings from
a distance, it warms my heart. There's a weather vane on the peak with a
rooster on it, just like in the old country. It's a gilded rooster. Those roosters on a weather vane like that perch. That's so they can swing around
and show themselves off to the world in all directions. And that rooster
pays 'tention to see if all the members come regularly. But the "come to
church" call is taken care of by the bells. The rooster can't crow.

We're really pleased to have a new church, and the dedication was impressive. The pastor preached on the word: "*Bis hierher hat uns der Herr
geholfen*, Hitherto hath the Lord helped us." It fit in real good. We took
that word and stored it up in our hearts.

At the same time we put in a new cemetery. At first we also wanted to
bury our dead up there on the hilltop, but they wouldn't get much out of
the view and besides there wasn't a whole lot of room up there. So we put
them in on the hillside. That way they'll still hear the bells and the organ.

So we have a gathering place for the dead and for the living, one right next to the other one. On a Sunday when a man walks around out there he knows where he belongs now, and where he's going to belong later. The way people are these days, it's good for them to walk through a cemetery every once in a while and answer the questions of the dead ones. One of them dead ones asks, "How are things *bei mir zu Hause*, at home, by my folks? Do you look after my children and my farm once in a while? You promised me that when I was sick abed." And the other one asks, "You've not been here for quite a while. What you been up to all this time? Surely, you haven't forgotten me?" And a third one says, "*Das ist nett*, it's nice to see you. You're probably here to pick out a nice spot for yourself."

My dear friend, I tell you that on Sundays a man has plenty to do, keeping track of the dead and all the promises he's made them. But when a mensch gets old, he has to take time for that. Otherwise he can't expect others to stop by and visit when he himself is living in the cemetery and wants to talk to them.

I made up a parable about this. It's like when I'm standing at the fence and a good friend comes up the road. I want to ask him something, but he just passes me by. Now here on the farm I can run after him. But when you're in the cemetery that won't work. You have to wait until friends come to see you. But you know, the dead like it when you love them and have a quiet conversation with them every once in a while. And besides, it's good for the living to think to themselves about themselves every once in a while.

Now, it's been a few weeks. I was telling you about our new church and the cemetery. Today, I plan to report on our church's new stove. It cost us two hundred sixty-four dollars. We fire it up on Saturdays for the Sunday services.

We have to have a stove. When you walk or ride five or ten miles in winter weather on our roads, you don't want to sit in church and freeze with wet clothes and boots. The dear Lord takes no pleasure when he looks down on a congregation shivering, with red noses and wet feet. You can't praise the Lord when your teeth are chattering.

This is our number two stove. Number one was cheap — it was made for a world with the wrong system. Instead of the smoke going up and out, it came in and around, and the heat went up and out the chimney.

So I and one of the other church council people went on a little trip. We wanted to look at land, visit friends, buy grain, and sell cattle. By the by, we also studied the stoves in other churches. It was just after New

Year's, which is a real good time to do that. We saw it all and believe me, I could tell you some stories about churches and their stoves. I don't want to name names, but I will tell one story.

In one church we visited on a real cold Sunday. Their stove was fired up and it was smoking. The stovepipe was kaput. Now the pastor was in the pulpit and was preaching on the Centurion of Capernaum and his servant. The air was blue. He was coughing away, and it was like his voice was coming out of a cloud.

A man from the church council stood up. He talked like a German, first from Schwaben, then from Pennsylvania. But he was a decent sort, belongs to our synod even though most of us are Low Germans. He was the one. He could see that this wasn't going to work. He had said to himself, *Das wollen wir fixen*, we'll have to fix that. He spoke into the smoke and the blue cloud, in the direction where the pastor was coughing and preaching, "*Bitte*, please, Herr Pastor, stop a minute. I'm going to fix that stovepipe." The pastor quit preaching, but he didn't stop coughing. The man from Schwaben called out again, "John, *tu man 'ne Bench angreife*, grab onto this bench." The two of them got the stovepipe fixed. We just took it all in. They knew 'xactly what they were doin'. We could tell that it wasn't the first time they had had to do this in that church.

When the worst of the smoke cleared out, you could tell that the man from Schwaben was real satisfied with his work. He even said, "So Preacher, now *kanscht weiter schwätze*, you can start to carry on." And the preacher got going again about the Centurion from Capernaum and his servant.

When church was out, we knew we had seen enough. We didn't travel any further. I said to Schröder, "Schröder," I said, "I'm telling you my opinion." He said, "You go ahead." I said, "The Centurion of Capernaum is long since dead, and the other one was only a hired man. But it wasn't right for them to have to wait until that stovepipe got fixed. These are holy people. If we keep traveling on, next Sunday this could happen to the holy Apostle Paul. Or one of the others out of the Bible could have to wait until a stovepipe got fixed." Schröder said, "Your idea is my idea." So we went back home and made a report at the congregational meeting. Everybody was amazed. They all said, "How is it possible?" See, now we have a second new stove for two hundred and sixty-four dollars.

Our pastor comes from Pomerania. By us in the old country, the girls on the street sang, "*Pommerland ist abgebraunt*, Pomerania had a fire, had a fire." That's where he hails from. He is a Low German and fits in with us just fine. His father was a farmer, that helps too. He is just like that old pastor Timmermann in Eldena — he also understood his people because he was a farmer's son from our village. Our preacher opens up his mouth and *bannig fix* out comes the Low German. But on the pulpit he is all High German. He preaches God's Word pure and undefiled according to the Scripture and doesn't take his time to do it. There's no second growth, no chaff, no human message mixed in. He gives it to us with a tablespoon, one good swallow after the other. He gives it to us just like old Doctor Steinfatt did in Ludwigslust. Steinfatt would prescribe a whole whiskey-bottleful at one time. For people like us, that's much better than a few drops that don't even get from the tongue to the belly. That's how it is with God's Word in this country.

We come quite a ways to get to church. We don't 'spect the pastor to get to the Amen in twenty minutes. When we sit down, we're there for a while. That's the way it is with us in church. So usually he preaches *eine Klockenigte*, an hour like the clock strikes it. My dear friend, I can tell you, he trumpets with power and majesty when he's on the pulpit. His words come without gloves — they are thunderbolts. He works on our ears and then on our hearts, till there's a glory in our souls. It's like the judgment of God coming with thunder and lightning. That's how he preaches into us. Our souls cry out for fear and sweat. He sweats too. He really gets worked up to give it to us.

He can hit that pulpit with his fist — you want to cover your ears. What it means is that he's beating up on the Devil. Another time it's like *Ja und Amen*: "This is most certainly true," the way Luther puts it. And still other times, he folds his hands and it's like he's got all our worries in those hands. And he's bringing them all before the Lord. Then we also fold our hands. That happens of itself, and it has to be that way. He just gets going and keeps on going into those devotions. Let me tell you, nobody's asleep.

When he's getting to the end, he gets quieter and quieter. The thunder and lightning pass. Then comes "the still, small voice, *das stille, sanfte säuseln*." That's where he resurrects his bush farmers, after he's thundered and lightninged them to death because of their sins. The women all like that part. They get something out of that. They'd rather hear this last part than all that thunder and lightning at the beginning.

One Sunday when I was in church and he was getting going into his sermon, it was powerful. He hit that pulpit then with his fist and a big hunk of plaster fell out of the wall. We were still in our old log church. My neighbor said, "Now look at that, he's got a sore hand for a whole week, and we get the bill to have that plaster repaired." But I had noticed that spot a while back. The plaster was already loose where that piece fell out.

For quite a while after that, I looked at that hole in the plaster. It was there as long as that log church was there. It had the shape of Mecklenburg on the map. Next to it, another little piece broke out — it was like the Island Pöl by Wismar. I really liked looking at that, because a man needs to have something familiar to concentrate on in church. You get tired of looking at the preacher all the time.

Our pastor brings us God's Word, that's why we honor him. And we honor him because he has to work so hard to get the Word into our *dicken Köpfe*, our thick heads. Furthermore, he doesn't run around all week in his preaching gown, and he leaves his pulpit voice at home. That's what we really like about him. Therefore we also do for him.

Now he was only getting four hundred dollars a year. So we gave him a raise. Besides his wife gets hams and sausages for her kitchen. When the pastor and the teacher understand us and get the congregation moving, we're ready to help and give money pretty generously.

He's never been away and had a real vacation. And we noticed he was beginning to get that real American-vulture look. That's something folks over here get who have to work all the time with their heads and never have a chance to get away and get a rest. Also his cheeks were gettin' too hollow for us. A pastor is expected to pray the Lord's Prayer, but you don't want to be able to read the Lord's Prayer through his cheeks when he's prayin' it.

In secret we all got together and came up with enough money for a trip to Germany. Looking at the money we said, "Should the man travel alone and the wife stay here? That doesn't make sense. She has to go along." So we made another collection and came up with eight hundred dollars in total. We all said, "Now let 'em go on this trip in God's name. Let them go on this trip and not have to come back for six months. Let 'em get some flesh on their bones and pink in their cheeks. Otherwise, they'll never be able to stick it out here by us. We're not going to go wild. It'll take more than six months for us to go wild. And if we do, he'll just have to thunder us back into captivity."

So they both traveled off. As soon as they were gone, we tore down the old parsonage and built a new one. The old house was in bad shape, a real broken-down shack. We built the new one down from the hill where the church stands. Also we put in a good big garden. By the time we got finished, the summer was pretty well gone. He got back just as things were dried off and didn't know about any of this. He wrote his last postcard in Bremen — he was staying at your son's house.

Our wives and daughters said, "This new parsonage looks pretty empty to us. We're going to put some flowers around, some garlands, and bright-colored signs. That will spruce things up." You see, my dear friend, that is a totally different nation that likes to play with flowers. My theory was, go ahead and make your garlands, but instead of using flowers, use sausage. And for those signs, use a bacon slab. That's pretty too, and it's good to eat besides. That's how it happened too. The new pantry made a ready-to-eat impression. Only on the front door did they finally hang some flowers. "Na, denn man tau, go ahead and do it."

Three boys were sitting on the barn roof. They were on the lookout for the mail wagon. We didn't have a train in those days. As the wagon pulled out of the bush, they waved their caps. Then we could see Pastor and his wife make big eyes. They were surprised and overjoyed. His wife two times more than him. The two times had to do with the pantry. She looked happy and pleased. Then Pastor made a little speech, a sort of thanks and praise speech. We took that in real good. The old Adam in us likes to be petted and tickled.

Now our pastor did put on a few pounds, and he did lose that vulture look. That's what we really wanted. By us it's not like some congregations I know, they only respect their pastor when he's good at piling up manure.

14

A New Church and a New Organ

In this new church we have a new organ. The old one squeaked too much. It was still howling after the hymn was done and the pastor was on the pulpit. The weather is what did it. That old organ knew the weather as well as did my grandmother's bones.

Our old teacher gave up playing it, so the pastor's wife took over until the new teacher came. He had the touch and immediately knew what to do to get music out of it, even if it was ancient. Only he couldn't get along with our old windmaker, the quiet old man who pumped the bellows. The windmaker guaranteed that the organ wouldn't run out of breath. He was one of God's servants and considered himself to belong to a higher order.

The windmaker insisted that the old organ was plenty good, it was just set up wrong, "I belong in the front because I am the organ's head. If I don't make the wind the schoolmaster can't play and the pastor can't do the service. That's why the preacher has to set his sail according to my wind, and that's why I belong in the front . . . *und darum gehöre ich nach vorn.*"

This was the windmaker's sin of pride, that and the top hat he wore to church. But he knew his way around that old organ, even when it played its worse tricks. Already on Sunday he would predict if there was going to be a shift in the weather. Once he even predicted a blizzard — not even the president can do that. Only thing was, the blizzard never arrived.

Because he had been doing this for years, he had pretty well figured out how many pumps went with any certain hymn. He was good at figures. And that all worked out so long as the pastor's wife and the old teacher were the organists. But when the new teacher-organist came, he didn't play as evenly as the other ones did. This new teacher got all kinds of tra-la-las into the holy music, before and behind, and even in the middle. That's when there was an explosion behind and before.

Granted, those tra-la-las were short, but when I tie together little pieces of string, it comes out to be a long piece, and that's what got to the old windmaker. He had to pump more than he was used to. The one on the organ bench was cut out of different cloth than his predecessors — he pulled out all the stops. He gave no thought to how old that organ was and that its lungs were rickety. It was getting short of breath, like old people do. And that was the beginning of a church war.

It got started one Sunday when the hymn number on the board was 183, "We All Believe in One True God." The old man knew exactly how many pumps went with number 183. But this was the first time the new organist played it in our church. He wanted to give God the glory and also get a little glory for himself. So he pulled all the stops and hung on that hymn every tra-la-la in his book. It sounded fine, but it didn't sound for long.

Behind the organ the windmaker was busy counting out the pumps for hymn number 183 and when he got to one hundred sixty-five pumps, that was it. But for him on the organ bench, it was only the third verse and now there was no more wind. He couldn't play another note. He got off the bench and went around to the back of the organ and started shouting. But the old windmaker had the wrath in his heart. He got real loud and said, "I know how much wind it takes to play, 'We All Believe in One True God.' It's one hundred sixty-five pumps. And I added five for the amen. That makes a hundred and seventy pumps. Für das Amen gab ich fünf zu. For the amen, I added another five pumps. But you want at least two hundred fifty pumps. Don't pull all the stops at once, as if that wind doesn't cost money. And, if you'd leave those worldly tra-la-las off those holy hymns, you'd get through real good with my wind. I have been a faithful servant of God at this church for many years. But I can't deliver any more wind for you than I did, 'cause my income won't allow it."

The whole congregation listened in on this. Then the two of them made peace. The one up front got friendly and agreed, and left off fifty pumps. The one in the back stayed stubborn and added just thirty pumps, including the amen. They both came together at two hundred pumps. So the windmaker went back behind the organ, the other one sat down on the bench, and we sang the third verse over. But afterwards we made it clear to the new organist that when he was practicing he could play any way he wanted, but during the service he didn't need to get so fancy. We wanted to praise God the old timey way. Which is what he finally did and got along with us real good. He was a reasonable mensch.

This new organist only made two mistakes. One was, he wouldn't say organ the way the Mecklenburgers do, *Orgel*. The other was, he liked to lift up his little finger when he drank coffee, as if to say, "Look here, I am not just a commoner. I belong to a higher order." But otherwise there was little of worldly pride in him.

He and the windmaker weren't all that different. The old fart behind the organ just thought that he too belonged to the higher order, even when he played for dances. At dances he played the bass. He didn't know a thing about it, but the young folk allowed him the pleasure because it didn't cost anything. He had made the bass out of an old sugar box. He cut a couple of holes in the top and pulled four thick strings over it. Then he stood in the corner and played until the dogs howled. He couldn't even keep time with the other music. Like the cow's tail, he was always dragging behind the dancers. But he wouldn't give in. He'd say, "The bass is my real instrument. People who belong to a higher order are peaceful like the bass. A fiddle doesn't fit in here — it's too squirmy. The bass walks along, slow and sure. The bass is true spirit-filled music."

This old windmaker also liked to sing when he played. He would half-close his eyes and out it came, like the arrow from the bow. But really, he only knew one song, and he sang that to every melody. It was enough to make the dogs yowl. He liked it though. He liked to hear himself sing, and that's why nobody ever said anything to him about it.

Now all the air is run out of the old windmaker. And sometimes I wonder if he pumps the organ in heaven, when on Sundays the little angels sit on the bench and play. It would grant him that pleasure, because he knew exactly how much wind it took to play number 183. But those little angels are a busy bunch and not slow and steady like us Mecklenburgers. And if they get all those tra-la-las in there, he won't be able to keep up. He is still one of the old-fashioned kind.

We cared for his wife after he was gone. She had always been a faithful member of the congregation, and he had had a spiritual office. Only there was no money, and after he died she and her children went through hard times. She gladly put her hand out whenever anybody offered something. If it was a little gift, she would say, "God bless you if the wind doesn't blow it away!" If it was a bigger gift, she would say, "Thank you in Jesus' name!" She was a pious lady. But to live from hand to mouth doesn't work well over time.

So we built her a little house and put some garden land to it. It was to help her till the children grew up. That's why she had no worries, and in church she could sit in her old place, in front of the pulpit. Sitting there is where she could watch her husband at work, and she surely was proud of him.

Only trouble is she nearly went blind. One of her daughters would take her by the hand and bring her to church. Always, she was one of the last ones in the door. The pastor had already warned her. She said, "Herr Pastor, when you wake up, you can see if it's day or night. I can't make that out any more. But when the day comes that the blind are made to see, I'll hurry me up — and Herr Pastor, it stands written, 'the last will be first.' When that day comes your sermon will not have to complain about me." He was speechless. And when we built her that house, everybody chipped in. Of course, there's always somebody in the neighborhood who's got plenty and gives little. You can smell how his greed stinks. I have a story for you about such a feller. But it's going to be a few weeks before I can get to it.

15

The Old Skinflint
. . . .

Stek di de Piep an, light up your pipe now — as we say in Low German — and *huer tau*, listen to me. You remember Hans Jahnke from Menkendorf. He was in school there. Old Karl Busacker hired him to tend cows. His wife comes from Tewswoos. He works in Milwaukee and lives five stairs up with a wife and six children. And he's just gettin' by.

Hans's uncle, Jochen Pennigschmidt, is rich and lives on a farm a few miles south of here. Well, the uncle visited in Milwaukee last fall and lived off his nephew for seven days. This is the man who brags about bringing in one hundred and fifteen loads of hay, worth twelve dollars each. But he wants to wait until he can get thirteen dollars a load before he sells. The cheese factory gave him a check for over nine hundred dollars. Then there's been money for corn, oats, barley, potatoes, and vegetables. As he told it to Hans, there are also investments paying interest. He sits there then, after counting up how well he's done, hands folded over his fat belly, and talks big about how God has blessed him. Jochen Pennigschmidt is a pious man, so long as it doesn't cost him anything.

Hans Jahnke scratched his head at all this and said, "Uncle Jochen, you're really sittin' in the fat, so then how much do you give to the church in a year?" Hans asked this because himself he is a God-fearing man and not only in words. Uncle Jochen stuttered around and finally said, "What do you think — I pay eight dollars." "What? Only eight dollars? And in my situation, I give some thirty dollars." This is when Hans began to wonder about his old uncle Pennigschmidt.

When Jochen left Milwaukee he hadn't even given the children pennies. He did invite the whole family to come visit. Hans's wife said, "Ja, I would like to see what a cornfield looks like again and have a taste of country butter. But your farm is two hundred fifty miles from here. If you can help us with the cost, we'd be glad to come visit. Uncle Jochen says, "That'll take care of itself," and off he goes. That next summer Hans's wife wrote and asked about coming. She never got an answer.

What happened was that another relative of Hans Jahnke invited him and his family for a visit. That relative sent money for the trip. The Jahnkes arrived and the children drank milk like newborn calves. Also, the Jahnkes visited at the pastor's who had seven children of his own. The thirteen girls slept in the barn on a straw stack. The pastor said, "Well, if we lose one in the straw, we'll still have a good dozen." Jahnke looked at the nest of kids and said, "Herr Pastor, the Lord has blessed your house. As the Bible says, 'your children are like olive shoots round about your table,'" "Ja," laughed the pastor, "the olive shoots are there all right, but we're running short on the oil in the kitchen and the flour in the bin." That's what he said. In those days he was still at four hundred dollars the year. Jahnke remarked, "You do have plenty farmers here who have meat in their soup." "Ja," said Pastor, "we do, but they don't put much meat in my soup. I know of one who put up a hundred and fifteen loads of hay and, on top of that, got a check for over nine hundred dollars from the cheese factory. Believe it or not, his name is Pennigschmidt [in German: a penny of a smith]." Jahnke said, "Believe it or not, he's my uncle." "He doesn't even have children," said the pastor. "Why doesn't he dig deep and give some away?" Then, the pastor laughed, "Before Christmas last, he met me on the way to town. He was hauling wood. Good dry, hard wood. I was on my way to visit someone in the congregation who was sick. He pulled up his team and said that he wanted to help me out this year, and maybe at Christmas he could do something for me and the Mrs. I've known him for years, so I said to myself: just wait, don't get your hopes up. Well, a few days before Christmas he unloaded a wagon full of wood at my place. Only, what wasn't green was rotten. Na, etwas ist besser als nichts, something is better than nothing. He also had something for my wife, beef, just butchered. But mistakenly it was all bones and no meat. "And that's the story of my family," said the pastor, "all bones and no meat. Well, we got one meal out of it, no more."

My dear friend and teacher, in Low German, glöwest du dat de Geschicht tau Enn' is, do you think this story is to its end? You're wrong. Just after New Year, Pennigschmidt knocked on the pastor's door. He was invited in and offered a chair. No, he didn't even want to take off his coat. He just stood there fidgeting with his hat in his hand, acting like a mensch with something on his mind. Finally, he came out with it, "Herr Pastor, I wanted to ask about that wood? I want to make it cheap for you. Four dollars for the whole load." At that he sort of looked away and right at a picture of Jesus. Too bad it wasn't Jesus cleansing the Temple. The Lord wouldn't have had to stand there scratching his head, he would have cleansed that Pennigschmidt right out the door, and that is written in Matthew, chapter 21.

The pastor was dumbstruck — he reached into his pocket for the four dollars. He's not the man with the right words for a scene like that. God willing, the wife came in at that moment. Anyway, she had been listening at the door, the way Sarah listened at the tent in Genesis 18. That was the pastor's salvation, because she knew all the right words that he didn't know. Anyway, it was not a good day for Pennigschmidt. He wanted out of the house, but she stood in the way, like the cherub at Eden's gate. "Well," she said, "surely we don't need a receipt to show how you got paid for your Christmas present." "Nein," said Pennigschmidt, "how can a Christian person say the likes of that?" "And besides," she said, "what do we owe you for those bones from your precious cow?" "Oh," said Pennigschmidt, "that good beef shan't cost you a cent." By that he looked away, again, and again right at the Lord Jesus. "Well," she said, "at least you think it was good. You should have heard that one sermon last fall. It was the Sunday when you had dinner at our table, with no receipt. It was the story about that old camel that wanted to get through the needle's eye and couldn't. It was the story about an old tightwad who couldn't get into the kingdom of God. Anybody can get some good out of reading that story." "Ja," said Pennigschmidt as he counted out the four dollars and put them in his pocket, "I agree, greed is the root of all beginnings." She said, "You mean, greed is the root of all evil." "Ja wohl, Frau Pastor, as I said, 'greed is the root of all beginnings.'" At that he walked out the door. At first, the pastor and his wife looked at each other, ready for a kill. Money was scarce at their house. But then they started to laugh. It was so bad, it was ridiculous. And it's good when you can laugh. It's better to laugh than to murder.

Nu glöwst du woll, dat de Geschicht tau Enn' is? Do you think this story is at its end? My dear friend, I can tell you that then you are of the wrong faith. 'Cause now comes the thick end of the story, that turned it into a joke for the whole neighborhood. It all got started when Jahnke heard the pastor's story about the Christmas present. So he schemed with his nephew to come up with a plan to punish the old tightwad and convert him to the real Christian faith. Because so far faith, hope, and love weren't making much progress with him. He needed to be converted, American style. In the next few days, Hans and his nephew made the rounds in the neighborhood and turned it into a real conspiracy. It was an expedition to give that old skinflint his due.

Now then things began to heat up and get lively. Pennigschmidt's nephew, Hans Jahnke, sent him an anonymous message: "Next Sunday, after church, expect company. We have been looking forward to making this surprise visit. We want to spend the day with you because we are such old friends. So we are planning on Sunday dinner at your house."

Behold, it was truly a mass emigration. On the next Sunday after church everybody took off for the Pennigschmidt place. Over the hills came all his friends and relatives. Pennigschmidt had eaten at everybody else's house in the whole county, and now it was tit for tat. It was a crowd of nearly thirty-five people. As they began to arrive, the frau met them in the yard. She was upset and asked, "What is it that you want here?" Somebody got down off their wagon, shook her hand and said, "We're here just to please you." The second wagonful said, "It's been so long since we've been here." The third questioned, "When are we eating dinner? And hopefully it's going to be plenty — we're hungry!" The fourth bunch said, "Hurry on up now, we can hardly wait." The house fairly burst with laughter and talking. But Frau Pennigschmidt ran to look for her husband. He was hiding in the garden behind the gooseberry bushes. He had no idea what to do.

Finally, the table was set, but with so many only half could sit down, the others had to wait. The house girl came into the dining room with one huge platter. The eyes of all were upon the platter, and they were curious eyes. What's going to be on that platter? One whole chicken and no more. That chicken held its legs up to heaven and lamented, "Don't blame me." Well, somebody said, "What's one chicken for all these mouths?" Somebody else complained, "This is more than my empty stomach can take." The third one, "Do I have to go home hungry?" The fourth one, "We want to get your ham and sausages into circulation, otherwise they'll spoil." At the end, they all said, "We can see that this is just too much for you two. It's only right that we should help, because we're the ones at fault." At that, they started to get into the pantry and brought out the ham and sausage. Somebody got busy catching the chickens that were running around in the yard, and it wasn't long before they were being roasted. Then everybody ate till they were satisfied, and then sat around talking till it got to be evening.

First, they ate because they were hungry, then they ate out of revenge. Third, they did it all over again. Pennigschmidt and Frau sat there with their hands in their laps and didn't say a word, all they did was look pale and helpless. Afterwards, as everybody began to leave, they all said thank you and praised old Pennigschmidt's hospitality, "You have a beautiful place, but isn't lonely here? We've had a wonderful time, and we'll come again. You are such sincere Christian people, and you're generous to a fault."

Pennigschmidt was done in and could only smile painfully. That next year he gave fifty dollars to the church instead of eight. By the grapevine he heard why they had butchered his chickens and robbed his pantry. And when we saw how guilty he felt, we all assured him that really, we were his friends, "We enjoyed the Sunday, and don't worry, we'll be back." The old man even finally got his church dues up to a hundred dollars. So you can see, what it means to be converted the American way. Ja well.

Dies ist eine wahre Geschichte. This is one true story, and the one who told it to me was right there when it all happened. You definitely can tell this story in our village. People can learn from it and take an example. It was a Pennigschmidt who did it and I'm sure you've got a Pennigschmidt or two over there in Mecklenburg. Only sometimes they have a different name.

My wife didn't go along for that Sunday dinner. She said it was shameful. But when I got home, she had a hundred questions about it, right down to the last bite of sausage. Frauenfolks have a healthy curiosity.

The Baptism of the Firstborn
• •

Our new church has four walls. Yours and ours are alike in that respect. Only here the four walls are closer together. That's why on Sundays ours is fuller than yours. It's also true that over here we have more interest in church. Here we don't only have to pay money, here we also get to make decisions. Here the pastor comes to the people. He doesn't wait until the people come to him.

We've got things in pretty good order these days. But in the beginning that wasn't so. My farm was out in the bush, and when the heir of all things arrived and wanted to be baptized, it wasn't easy. Because if you're going to have a baptism, you need more than the baby — *da ist auch ein Pastor nötig*, you also need a pastor.

The baby was there, all nine pounds. But no pastor. That made for a bad situation. Now there was a Methodist reverend in the neighborhood. Only he had the habit of moving every two years. He told me that it was God's calling. You know what I think? I think he has a hearing problem.

The wives of these Methodists really have the problem, because they have to do the packing. These preachers' chickens even know what's coming, when somebody strange comes to look around the barn: the chickens lay down on their backs and put their feet up. They say to themselves, Now this miserable moving is going to start up again. We want our legs tied up right now, so we'll be ready to go.

There needs to be something said about the Methodists because there are so many of them around here. I've been to some of their meetings where the preachers shout, "Repent ye sinners for the end is near!" They tell stories about conversions and let 'em have it about the end of the world and about the fires of hell. The women are hollering and singing, but nobody's being converted. So they preach longer and shout louder.

You could hardly understand anybody. They're all sweatin' and moaning, especially the preachers.

At the end, the head one told *greuliche Geschichten*, horror stories about folks that don't want to repent. The Devil comes with the stink of hell and takes their souls so that they die in their desperation. Then finally two or three old ladies came forward. They bawled and whined and threw themselves onto the sinners' bench. Well anyway, that was something to behold.

One of those Methodist reverends came to call on us at home. His idea was to convert me. Well, like a good Lutheran *hausfrau*, Wieschen set him out some lunch. He *jammerte über meine Seele*, bemoaned my soul and worked himself up into a real heat. I noticed though how he was eyeing Wieschen's ham and sausage. First he looked at one and then at the other. Finally he leaned into me real good and was going to take me by force, but he speared a few of those thick ham slices on the way.

So finally I said, "I see that you like ham the best. But, you know, if you're going to be one of the Spirit, be of the Spirit. Or, if you're going to be of the world, be of the world. But spiritual and worldly in one pot — I don't approve of it." That's when he let up with his converting and bemoaning. He just had a few pious words for me, to edify me. He was a reasonable mensch, and he even praised Wieschen's sausage.

No, that's not what we had in mind for a pastor that would baptize our boy. We were Lutherans and we wanted a Lutheran. So when Wieschen got back on her feet, we started off. I went first with the baby, she followed after me. We walked for two days. That first night we stayed by a farmer who came from Norway. We didn't even know him, and we've never seen him again. He took us in. His wife was good to us.

In the morning we got going again. The road was awful. The road was like an angleworm that lost its way. One minute we were off to the right through a swamp, next we were off to the left through the bush. Then again we were going through a forest of tree stumps, thick ones. I said to Wieschen, "That one stump is so thick we could dance a *schottisch* on it." But Wieschen didn't want to.

We ran into as many wagon trails and tracks as there are at the train station in Chicago. They were running wild, one into the other. There was no law and order to them. And the holes in the road kept us from going at any speed. It was a bumpy way to go. As quick as I got my left foot out of one hole, I already had my other foot in the next one. Wieschen had to be helped out, and then I had to be careful not to let the baby fall. This is how we moved forward, and by evening of the second day we were at the pastor's house. He was away, ten miles to the east, to visit the well and the sick.

But we were in luck. We slept at the pastor's house and his wife gave us more than friendly words, she gave us something to eat. The next day we had even better luck. The pastor himself arrived and the boy was baptized. Now that was a joy, and now we could go home. But that didn't mean the road had gotten any better because the boy was now a Christian. Anyway, he was yowling like a heathen. He didn't like this going on another trip. But the worst was yet to come.

When we were back in our log house, Wieschen fell to pieces. It was all too much for her. She slept for a whole day and that helped. But the baby cried, the cows bellered, and the pigs grumped that this was no way to do farming. "How are we supposed to put on ham and bacon when you treat us like this?" I went to work. I scratched me behind the ears. . . . After that I said to myself, Jürnjakob Swehn, scratching won't help here. *Riet di man leiwer tausammen*, pull yourself together and give them animals and people their due. So I got going. I milked cows and fed 'em. The pigs got their grain and water, which shut 'em up. Then I made a sugar-titty for the baby, which worked fine for him. I cooked a soup for Wieschen, sat me down on the edge of her bed, and chewed on a piece of bacon like old times. Ham and bacon make good company for a lonely soul. Ja, here in America, in the beginning, having your child baptized a Lutheran could get real complicated.

17

In the Beginning

· ·

My dear friend, I still have much to tell about how we got started here. Even when the pastor and the church were no longer so far away, it happened that he would meet me as I was coming to church. He wasn't just being polite — church was over. I just couldn't get there any earlier. Now this didn't just happen to me. There were others in the same predicament. Once in a while, just before the pastor finished his sermon, we would hear a team of oxen in the distance. Slowly they would get closer in. It was Heinrich Tiesel. He lived some twelve miles north and his road was nothing but bush and swamp. And with a road that was nothing but holes and bumps and mud, oxen worked best. Only, you have to shout at oxen, otherwise they don't understand you. Now Tiesel had good lungs, that's why we could hear him from quite a distance. Right around amen time he would make it to the church. The pastor would call for a long closing hymn so Tiesel at least had something of a Sunday and didn't come the whole way for nothing.

Myself, I had some bad times in church at the beginning. On the hymn board stood number 401. Ho ho, I laughed to myself, this is one you learned to sing by heart when you were in school. You don't need a songbook for this one. I sang out in good voice, "*Ein feste Burg ist unser Gott*, A Mighty Fortress Is Our God." But my neighbors looked at me strangely and poked me a good one. They were singing, "You Are Mine and Will Be Mine Forever." Just think, in America that's hymn number 401.

On one other Sunday, number 359 was on the hymn board. I gave it no never mind and laid right into that hymn, "*Wer nur den lieben Gott lässt walten*, If You but Trust in God to Guide You." But this time, Wieschen gave me a poke 'cause everybody else was singing "God Lives, Oh My Soul, Why Are You Heavyhearted?" It's too bad that the one world doesn't have one tongue, one language and one songbook. I really knew the numbers for those old hymns, but I have to be ready for a new education every once in a while, even when it comes to hymn numbers.

Our pastors in this country have an uncomfortable life. They all look pretty lean. In the beginning our pastor worked mostly as a circuit preacher. He preached four times a week, two times on Sundays and two times during the week. He came to our place on Tuesdays. And you had to keep up with things real good, otherwise you made a Sunday out of Tuesday.

Seven miles a day on horseback was how our pastor did it. He would get here early and have church until noon. Then he did Bible history with the older children — we also stayed around for that. Later on he got himself a wagon and came by more often. Mostly he came toward evening because he would find us home.

At first he was on horseback the whole day, going from farm to farm. That meant he'd only get to see the younger children. The big kids and their folks were in the field. So he started Bible classes for the little ones and confirmation for the big ones. He would teach school in town for three days and in the country three half-days. Our children learned Bible, catechism, and hymns.

Most of the children still couldn't read. They could plow, they could mow, and they could ride, but they couldn't read. Reading is harder. Ja, if you could only mow and rake those letters into some kind of sense.

The pastor would read out loud and the children would repeat it after him until they knew it. So in two winters they did learn their ten hymns and then some. They even sang them. As time allowed, they learned from him to read and write and cipher.

You couldn't keep it up, though. He tried hard enough, but the kids were getting big as fast as the calves were. He just couldn't hold out much longer. There were too many difficulties. Once he got lost in the bush and had to sleep out overnight. He didn't have as nice a weather as old Jacob in the Bible. He got wet to the skin. It was pretty cold too. If the weather had been this bad for Jacob, he wouldn't have dreamed of a ladder to heaven either.

On one excursion he and his good brown horse forded the river. But on the way over the water, either he lost the horse or the horse lost him. He hardly made it to the other shore. Only trouble was his horse went back to where they just left. The two looked at each other across the stream, while the packet with his holy robe was on its way to the ocean.

Then one time he tipped his wagon over. So he just let it lay there and arrived by us with the two horses on the reins.

He spent one night in a broken-down old log house. Nobody had lived in it for years. There were so many holes in the roof he had to sleep under his umbrella. You just can't keep that up for long, even if you are an American pastor. But we honored him for all that he had done, and we were thankful.

As more people moved into the neighborhood, we changed our ways. The pastor was there for Sunday. Those of us who lived in the middle of about a ten-mile area took turns having church. A few times we even had church in our old log house. I had caulked the logs on the inside real good. The sitting room was the church, and we added the kitchen. I dragged in some blocks of wood and laid boards over them for a table. Wieschen put a white cloth over the boards and there you have it: church.

In the morning they started to pull in, some on foot, others by wagon. Some of the women even came on horseback because the road was so bad. It was winter, and it was a cold winter. Na, well as a remedy for that we had a hot stove and hot coffee.

To begin with, we sang, "Ich singe dir mit Herz und Mund," "Oh Lord, I Sing with Lips and Heart." We made the walls ring. It was good, but when the end of the verse came we were straggling all over the place. Some were fast, some were slow. The fast ones, though, held on to their notes till the slow ones caught up.

A Dane was there. He came from Nästved. It's a town over there behind Rostock. He sat in the corner behind the stove. That's where it was the warmest. There he sat on his log end. He sweat American and sang Danish. What was good was that he did what the hymnal calls, "In eigener Melodie, this hymn has its own tune." Ja wohl, he sang according to his own tune and that was real Dane. My dear friend, you know what I think? I think the dear God had second thoughts about his bush people that Sunday.

The Sunday I was the elder, I went around with the Klingelbeutel, the collection bag. It was my old straw hat. Wieschen said, "You cannot honor God with an old hat like that." I said, "Wieschen you have the wrong faith. An old straw hat can honor God because the Lord looks on the heart. The Bible doesn't say anything about the hat, whether it's new or old." She said, "It's not been new for a long time and the holes in it show how old it is, and when somebody puts money in it, the money falls through the holes and rolls along the floor. Then you have to get down on your knees and go looking for it. That doesn't do anything for anybody's devotion." I said, "Wieschen, even if you're right, I'm still gonna use my old straw hat because it's black and that makes it spiritual."

And so that old black hat got ordained as a klingelbeutel. Only it didn't have a little bell on it the way the collection bags do in Mecklenburg. In the worst way, I wanted to klingel that little bell.

So I started to make the collection and nobody shook his head at me, they all contributed. The pastor got over fifteen dollars. He was pleased. I was too, and Wieschen was proud of me. The old sinful self likes that proud feeling, believe me. Even the Dane from Nästved who sat on the block of wood behind the stove gave a dollar. He said to me, "I didn't understand a thing but it felt good and I was edified. If you don't mind, I'll come again."

The pastor preached about Jesus feeding the five thousand. The cows and the oxen groaned, the pigs squeaked, and the roosters crowed. It was good background music for that text. Because the birds and the animals praise God with their voices just like we do. All according to their kind.

After the amen, a woman came forward and wanted to be baptized. Who do you think it was? Dürten Fründt from our village. She married Fehlandt's second boy. And I'm the godfather to their little girl, Wieschen is the godmother.

When all that was over, we picked things up and moved the tables together. Most everybody stayed and ate with us. My dear friend, I tell you there were some different eats served up there. A poor man could come to that table. But you can believe me, we all ate and were satisfied. Folks said, "*Danke, ich habe* plenty." I was terribly proud of my Wieschen.

We all sat around and told stories. First we talked spiritual, then we talked worldly, afterwards we came back to the spiritual. It was all very nice and it lasted a long time. We didn't get together very much in those years. But when we once got sat down, we stayed that way real good.

First we talked about the dead. Now one of us had a grampa buried in the cemetery at Picher. The other one's dad is buried at Konow and mine is buried at Eldena. The dead are neighbors to one another in the old country, as their children are neighbors in America. The one buried his first wife somewhere in Hanover, the other one has a boy buried in Holstein, and the pastor spoke good words over all of this about life and death, and about the resurrection.

First we talked about the dead, then we talked about the living. *Denn was dem einen recht ist, ist dem andern billig,* 'cause what's good for the goose is good for the gander. Pastor himself told stories from the old country . . . and out of his best books. It was a real joy, and our eyes sparkled.

Then one of us had to tell about mowing beans in Holstein, and what hard work that be. Another had a story about that three-cornered wheat on the Lüneburger Heath.

All of a sudden, we were back in our childhood and we began to talk about home and about our school. Next, we were on our farms, and the one sold last year's pigs all over again. The other one began to thresh the coming wheat harvest, which he didn't even have in the ground yet. The number three talker was cutting wood, and number four blew out the stumps with dynamite. Everything *auf Plattdeutsch,* in Low German. Only this didn't last long, because we do it around here all the time, and on Sunday *der Mensch* wants to hear something different.

By golly, one of us even got to talking about his army time. He was a dragoon in Ludwigslust. Another guy was an infantry man in Rostock. A third one stretched out his crooked knees and showed how a Schweriner grenadier marched. So we all got to putting on a parade for the grand duke of Mecklenburg's birthday. This meant we had to take Wieschen's broom and make believe it was a gun.

The dragoon started to sing: "*König Wilhelm sass ganz heiter*, William the King sits high, and he's happy!" He couldn't get much further than verse one, but that's no problem because by then we were in the war. We were capturing Sedan and Strassburg and Metz and Orleans. But when we got to Paris, the broomsticks were wandering back into the corner. Old Schuldt had already started in with his *Häih?*! That's proof that he's tired and wants to go home. The women all said too, now it's time and began to act as if they were going home. It was getting dark.

Wieschen cooked another pot of good coffee and when they had emptied their cups they began to load themselves on to the wagons. Everybody said: So *einen schönen Sonntag*, such a nice Sunday. We haven't had a Sunday like this for a long time. It's what we've wished for, because a mensch isn't only in the world for work. With that they drove off, and we went to bed. That was a real nice Sunday. Ja well.

For quite a long time this is how we did church, once by us, then by them, and then by the next ones. But after a while this didn't work. We got to be too many. Our log houses weren't that big. *Wat nu*, what now? We discussed it two times the length and once across. But when it comes to talk, not much comes out of it. Even less comes into it, if you don't know where you're headed with talk. You might as well stand in front of a mirror and work your jaws.

When our turn came up again to have church, I said, "Wieschen, this Sunday you'll have to cook the best you can and cook plenty of it. Because I have a plan and you can help me with your cooking." Wieschen perked up her ears. She said, "*Woso und woans*, how and what are you up to?" I said, "'A virtuous wife is her husband's crown but many questions exhaust the flesh.' You'll see what I'm up to when we're all stuffed full of good eats."

Church was over and everybody had eaten, . . . and they had eaten till they were out of breath. Wieschen had done exactly as I planned. So I started off, "Dear friends, neighbors and all you Low Germans. Our congregation has grown big and our houses are still small. Therefore let us build a church."

On the spot, many were in favor. They were the ones I had talked with beforehand. And the ones who had eaten the most also supported my plan. You know when a mensch has a full stomach, he'll agree to most anything. That's why you talk about something like this after dinner. But a few disagreed. They wanted out, because their money was too close to their hearts. We had a plan for them: we'll do most of the work ourselves, with our own hands and our own oxen. Because to start with, this is going to be a log church. One like that costs hardly anything. And we can put it up ourselves. There's plenty wood around here, and if we get busy with it now, we'll be finished by Easter.

Old fat-assed Meier disagrees. But he doesn't say a word. He just puts his hands in his pockets and sort of grumps around. We woke him up from his afternoon nap. That was a mistake — you can't do a thing with him then. But I know him only too well. I say, "Meier, I want to tell you something. It's been bothering me that you can't find a decent place to sit here. Our benches are too narrow for you — you always have to sit sideways. In this new church we're going to build such wide benches that everybody can sit comfortably on them. And there will be one especially wide, just for you, so that you can praise and give thanks with good feelings. We will put it in writing that this is your bench. If this seems right to you, you go ahead now and sit behind the stove and enjoy a snooze. . . . Wieschen, *stell Meier den Stauhl doch en beten achter den Aben*, put Meier's chair a little ways over there, behind the stove."

I say this because I know he likes to sit comfortably. He also likes to hear about a broad bench. And at that he quit grumping. Only, he still had his hands in his pockets, which means he was only half won over.

At that I said to his wife, "We have to have a church. *Das geht nicht*, it doesn't go that we get snow on your beautiful rugs and bring so much dirt into your nice, clean home." Now she understands that because she is determined to keep the house spic and span. So she gives her ja, which means old fatty Meier is now on our side. He takes his hands out of his pockets and sits down behind the stove. He is a reasonable human being, a mensch. But in some affairs, his wife is the man, and his household sometimes is of the upside-downside world order.

There were also others who didn't want to take the bait. Rugs and shining floors were wild ideas to them and their floors never looked scrubbed. To them it makes no difference if another inch or so of dust and dirt piles up in the corners. But they are good people. We love them. They belong to our church. They are not Mecklenburgers, but they live in the neighborhood, and if we don't welcome them, they'll run to the sect churches, which we're trying to ignore. You have to treat them different.

Then I said, "You'd like to hear church bells?" "We'd like to," they answered. "When we were in town three weeks ago and met, you said, 'We'd be happy to hear church bells.'" "Me too. I really like bells." "Well, then you ventured the idea that it would be nice if we had some." "That is still our opinion." "Ja, where are we with those church bells? We can't hang them on the roof of the house. They won't go on a tree limb either. A bird might easily drop something on them, that wouldn't be fitting for holy bells. Besides, what would that look like? If somebody'd happen by, saw it and put it in the newspaper, the whole county would have a laugh on us."

At first nobody really wanted to get behind this. They said, "That business with the birds makes no sense. But we don't want to get into the newspaper." So at the end, we got them all thinking: if we're going to have bells, then we have to have a tower. You can't have one without the other.

Good is what I said. "But are you going to put that tower up on top of the hill? There's where most folks pass by when they're on that road. They stop there to catch their breath, and when they've got it, they'll look around and one of them will say, "Nu seht mal bloss, just look, isn't this crazy. They put up a tower with no church." The other one will say, "They must be the kids of that farmer who wanted to buy a woods. But it was too expensive, so he bought himself a beanpole." A third one will say, "That must be the man who wanted to buy a farm. But it was too expensive, so he settled for a head of cabbage." By that a fourth one will say, "Or that's the man who found a button and now is waiting for somebody to bring him a pair of pants."

"That would be a laugh on us. A few days later people will read it in the newspaper and it will really be a laugh on us. So if we build a tower, we have to build a church. Otherwise, we'll be the eulenspiegel, the jokers of the county. Only a tower is neither shirt nor pants. So you tell me, what is your opinion?"

At that they had a good laugh and said, "Our opinion is, you have put one over on us. You started with talk about building a church, which is where most people stop. But because we said church bells sound really beautiful, you've got us actually building a church." At that we agreed and got busy with the business. In the next few days we started — we already had the spot picked out. We cut down the trees that would work for the timbers: supports, beams, braces, and boards. We measured and we cut. But for the floorboards and for the inside trim and wainscoting, we took maple. That was *ein saures Stück Arbeit*, one sour piece of work. The wood was hard and it sawed like iron.

The stones for the foundation went up the hill headfirst. The work went well — we worked for the joy of it, not with groans and regrets. When Palm Sunday entered the land, the building stood there for all the world to see. On Easter we had church in it, even though the building wasn't finished. Pentecost we rang the bells for the first time. We all stood in the yard, took our hats off, and prayed. Then we rejoiced and felt a deep satisfaction. We were pleased. Even fatty Meier liked his outsized bench.

Only one of us wasn't satisfied. That was old man Krüger. He had opened up a saloon and had offered us two hundred dollars to help build a church if we'd build it closer to his place. He even wanted to give us some land on a beautiful hillside, right on the road. We could also mark off the lot for the church as big as we wanted it. But we turned him down: Christ and Beelzebub don't go together, they need to be kept apart. For a while he was mad, but then he got over it. He's also got a store, and we're his best customers.

This was our first church. After a while it got too small, and so we built the beautiful new church out of stone. For a while the old one served as a school. But the tower on the old one didn't have to be taken down, a storm did that job for us.

We still like to think back on those Sundays in the old church. It was the first one, and we built it with our own hands. There is where we heard the Word of God, and from there we received many blessings for our farms.

18

It Takes All Kinds to Make a Church
· ·

Three months back I wrote you about some of the people we made into Lutherans, and how we converted them into helping build the church. Today I'm going to write you a story today about one of them.

Wieschen is in the midst of housecleaning, and there's no talking with her. Because the whole house smells like water, I said something about Noah's flood. Her reply was that I could just go ahead now and build myself an ark and sail far away. Ja, those are the ways of the womenfolk, *so sind die Weiber.*

The man I'm writing about is Schwenske. He and I were together on the church council for a year. His house is a real pigsty. In my life, I've never seen such a dirty place. Dishes were stuck to the sideboard. Regiments of bugs were exercising on the walls. Only they couldn't move — they were in dirt up to their belly buttons. Na, there are different kinds of bugs on God's green earth. Some like to sit in apples, others in dirt. They are by nature different, but they are all bugs.

Then the pastor came to visit them. The mister wasn't home, so the wife came in. She had been in the barn, forking out manure. You could see that, and she smelled like that. Without as much as washing her hands, she put out the bread and butter, and some cheese. Pastor had to eat, even though it gagged him. It didn't want to go down. He even had to take a big hunk of cheese as a gift. He was just happy to get out of there without having to drink anything.

When he got home, Pastor set the cheese on the desk in his study. As he came back into the room, his vicar was slicing off pieces with a knife as big as a sword. Now this vicar was quite a fine young gentleman whose father was a college professor. He also had visited at the Schwenskes and afterwards couldn't eat for a whole day.

Pastor walked in on him *so emsig essen sah*, and caught him busy eating away at that cheese. Pastor said to himself, "He wants to be a pastor, which means he has to learn to eat with all kinds of people. Otherwise, they'll feel insulted. Now this young man is real picky in what he eats. He needs to learn to eat with the common folk. And this is the moment to convert him."

Just as Pastor was holding this thought, the vicar commenced to praise the cheese, saying that this cheese surely had an unusual smell. "Ja," said Pastor, "it's from Frau Schwenske." Hearing that, Mr. Vicar stopped chewing. He laid down his sword. He got pale in the face. He ran out of the room. The cheese also ran back into the fresh air, and the vicar's supper followed right after the cheese. That's when the pastor gave up on trying to convert the vicar.

These are the stories we tell around here. Finally Schwenskes sold their farm for a good price and moved across the Missouri River to Nebraska. Along with them moved a neighbor whose house was spotless. After they were gone, folks around here came up with a saying "Hir *schwemmen wi Appel*, away, away swim we the apples, said the Gravensteiner to the Horse-Apple [horse-apple: a German expression for horse manure], and down the creek they went." Them that bought Schwenskes's place worked for half a year cleaning it up. The Mrs. had to shovel the worst out of the house.

Wieschen said, "Don't write things like that. It's disgraceful gossip. And it's against the eighth commandment." I said, "Wieschen, that's not so. I'm writing this so that over there in Mecklenburg they know what things are like here in America." She said, "You're not writing any stories that embarrass you, why would you write them about somebody else?" "Ho ho Wieschen, I will write them too. I shall write about life here and paint it like it is. I have to do that, whether it embarrasses me or not." "So, tell me, what are you writing about yourself?" "How I got scolded from the pulpit." "Ach forget about that. It's been years, already ten years ago." "It's a good thing, Wieschen, that it didn't happen last Sunday. Otherwise I wouldn't be dipping the pen in my ink but in my anger." "It's not anything a Christian would do. I could set you the best meal, but you'd get up and walk off." "You're right, Wieschen! A meal of kraut made with love is better than the fatted calf cooked with hatred. Proverbs 15." "Na, let it be. You've never been one for kraut, period."

Now Wieschen is away, and I'm going to write you the story. There's nothing to it and it's been quite a while ago. But listen here, you don't have to tell this in the village.

We were having a little party with friends and relatives. Everything was going along fine, until at the end it started to get loud. A young man came by who had had a little much to drink. Now Wieschen had given him the word once before, a little earlier in the evening. He was being obnoxious and talking out of line. Now he started to work on Wieschen with words that rub hard. She looked to me for help. He kept right on picking and scratching. First he used needles, then he resorted to darts. Everything quieted down. I said, "Let it be now, or I'm going to give you one. You're not going to get away here in one piece if you don't let it be." It didn't help. The varmint just kept it up. Wieschen was embarrassed in front of everybody. I stood up. I went over to him. I raised my fist. Yes, I did it. But Wieschen got between us. Then one of the neighbors threw him out the door. I forgot all about it. But his dad went to the pastor and complained about me. That is part one.

Now comes part two. On New Year's Eve I was sitting in church. The pastor had a good sermon, "My Times Are in Your Hands." At the end, he made an announcement: "In our congregation there is a man who has raised his hand against one of our younger brothers. The man hasn't asked for forgiveness. So at the close of the year, let us all together make prayer for him."

Well let me tell you, they prayed for me and I didn't like it. As they were praying, I was thinking some unchristian thoughts, things you're not supposed to have in your heart when you're in church. So I prayed too, "Father, forgive them for they know not what they do." Afterwards, I went to see the pastor and told him about my prayer, and I also told him the whole story, all about what had happened. My heart is not a den of murderers. I also told him if he prays again from the pulpit for somebody in the congregation, he'd better find out what really took place, so that he doesn't pray past the truth.

So war alles wieder in Ordnung. So, now everything was again in order. Only the pastor got red in the face. He gave the boy and his old man a good talking to. The boy even excused himself by Wieschen and since then has behaved himself a lot better.

Na, this happens, "To err is human." In fact people even err when they're on the pulpit. But a mensch always stands in need of prayer. If it doesn't fit for him today, it will fit tomorrow. I think the dear God stored up those New Year's Eve prayers for me, so that another time they'll stand me in good stead. But when it comes right down to it, it's necessary that squabbles and misunderstandings be cleared up. And all this was cleared up.

Try Anything, Once

. . . .

Oha, yes, some unusual things used to happen in our churches. That was when we were scattered out, all over the countryside. There's a church story from those days that took place in a neighboring congregation, about twenty miles west of here.

Those folks over there had a good pastor but poor crops, three years in a row. Everything dried up and saved them the trouble of harvesting. Their cows looked like greyhound dogs. Those folks survived the first year, but when the heavens closed up for two more years, they all met together and lamented their troubles. When they had done that, they decided that in times like these they could save some money by not paying the pastor's salary. So they went to see him. First they talked weather, like people do when they see each other. Then one gave the other one a poke in the ribs, and finally the elder on the church council came out with it.

That's the feller from Buxtehude, the elder. He came from over there on the other side of Hamburg. That's where the rabbit and the hedgehog ran a race, and the hedgehog beat him. *"Herr Pastor, sagt er,* you have been preaching God's Word to us for some three years now, and we've gladly paid your salary, with no complaints. But now, in these bad times, we have to conserve. The congregation can't raise the money, and we're not going to be able to pay you. We've decided that for a while we're going to try to get along without you."

At that point ol' Buxtehuder stopped and looked around at his fellow congregants. Nobody helped. His temperature was rising, and he began to sweat. It wasn't easy. The pastor was standing, looking out the window. He didn't say a word. Ol' Buxtehuder started over again, "We been think-ing over that word you preached to us, '*Gott ist in den Schwachen mächtig,* God is powerful in the weak.' That's true for these dry years. Particularly when the weak ones are more than just a few. And, we have prayed for

God to bless us. Now we are twelve church council members. We thought for a quarter of a year we'd take turns. Each one of us would do a Sunday, and we would give a spiritual lesson in church, the way you do. Only shorter and with more power. It would be one of us after the other, so that everybody got a chance."

It got quiet in there. Ol' Buxtehuder was really heatin' up. He had to wipe off the sweat. The pastor was still looking out the window and hadn't said a word. Then Buxtehuder started over, "You have faithfully preached God's Word to us. We're thankful for that. But now we're in big trouble, and we want to thank you if you'd look for a new congregation. Our dear Lord will help you, and we will pray for you. If God listens to us and sends rain, we'll get you to come back." Er hustet, he coughed, he shuffled his feet, he was finished. The rest of them all nodded their heads and thought to themselves, Du hast deine Sache gut gemacht. You've done a good job.

The pastor was also done looking out the window. He turned to them and said, "Ja." Then he rubbed his hand over his mouth and chin once or twice. "Ja, if you believe it's necessary, and you can get by without me, don't worry. Things will work out. Today is Monday. I'll go next Thursday and you can start that following Sunday. Only let me leave my things here for a few weeks. At this moment, I've no idea where I'll be going." All twelve of them nodded yes and left. Pastor called out after them. "Until we meet again, God bless you all and pray, send us the rain." "Ja wohl," they chorused.

Outside the house, the one said to the other ones, "When he said rain, he put his hand over his mouth, but in his eyes I think he was laughing. And what's he got to laugh about? But you tell me, what's he rubbing his mouth for?" "Let him rub," the other ones said. That next Thursday the pastor left.

In those days, nobody on the farm thought they needed a telephone. In the next little while this story made the rounds of the whole neighborhood. "Over there, at that whatchamacallit church, they fired their pastor. When the years get dry, God's Word gets too 'xpensive for 'em. Next Sunday one of the council members is going to give a spiritual lesson to the congregation. It's going to be short and with power." Them's the words that made the rounds.

That next Sunday was there before you knew it. Anybody with legs was in church, and that included me. I said to Wieschen, "I have to hear this." She said, "Those people made a dumb mistake, and the one they'll make on Sunday will be even dumber. If you can believe that. For what good reason are you running your shoe soles off to hear that?"

But when it got to be Saturday, I walked the twenty miles and by evening I was there, and I was done in. On Sunday morning the church *war proppenvoll* — it was packed. It hadn't seen it that full for the pastor for a long time. The lectern stood in front of the pulpit and the Buxtehuder sat in front of that. He had his Sunday suit on, but he wasn't wearing his Sunday face. His behind went first one way and then the other way on the pew. Na, I said to myself, I'm glad I'm not in your skin today. *Wo dit woll moet*, how's this is going to turn out?

The hymn was 288, "Why Are You, Poor Sinful Lump of Clay, So Proud in Your Iniquity?" It's a long hymn, 13 verses. It was over before you knew it — but then he had us sing a second hymn. The congregation was puzzled. Usually he was not all that much for music. Finally we got through that. One more hymn? No, that wouldn't work.

Finally, he got up and walked over to the lectern. The eyes of all were upon him. Some were curious about what was going to be. Others were totally awestruck. Ol' Buxtehuder was shaking in his pants, and he was sweating bullets.

We stood up to show our respect. He opened the Bible to Matthew 23, "Oh ye serpents, ye brood of vipers, how can ye escape the damnation of hell?" We sat down. Then we all had a good cough, so's we didn't have to interrupt him later on. We sat up straight, and I said to myself, *Alles was recht ist!* That's a good beginning for a short sermon, with power. Now farmers like us, we're hardly serpents and vipers. That's a little much. But he's the preacher. And, besides, there's a lot of serpents and vipers in the Bible.

The congregation coughed good, . . . so did he. Then he sort of shook himself and believe you me, he started in. My dear friend I can tell you that what happened now was something I had never heard before in all my life, and I've been in church a whole lot. It wasn't of the Spirit and it wasn't of the Word. It was of fear, and it was of pure nonsense. He started in: "My dear Christian friends, or as the Apostle says, 'You serpents! You brood of vipers! . . . You snakes in the grass!'" That's what he said. "You vipers and serpents! You vipers! You serpents!" At this he began to shout and hit on the pulpit with his fist. But it was out of fear, not out of strength. He tried to work up some courage. No luck. Then ol' Buxtehuder got really stuck. He looked into the Bible, he turned the pages, he started over again, "You brood of vipers! You snakes! You crawl in the grass! You grasshoppers!"

It was all over. He stared at us, we stared at him. We sat there in total silence. Then once more he got going, "You snakes! You snooks! *Ihr, scho-*

lettern und zangen! You wippers and snickers!" Actually, he got to sounding pretty good. Then he stopped dead. His short, powerful spiritual lesson was at the end. He looked like somebody in trouble.

One of the council elders was there. He was up for the next Sunday. He could smell the sweat and the fear, and the way ol' Buxtehuder was mixing up the reptiles and the insects. No question that today's spiritual lesson was done. He whispered loud to Buxtehuder, "Just say 'let us pray' . . ." Which is what this preacher needed to hear and do. So for a minute Buxtehuder searched Matthew 23 for a prayer start. Nothing. Besides that, he was done in, soul and body. He could hardly open his mouth. Finally, he folded his hands and said, "*Lasset uns beten*, let us pray: Woe to you scribes and pharisees. Amen." With that he sat down, wiped the sweat off his face, and said: "Hymn 346, *Nun danket alle Gott*, Now Thank We All Our God." With that church was out.

The devotion had ended a long time ago. You know what? I wonder what God in his mercy had to say to the Ol' Buxtehuder about that spiritual lesson?

All the church council elders met and resolved, "We want to find where our pastor is and ask him to come back. It's harder than we thought."

The pastor hadn't gone too far. He figured that's probably how this was going to end up. Already the next Sunday he was on the pulpit, and again, the church was full. Everybody thanked him and asked that he forgive their stupidity. They'd rather go through another dry year than through another sermon like that.

Ol' Buxtehuder had to apologize publicly to the congregation. He said it was because of fear, and he was sorry. But he couldn't keep from adding, "You wouldn't have done any better." Anyway, they asked him to resign from the church council because he did it in front of everybody, even before God the Almighty. From then on, *if* you even mentioned his reverend experience, he'd get all wild and worked up.

After all of this, the pastor and the congregation got along real well together. No matter how dry the year, nobody ever asked him to leave again.

When I got home, I set my walking stick in the corner and said to Wieschen, "Again, you were right. In a dry year, it's better to eat sawdust than to stand before the altar and not be able to do what the reverend does." Wieschen thought out loud, "I told you so." But then she wanted to hear the story and every grim detail.

20

Working Up the Corn Crop
· ·

For years and years our corn harvest has been good — it only got rained out one summer. Corn likes to stand in the sunshine. A bushel of corn weighs almost as much as the little Rostocker measure in Mecklenburg, about fifty-six pounds. Right now a bushel of corn brings seventy-five cents — that's a good price.

Here by us in America a bushel doesn't always carry the same weight. A bushel of wheat weighs sixty pounds, a bushel of potatoes is about the same. You figure corn differently — it depends on whether it's on the cob or off the cob. With cobs, a bushel of corn is about seventy pounds. Without the cobs, the way it comes to you over there in Deutschland, it weighs about fifty-six pounds. There's not much difference between German pounds and American pounds — a hundred German pounds comes to about a hundred eight American pounds.

We use the corn stubble, and we use the cobs after they've been shelled. We use 'em both, ja well. We stick 'em in the stove. They heat better than hard coal and hold the fire real good. You can't leave the corn stubble in the field. That won't work. If we waited until it rots, we'd be as old as Methuselah. And they're hard as a rock. If we want to break 'em up we take an axe.

Das Korn macht viel Arbeit, there's a lot of work to corn. Those first years we did it all backwards. We'd haul it together in one big pile. There we'd shuck it, stack the stalks, and rub the kernels off the cobs. We'd leave the house before four in the morning — even Wieschen got up to cook coffee for us. The horses also had to have something to eat. The way my head works, I'd wake up at the right time. I remember when I worked for Hannjürn there by you in Mecklenburg. We had to thresh quite a few bundles of rye before we'd even get to eat our flour soup, and that was breakfast.

We did our corn that way year in and year out, until we got smart and changed our life. We quit getting up so early. We started hauling the corn home, and we'd work it up there. Sometimes we did it by daylight, otherwise in the evening.

The family would sit together in the kitchen and shell corn. You'd rub one ear of corn on the other and the kernels would jump right out, like crickets. It does take time. Nowadays it's only the small farms that do it that way. The big farms do everything with machinery.

Out West and in Canada they do it with steam power. At the same time they chop up the leaves and stalks for fodder. We even feed quite a bit of green corn. We bring it in and pile it high. Then we close it off airtight. That way it keeps real good, and the livestock loves it.

In winter, working up corn the old way gave us something to do. It was a time for telling stories and reading out loud. We heard news from the old country and from the new. We heard about the just and the unjust, about getting rich and getting poor. We heard the good and the bad from all the directions that the wind blows, *aus allen vier Winden*. Mostly the news came from the East. About four miles north of us, a main road goes by our farm. It runs west into the country. Every once in a while, somebody going west falls off the edge and drops in on us. They're tired of wearing out their shoe soles. Sometimes they are without shoe soles.

If those drop-ins looked decent, they could stay. Wieschen would feed 'em and give 'em a bed. Then evenings they'd help with the corn. They liked that, and so did we.

That's when they'd tell their stories — they liked that too, and so did we. Mostly they had seen and experienced a whole lot. Some of them could talk nonstop for eight days. You got to hear it all *und wurde nicht dummer davon*, and it didn't make you any dumber.

It was the old ladies who really liked to tell their stories. When you got them together, as one was talking the others had their mouths in gear like they were nibbling on something. One could hardly wait for the other one to finish, so she could take her turn.

Them stories were the best. The storytellers came from Russia, from Galacia, Bessarabia, and whatever you call those places. Our boys couldn't even find them on the map. Sometimes the country was so small I could cover it with my thumb. You can hardly imagine that there are people living there, people with stories. You get to thinking those maps are only for school kids to study. One place is yellow, the other blue or brown or green.

All of a sudden, then somebody was sitting with us around that pile of corn who came from one of those yellow spots on the map. It came to life.

People lived there, people like us, only different. Years later we'd often say, "*Haha da was ja der her*, that's where that one came from who told about the Polish Jews." Or, "Wieschen, that's where the woman lived who had those two boys — evenings they would sing the most beautiful songs, nights they'd wet the bed."

There we were, sitting around that pile of corn, some talking and some taking it all in. We drank coffee and we smoked until the air was blue. The corn moved right along until about nine o'clock. Then we started with our prayers and devotions — after that we went to bed. The next morning the company said thank you and left. Of course, some stayed longer. If only for one winter you could have heard all that talk and written it up. Those were stories. They would make quite a book.

Working corn up this way doesn't happen anymore, but you still have to come visit us. You'll sit at the head of the table, and in the evening read

the devotions. If we can't get to church on Sunday, you'll read us a sermon. Just think it over, but don't take your time. You have to come over
here right away soon. Until then, I'm going to tell you some of our cornshelling stories to whet your appetite. Wieschen said, she's going to
do everything in her power to make it a pleasant stay for you, and she
said, you're going to like it here. *Das glaub ich auch,* I believe it, because if
Wieschen says it, you know it's true and it's going to happen.

It was a beautiful afternoon when she came to us. I could see her coming while she was still quite a ways off. I thought it was a party, not just
one person. But that can happen to you when you're working the corn.
She turned out to be alone. All alone, she was jabbering and arguing with
herself. *Das hat der Mensch gern,* a person likes to do that in order to make
thoughtful conversation.

At first she put on like a scared chicken and looked at us as if she had
strayed into the hands of the robbers and murderers between Jerusalem
and Jericho. While we were eating supper, she looked us all over pretty
careful. I said, "Go ahead and eat, there's no poison in it. We're all sticking our spoons in the same dish." She got to eating pretty good. She
talked enough for three people, but mixed stuff together so that you could
hardly stand to listen to it. It was like somebody was after her with a buggy
whip. It was like, for a long while, she was scared and running away from
something.

When she first came she sat down behind a corn shock and got real
quiet. I said, "*So, nun siehst du,* so now you can see that you are among
normal folks. Nobody's going to hurt you. Behind this corn shock you're
as safe as in Abraham's bosom. And now tell me how you got here, only
get it all in the right order. So talk now and give us your story. Tell us what
your name is, where you've come from, and how you got across the border, since you obviously don't have a husband.

Then she told her story. Her name was Etelka Bräuer — she was from
Hungary. Her mother and father were Germans. The boys found Hungary
on the map real quick. So far, she was right. Then she really got going,
"Ach, I am so happy that I've come to you and that, excuse me, I have
escaped Satan's hand."

"You're going to hear how I got across the border. You only have to be
good-hearted and bold, because the Lord is generous to the upright. I
made up a name for myself and got as far as Teschen. In Teschen they
asked me, "Where you headed?" I said, "To Oderberg."

My firstborn pointed it out on the map to me, "Father, here it is." Then
she said that they asked her, "No farther than that?" "No!" So in God's

name I went to Oderberg. In Oderberg, they asked me, "Where are you headed?" I said, "To Ratibor." "No farther than that?" "No." So I went to Ratibor. "Father, look here is Ratibor." In Ratibor they asked me, "Where are you headed?" I said, "To Berlin." "No farther than that?" "No." So I got as far as Berlin, and then nobody asked any more. So I went on to Bremen. With God's help I managed to get all that way. You only have to be good-hearted and bold, because the Lord is generous to the upright."

I said, "Your Christianity is of a sort which isn't proper for true believers. You bluffed your way through all that and then you say 'God helped me.' With all that good-heartedness you're in a snarl, and you're in trouble with the second commandment." "Ja," she said, "that's how it is, God is generous to the upright, that's how I made it through." "Na, then get on with your story, but this time please leave God out." And, so she kept on.

In Bremen there was a man at the railroad station with a blue uniform and a number on his cap. He grabbed at me and wanted to take my things. But I held onto them, and I said to him, "Get behind me *Satanas!* I am going to see the high and mighty Herr Pastor. I am of the evangelical faith. I was born evangelical and brought up evangelical. And if I'm in the faith, well then I'm in the faith." At that he backed off and only turned around once to see where I was headed. Ach, it is really too bad to fall into Satan's hand. Excuse me.

I saw the pastor, and he handed me over to Herrn Missler. Then is when I got a still different name. You only have to be good-hearted and bold, and you need to put your money in your stocking. Excuse me. I have had to make my own way, and it's been hard. My husband was a Satan, excuse me, and my boy ran off with all my money. I can't believe that I've survived all this. Excuse me, but I don't want to sleep in a hotel, I want to sleep in your kitchen.

Na, I said, about putting your money in a stocking, that pleases me. I'm not impressed though with that business in your story about being good-hearted. At the train station in Bremen, Satan does not wear a blue uniform and a cap with a number on it. "Wieschen, where are we going to put this one up?"

Naturally, Wieschen found a room for her. She went to bed, and we sat up by shifts to keep watch. It wasn't long before there was quite a noise in her room. She screamed, "Help! They trying to poison me. I have fallen into Satan's hand." Wieschen got up and went into her bedroom. Everything *war in Ordnung*, was in order. But she said, "No, there is poison in the air. Satan's hand is in the air in this house. I can smell it. I have fallen among robbers." Wieschen said, "*Dummen Snack*, that's dumb talk." And then Wieschen sweet-talked her into going back to bed.

Not much later, she started up again with that talk about poison. Wieschen got out of bed and comforted her again until she fell asleep. "Wieschen," I said, "this could be a short night. That old lady is not right in the head. No reasonable human being would think we've put poison in the air. That would poison us. Such talk brings no honor to our house."

"Jürnjakob, calm down!" said Wieschen. "Do you think there are curious people standing around outside our house, listening to what's going on? This woman has had some bad days in her life — they have made her fearful. You just turn over on the other side and quit the talk." So my dear friend, upstairs we've got one screaming in Hungarian-German and downstairs one is growling in American-German. That's plenty for one night.

With that sermon over with, I was amazed. I turned over and went to sleep, thinking to myself, "That is the longest speech Wieschen has ever delivered in her whole life — and in the middle of the night. And it's because an old lady upstairs has a heart full of complaints. All that Wieschen gets out of it is running upstairs and downstairs. It's truly a remarkable race of people that has mercy on their own kind in the middle of the night."

Two more times the one upstairs noised her complaints, and two more times Wieschen got up and looked after her. Finally she fell asleep, and so we also could fall asleep. It didn't last long, soon daylight was peeking in the window.

Afterwards, when we all had our breakfast coffee, I went upstairs with her. That woman could not get it out of her head that there was poison in the air. I put my nose to all four walls and sniffed upwards and downwards. There was no poison that I could smell, but I did figure out what she was talking about. I told her as much in Hungarian-German. "No," I said, "there is no poison here, it's the smell of American soap that you're not used to. I can see on your neck and behind your ears how long it's been since you and soap have had a meeting. You also haven't really combed your hair. You'll have to get used to doing that in this land of America." She promised as much, and afterwards she happily went on her way, satisfied that it was only soap and not poison, and also not the hand of Satan.

Ja, *erzählt hat sie genug*, she told plenty enough, and we have experienced more than enough with her. But she didn't show us much with the corn.

She had no quiet mind and that's why she was missing a quiet busy hand. My friend, what I think is this. She will risk it all again. I think that she thinks that the Lord God will help her with words. I think there are Christians of a different sort in Hungary. Now this was number one.

Next comes number two. I let him sit in the big chair. He won't get a job here shelling corn — he's too old. Two years back he came through here. Then he was counting up to seventy-eight years of life — now he's eighty. But he moves along quick, like a squirrel.

He was headed for the Hanover area in Germany to have someone look at his eyes. There's a city there named Göttingen. A good eye doctor and spectacle maker lives there. On the map Göttingen is nothing but a dot.

This man at eighty years still has all his teeth and his hearing is real good. His only problem is that to read the Bible or the newspaper he has to hold it at arm's length.

Now he is on his way to Göttingen for spectacles that will bring his Bible and his newspaper closer to his nose. He also wants to visit his relatives.

His boots brought him to our house, and then after a good fourteen days over there in Deutschland he got the right prescription for a pair of glasses. This was all two years ago. Now he is back again and this time everything is going the way it went the first time. "Na," I said, "*da bist du ja auch schon wieder*, so you're back already." "Ja," he said, "I have to go to Göttingen again and have them put new lenses in. In my old days, the glasses wear out like the soles on a boy's shoes. And with worn-out glasses you can't see. That's why I'm going back over there, besides the American glasses aren't any good."

It was about two months when he got back, and he was very happy. "How did things in the old country please you?" "Oh," he answered, "it was good by the eye doctor. He was pleased to see me. He knew right away who I was when I told him. Ja, that's a friendly man. And his little wife was friendlier. When she heard that I was from America, she served me coffee and cake. After I told her about being eighty years old, she extra put a nice soft pillow behind my back. They are friendly people. Ja, well."

"Now then, tell me about the family." "Well, that was so-so. I was glad to get away from them without losing my life. They're nice people but not my kind of nice. Nice to them means that when the American uncle comes to visit, 'the eyes of all wait upon thee and thou givest them their meat in due season. . . .' At first they celebrated and baked me a cake. It tasted good. And I was 'dear Uncle' this way and I was 'dear Uncle' that way. I liked hearing that.

"All at once, they started talking about how old I was and they got real serious and Christian about death and funerals. At the end they got to the wills and heirs. Even in the morning they were singing hymns. I didn't like it. When they noticed that, they quit with the death talk and the hymns. They started wanting me to go with them to Hanover. One needed a dress, the other one a hat. The next day I even bought the man a gold watch. They about broke me. They did it with love and holy talk. I couldn't say no, and I didn't say no. Only when I ran out of money, they ran out of love. Their face wasn't what it was yesterday and the day before.

"That's when I put on my traveling socks. Everybody had a Bible verse for me, and they hoped there would be a *Wiedersehen*. Me, I felt around in my empty pockets and said, 'Ja, I hope that too. It's been good here and I want to come again. The next time I come, though, you have to preach to me on a different text.' They all said, 'How so? What do you mean?' 'Ja, well, this time your sermon was on the verse, "a living dog is better than a dead lion," Ecclesiastes, the ninth.'"

Once he got his pipe smoking again, I said, "Na, you better stay home and forget the traveling." He didn't agree, "Ja, *fürs erste*, first off I want to do that. But when I have to have new glasses, I'll go back over there. Them American glasses aren't any good. Going on a trip makes for fun, only next time I'll need to put more money in my pockets." At that he shuffled off to bed.

Two years went by, and I began to look for him. He'd be needing new glasses now. He didn't come and he didn't come, and I never heard of him again. I think the friendly doctor folks in Göttingen won't get to see him again either. I think he's made a trip to the land where he won't be needing glasses from America or from Göttingen.

Numbers three and four. Now come the episodes involving two men. It's a noteworthy story. My dear friend, I can tell you that nowhere is there more excitement than here in Iowa. One day two men came to our door unannounced — they were real tramps, hoboes. I looked them over good, but in winter a person likes to see a new face every once in a while. At first I was tempted to send them on their way. They looked to be in pretty bad shape, and you know what that kind brings in your house. It jumps around in your britches even when it's ten below zero. But I recognized the flavor of their German, and when I looked sharply at the youngest, he seemed to be someone I had met before. I just couldn't place him.

So we took them in, and they ate like workhorses. When foodtime was over, they looked different to us. One big concern in life is are you hungry or have you had something to eat.

That evening we sat together behind all those ears of corn. I asked them where they were from and where they were headed. The big guy did all the talking. Once he got started, it was nonstop. He had it with words the way a squirrel has it with his tail. He said, "I come from Berlin. Times were bad there, so I left and went to Wittenberge in Mecklenburg. The food was bad there, so I went to Grabow." When I heard Grabow my ears perked up. Grabow is my country, those other places are foreign territory. "From Grabow," he said, "I moved on to Ludwigslust." That's when my ears really perked up. He kept right on with his story. "After hiking the road from Berlin to Hamburg, I had a thought. I know Berlin, but I don't know a thing about any of these Mecklenburger villages. Maybe I could strike it lucky here. So I turned off at the next country road and arrived at a place called Hornkaten. It's one of those villages that is stretched way out along the road. Everybody lives on his own little piece of ground. But the dogs didn't approve of me, so I kept on going."

My dear friend, just think about this, our long-legged friend from Berlin actually stopped off at our old village. Can you imagine that? And he mentioned it as if it was a nothing, as if he had been in some town in Asia.

When he said he had been in Hornkaten and then had moved on further, I stood up, went over and looked out the window. It was already dark, but I could see the light. I said, "I enjoy listening to you. I see that you're from Berlin and that you know your way around in the world. Let's hear more."

At that, he got real friendly. "I sure do know my way around. As a kid from Berlin I know how to strike it lucky any place, even in one of those Mecklenburger one-horse towns. That's how I got myself a job, working for the Mayor, the Bürgermeister — in Low German, the Burmeister.

"What I did was get the young ones into *Schwung*. When it got to be evening I would drum them out into the streets. There, I'd get them into a parade march, you know, get them to goosestep. Then we'll all end up at the tavern and get the beer bottles marching. I figured that if I worked it right I could get to be the mayor of those farmers and teach all of them the parade march, including the beer bottles."

I just stayed by the window. It was dark outside, but inside I had a good laugh. He was giving us the Berlin treatment. I thought to myself, the human mouth is a street traveled by the many. I said, "Doesn't the Burmeister have a daughter? Just think you could have married her and got yourself in line for the old man's job." "No, there was no daughter around and besides, I didn't like the work. You have to wait until harvest before you get any money in your pocket. That's not for me. I'm a kid from Berlin and know my way around. That place didn't even have one lantern on the street in a dark night. It was nothing for me. So, I moved on."

"Did you go through Ludwigslust?" "No, I went through Dömitz. I wanted to see the Elbe River. Why? What's it to you?" But his voice sounded uncertain.

My voice sounded real certain. I got a chair and set myself right across from him. On one side was the stove, on the other that pile of corncobs. He was walled in — there was no way out. Then I said, "What happened to the hundred eighty-five marks? The money you got in Dömitz for the mayor's calves?"

My dear friend, I can tell you that I have seen faces in my life, but never one like his when he heard me say that. He jumped up off his chair and looked for a way out. I grabbed him by the collar. I set him back down, gently. I said, "The Philistines have got you, Samson. If you make one move that looks as if you're running off, I'll make your hide look like the map of Germany."

After that I turned to the other one, his partner: "I recognize you too. You're Wickboldt's hired man. Your boss had you take two calves to Dömitz — you got three hundred fifty marks for them. You're another one who couldn't find his way back home with the money."

The two of them sat there like Lot's wife from Sodom and Gomorrah. Their mouths went open and closed, open and closed. The short one kept clearing his throat. The big fella's eyes studied the walls and the ceiling. And I said, "Just don't try to run or I'll make *Kloppschinken*, tenderized pork steak out of you."

Then, my dear friend, I got the letter out, the one where you wrote me the whole story. I was ready to hear their confession and their promise to repent. I gave it to the Berliner first, "You came to the village hungry and in rags, *ein Lump*, a real good-for-nothing. The sheriff's mother fed you up and he found clothes for you, so that people didn't think he had brought a scarecrow in out of the garden.

"First off, you were supposed to unload some barrels off a wagon. You bragged that in Berlin you wore something like that on your watch chain. But your big mouth couldn't get the barrels down, the *schulze*, the sheriff had to do it. Evenings, you were always out on the street and carrying on in the saloon.

"You have forgotten how the *schulze* used his nightstick to break up the rowdies, and how you got to feel it the most. Our *schulze* is a righteous man." My dear friend, I had your letter in one hand and his arm in the other. After I read him a few words, I'd pinch his arm good and he'd roll his eyes. We took turns on that, I'd pinch and he'd roll.

I said, "You got paid the money in Dömitz all right. But then you talked that one over there into going with you to Hamburg." I pinched again real good. He rolled his eyes. I said, "You don't have to put on an act here with that eye-rolling. I'm not buying any ticket."

At that I turned to his partner. "Nu kommst du, now it's your turn. Du bist auch dümmer als dumm, you are the biggest dummkopf of them all. If you were as tall as you're dumb, you could kiss the moon. You're also evil. The Brünings needed those three hundred fifty marks to pay their rent. You brought a great sadness into that family. The harvest was not good and money was scarce. Brüning had to borrow the money. Where is that money? What did you do with it?" At that, I squeezed his arm real hard. He cried out, "God help me!" I said, "Don't you bother our dear God, for you it's against the second commandment." I slapped him a couple times, and that was not breaking the ten commandments. I gave the big one a couple too, just to make sure I was being fair to the two of them.

After that was taken care of, I made a decision. "I should send the both of you back as criminals, so that you could serve time in Grabow. But that's all it is, time. And what about the money? So we're going to do it a different way." "You," I said to the big one, "in the morning, you write to the schulze and see if he will forgive you. The letter said that you scrammed out of there before you got paid. Probably that got evened out. But now, you're going to work for me as a hired man until the schulze writes back. If after that everything is all right, you can go. If you run off, I'll send the police after you. Nun weisst du Bescheid, now you know what it's all about."

Next, I said to the other one, "You're going to work here too until those calves are paid for. Then you're free to go. I'll send the money to the teacher tomorrow and he'll see that Brünings get it. Then you'll write them and ask them to forgive your Dummheit. Just write Dummheit, it's no lie."

That's how it all happened. The one from Berlin left after two months. The other one had to work three-quarters of a year. I read him your letter about how you brought the money to Brünings, and how the Mrs. cried tears for joy. That good-for-nothing got tears in his own eyes. He's not a bad person, just a real dummkopf.

That year the corn did its work real good. They could feel in their bones that they had to go from Dömitz to America before everything got evened out. When the big feller left, I said to him, "You could have settled all of this with a lot less geography if you had taken care of it in Dömitz. And, I'll tell you, the Berliners are not going to put up any monument for you." It's good that now everything has been settled, it's in *Ordnung*.

Now we're at number five: another Mecklenburger. It was afternoon, and we were shelling corn. The pastor sat on the sofa with a grog. The weather was cold and unfriendly. All to once, the door opened up and in came a mensch, a type with corners, built that way. That's also how he came into the room. When he closed the door, he turned around, took his hat off and began to speak: "Excuse me, my name is Drögmöller. May I introduce myself. I'm from the Singer sewing machine factory. These machines are famous worldwide. Every house has to have its Singer. Excuse me, but a sofa is not absolutely necessary. A piano is not an absolute necessity. A sofa goes out of style. A piano gets out of tune. But a Singer sewing machine will not go out of style and will not get out of tune. That's why you want to buy a Singer. You will never regret it. There is nothing better you can do for the happiness of your lovely wife. That way you will save yourself the cost of an expensive vacation trip, which is why you will want to buy a Singer sewing machine. We offer the most advantageous conditions and will always consider it an honor to count you as one of our customers."

After he got started, we all sat there like mummies, even the pastor. Then I got a hold of myself and said, "Na, are you all done now, Drögmöller? You've memorized your speech real good. We don't need to buy a Singer, though, because we've already got one. It's standing there right next to you. You missed seeing it because you were so busy saying your piece. But you're a Mecklenburger, so you're up for a grog. Wieschen, my lovely wife, please get the gentleman a grog." Wieschen went out to the kitchen.

It was his turn next, because he wanted to know how we knew he was a Mecklenburger. "That's an easy one," I said, "your speech betrayed you. All different kinds of people pass through here with all different kinds of languages. Some we can hardly understand, and some we can't understand at all. That's all the fault of that *dämlichen* Tower at Babel. But the Mecklenburgers we understand. That's because we write the same way they do. Now, enjoy the grog. It tastes. This dogged weather has nearly frozen your hands. After you thaw out, and if you don't want to go further on, you can stay here overnight. That's why you'll help us with this cornshelling. You'll save your shoe soles, and you won't have to pay for a tourist room somewhere."

He agreed. So the pastor and he sat there with their grog, and we shelled more corn. The rain was splashing on the windowpanes, *es war sehr gemütlich*, it was real homey. Conversation got around to the old country. When two real Mecklenburgers get together, they *klönen*, they talk a long line about home. From there we got onto the pastors, and Drögmöller told about this Pastor Brandtmann and the neighboring congregation. He had nothing but praise for Pastor Brandtmann: "That was a man with a heart for the people. He cared about the poor. He knew the peoples' troubles. When I went to him and asked for help, he reached into his own pocket and said, 'My brother in Christ, here is a dollar.'

"My own Pastor Brümmerstädt never helps. He has no compassion. The troubles of the poor people mean nothing to him. When I went to him and asked for help, he'd put both hands in his pockets and say, 'Drögmöller, go to work in the stone quarry, make little ones out of big ones. Then you'll have bread and *brukst nicht tau snurren*, won't have to make a pest out of yourself.'"

I said, "Your Brümmerstäd's advice sounds better to me than your Brandtmann's dollar." "That's what you think," he said. "How would you explain that?" "This is what I mean, Drögmöller. When you go to the quarry and do a day's work, you earn your own bread and you get a strong arm and some will power." "And you get blisters on your hands," he said and looked at his own hands. They were soft and had no blisters. I said, "It won't hurt you. You can be proud of work. Blisters are better than handouts. Anybody that lives off other people's money, anybody who is healthy and has his hands in other peoples' pockets is a *Lump*, a good-for-nothing."

That pastor nodded in agreement, and Drögmöller said, "That is very interesting what you're saying. Do you really believe that work in the quarry gives you energy?" "Ja, I really believe that. But it's not only the quarry that does that, any honest work will give a man energy and will power."

Drögmöller thought about that for a quite a while. Then he took another sip or two of his grog. Wieschen put more coal in the stove, and *es war sehr gemütlich*, it got quite homey by the Swehns.

When he came to the end of his thoughts, Drögmöller started again: "In my younger years I felt I had a higher calling. First of all I was in the college at Lubtheen in Mecklenburg and wanted to be a teacher. That didn't suit me after a while. Then I wanted to be a pastor in America. So then I wrote to Pastor Brümmerstädt that I was a person of many gifts and felt that I had a higher calling. And what do you think, Herr Pastor, what the man wrote back to me?

"He wrote: 'My dear Drögmöller! It is truly wonderful that you have discovered how gifted you are. Now it's always better when other people also notice that and talk about it. Otherwise it's suspicious. I know a man that the good Lord Himself called to be a preacher. You know he had to be very gifted. But he answered and said, "Ach, Lord, I'm not fit to preach, I'm too young." If you want to know more about this, open up your Bible to Jeremiah 1.'" I asked him, "Did you do that?" "Ja, I did do it and I got as far as the boiling pot that faced north, but I also left the seminary behind. Being a pastor didn't really suit me either. To work on a farm, milking cows and moving manure, was also not my idea of a life. Then I wrote to my friend and supporter who is the missionary to the immigrants in Bremen. He in turn wrote to a bank president in Schwerin who wrote me and invited me to come and introduce myself."

"Well, what did the bank president say to you?" "Ja, das war ein lustiger Herr. He was one of those jolly gentlemen — short, round — and at first real brief and real serious: 'Did you bring your papers?' I handed the package over — everywhere I've been, they've written me a recommendation. Sunday afternoons, I enjoy reading 'em. It's a joy to see what people have said about me. Na, the bank president weighed the package in his hand, looked at me pointedly, and said, 'You evidently like to walk?' 'Not at all sir, I have flat feet.' He laughed loud and hard at that one. He laughed until he ached. Why did he laugh, Herr Pastor?" "He thought you moved from one place to the next a little too often." "Ja, that's what I thought. Well, we had quite a good talk after that, and finally he says to me, 'You know about as much as any good student. Let's give it a try.' Where and how did he come up with that? He hardly looked at all my recommendations." "He got that out of the conversation." "Ja, that's exactly what I thought. Well, anyway, he put me to work selling sewing machines."

"Herr Pastor," says Drögmöller, "I feel that I can trust you. I respect you. But I don't respect my boss. Look at this letter the man wrote to me. I don't sell enough sewing machines to satisfy him. But the man obviously neither knows any grammar nor does he know how to spell. How can a person respect a boss like that? I'd like to know your opinion. I would like to hear what you have to say about that?" "Ja, Herr Drögmöller," said the pastor, "that all depends on what you wanted to learn from the man. Did you want to learn grammar?" "No, not at all." "Did you want to learn orthography from him?" "No, not at all." "Did you want to learn from him how to sell sewing machines?" "Ja, he really knows his sewing machines. And that man knows how to make words. He also knows how to do business." "Then pay attention and respect him." "Aber, Herr Pastor, the man neither knows any grammar nor does he know how to spell."

"You tell me now, Herr Drögmöller, do you know about Charlemagne, the great king?" "Yes, I do, 768–814!" "Do you respect Charlemagne?" "Very much." "Now, that man did not know how to write. He made more mistakes than any child makes in school. But he's still Charlemagne." "That's impressive, Herr Pastor. That makes sense. Na, denn when my sewing machine uncle makes a mistake, I'll think of Charlemagne, and I'll respect him as my boss."

"Then, man oh man, you'd better do it," I said. The pastor left, and Drögmöller joined us around all those ears of corn. I was beginning to understand him better, and I liked him. He said right out what was on his mind. What other people said about him, he also told right out, even if there was no honor in it for him.

He told more of his story. "Pastor Brümmerstädt always compared me with Joseph. He said to me, 'Drögmöller, whenever I lay eyes on you, I think of Joseph: 'Behold, here comes the dreamer.' That was what I didn't like about that man. He was downright impolite." "Oh, forget it," I said. "Joseph was a real holy man, and he's in the Bible," "Well, he still wasn't being polite." "Na, say it yourself, were you kind of a dreamer at that time in your life?" "I can't deny it. And it was a good time in my life. Once back then Brümmerstädt had to be in Hamburg, and I had to go along. He even took me along to the zoo. The two of us stood there for quite a while watching the lions. Pastor lectured about lions, and I daydreamed about all the lion stories I had read. He finished about the same time I woke up from my visit to faraway places. I spoke up first, "Herr Pastor, are those real live lions? Oh, he was angry. He even scolded me in High German, which is something he never did.

"One afternoon I was standing behind the barn making a visit to those faraway places, thinking about myself and my future. Nature has always been an inviting escape for me. When here comes the Frau Pastorin, who says, 'Drögmöller, the cows are bellering so loud I can't stand it. They probably didn't get any water again — Drögmöller, Drögmöller what are you always daydreaming about?' I brought myself back down to earth and answered and said, 'Frau Pastorin, I'm always learning new things.'"

This Drögmöller saved his money, and that's something I like. He's selfish with his money, and that's something I don't like. He was already in his middle thirties and had precious little income. But he's got three thousand marks in savings. He told me that himself, and I believed him.

For years he lived in Lübeck and went hungry. Once a year, on Old Year's Night, the tightwad turned into a wastrel.

"Ja, that night I lived it up. I bought myself a choice piece of smoked eel for half a taler, a butter cake with raisins and korinthers, an extra pound of butter, and a bottle of port wine. I set it out on the table and put myself behind it. Ja, I devoured it, and later on I even ate the skin of that smoked eel — it was so fat and good. Only trouble was, in the night I had one terrible stomachache. Now, where do you think that came from?" "Na Drögmöller, wenn du dat all inpakt hest, when you loaded yourself up with all those groceries and then set them to swimming in that port wine and butter, and then you topped it off with the eel skin, not even a prairie buffalo can digest that."

"Well, that's what I thought too. Otherwise I have a strong stomach, going hungry has always agreed with me. But I must admit that from St. Martin's Day on, I always looked forward to Old Year's Night. I lived in good fashion and high times, like Moses and the three fat years of Egypt." "Now listen," I said, "and don't take me wrong. It wasn't three fat years, it was seven. And, Moses wasn't even there. Furthermore, the 'good fashion and high times' isn't about Moses, it's the story of the rich man in the Gospels. You don't know your way around in the Bible as well as you think you do. You haven't got the right Schlagordnung, order of events. But let's read Jesus' story about the rich man for devotions and then let's hit the hay."

He still had something on his mind and finally came out with it. He asked Wieschen for a favor: "Can I use your kitchen to put on a clean shirt? It's nice and warm there and tomorrow is Sunday." In her lifetime Wieschen had not heard the likes of that, but she said yes. He said, "In Lübeck my landlady always let me do that. That saved me from building a fire in the stove in my room. So Saturday night I'd take my shirt into the kitchen and she'd excuse herself. When she was out, I'd take off my old shirt and sit for a while right next to the stove. It was real warm there and a good place for daydreams. After I got good and warmed up, I'd put on the clean shirt. Ja, das war eine schöne zeit, those were good times." And those were his stories. Wieschen sat there and made big eyes.

On Sunday he was still around. He got to talking about his mother. He thought a lot of her, and she of him. He was the only child. Once she came down sick and was in need of money. He held on to his money real good, but he did take three hundred marks to go back to Germany to see her and nurse her back to health. I sure approve of that. Anybody who honors his mother must have his heart in the right place. He keeps the fourth commandment.

He took off the next day. I think he probably won't sell many sewing machines in this land of America, even if he says his piece without a mistake. I think that in his head he's just a little too stiff. On top of that, he's lonely. He's not the kind who makes it in this country. But he's like a child — you can't help being good to him.

Wieschen gave him the best advice: "The thing for you to do is go back to Mecklenburg and marry a girl who owns a little land and has two cows." He didn't want anything to do with that. His idea was that in America money lies around in the streets. All you have to do is stoop over and pick it up. So Wieschen's suggestion will have to wait.

When he stoops over to pick up the money, he first has to have a daydream. In the meantime someone else comes along and walks off with the money. I feel sorry for him. When he left, our thoughts and prayers went with him. But they returned without him. Once in a while they go after him again, without success. Maybe he took Wieschen's advice, after all.

Next is number six. The last one. Seven winters back, I wrote to you about him. I recognized him the minute he stepped in. I looked at him and I said, "Die Welt ist bannig klein. Oh, but the world is small." I would walk the fence to Chicago if that ain't the Frenchman doctor off my ship. And he was it. Now listen while I tell you how he looked.

His head is about as big as it was when we were on the boat for America. But now you can read the Lord's Prayer through his cheeks. Back in old Mecklenburg Krischan the baker would have been ashamed to wear his hat, even though Krischan wore any hat a farmer would put on his scarecrow. He was still wearing that coffee-brown overcoat, but down below it was looking more and more like green. Before and behind, it was patched with every color you can imagine. But that was mended a long time ago, and the patches hung down like mourning banners at a funeral. Over his coat he wore a cape. It seemed to me that it was hardly more than seams and threads. I don't think he had a shirt on. I asked Wieschen, and she said the same thing. And here we were in the midst of winter, a cold winter. He wobbled around on legs that could hardly hold him up. His britches were nothing but rags — you could hardly hold 'em together. Rope served him as suspenders. He had tied his shoes together with string, but the front ends had their mouths wide open. He had a chest like a rooster — it hung on his shoulders like a birdcage. The man looked like one of Pharaoh's seven hungry cows. You don't even want to talk about the live things crawling around on his coat collar. But they were also mentioned 'mong Pharaoh's plagues. The women don't approve when you bring them into the house. They're all like that, including Wieschen.

To begin with he didn't talk much, outside of a few words about the bad weather and about being hungry. I said to myself, Put this man in a wheatfield and he'll keep the starlings away. But you can't do that, because first of all it's the end of January, and second, he's a human being, created in the image of God, even though he's not exactly what God intended him to be. He's a man in trouble, and if you send him on his way, you'll find him lying behind the fence. You'll also find him lying on your conscience. On top of that, he's a German, even if he is one of the worst kind of Germans. Wieschen will probably feed him, and he can spend the night in the warm straw, so he can rest his tired bones. Only he'll have to get rid of those lice or Wieschen won't let him in the house.

Well, I took him up to the house and presented him to the wife. Wieschen looked him over. Wieschen looked me over. Wieschen looked him over. But she didn't look me over again. That was good. She didn't say a word. He didn't say a word. So I said, "You sure were in a hurry this morning, couldn't even wash up. Couldn't eat. We've got plenty of everything here and after a little soap and water, you're welcome.

I gave Wieschen a wink. For him I poured two buckets of warm water in a washtub out in the barn. Wieschen fetched him some old clothes — she even found him a shirt. I picked up his clothes with a manure fork and buried 'em behind the barn. When he came out, his outer person had a different look. Only my coat was way too big for him.

So, I said, now the inner person has a different look, because *Ordnung muss sein*, there has to be order in life. Wieschen set out a good piece of bacon and I cut him some thick slices of bread. She poured him hot coffee. She kept walking around him like in a circle. I knew what was going on. She believed in lice. Not me. He itched himself every once in a while, where you itch for things like that. It was only a habit of his hands and his thoughts.

Then he ate. My dear friend, I can tell you this — the man ate. My good luck has been that when we're shelling corn, people really have an appetite. Some of them haven't had anything between their teeth except their tongue for a long time. Finally, he had enough. He perked up a little. His eyes had got a different look. Do you know what I believe? I believe that if people had enough bread and bacon, there would be less hunger and less misery in the world.

Afterwards he napped a little, woke up, and I offered him a pipe. That really woke him up. He sent out clouds of smoke like Father Köhn's bake ovens at Pentecost, when there wasn't any dry wood left. He slowly thawed out and began to talk. Hunger and exhaustion had temporarily stolen his voice.

After he had rested, I put him on a chair behind the corn and said, "Now you've eaten and you'll also be free to sleep here. Now is the time to help shell corn. It's *schön gemütlich*, nice and comfy here by the stove and it's a good place to listen to stories. So tell us, where are you from and where are you headed?"

He worked on his corn. He was slow. After he started to talk, he picked up a little speed. His German sounded good, so his tongue wasn't lame or helpless. The more he talked, the more he sounded like the Frenchman doctor that I met on my trip over the big water. He waved his hands around, and in one hand he had two ears of corn and in the other, his pipe. In his head he was making plans. The children puffed their cheeks and wanted to laugh. He was putting on quite a show. Finally, I sent them to bed and thought my own thoughts. He was telling what his life had been like. He knew his way around in the northern states and in the southern states. He had been in the East and he had been in the West. He had seen everything, and he amounted to nothing. Now he wanted to go back to the big city. Think about that, this old boy wanted to go to New York and try his luck. And buried in the barnyard were his rags and lice — they argued against him. He wanted to make his way in New York, dressed in rags and crawling with lice. Wonder what people would have said when they saw him coming?

So I finally said, "*Da war es man gut*, it's surely good that you're starting out here. The way you were dressed they wouldn't have let you into New York. Whose fault is it that you're in such a pickle? My guess is that you're a little shy of work — you've changed jobs too often." At that he got real worked up and talked big. "Work? There's a difference between work and work. Some work like oxen, like they've got a plow to pull and rocks in their heads. Then there are some who work like they've got a brain in their heads and they're the ones who set the pace for all the rest. That's the way it's always been, and that's the way it will always be. Now me. I've got a head full of real brains. Just look me in the face!" At that he tapped himself on the head with a corncob. "Right now I'm down on my luck. Here in the West people are dumb and backwards. They're not ready for anything new. But for me, this is only for the time being. You just wait and see, in a year every kid on the streets of New York will know my name."

He kept it up, moving the air like a windmill. I panicked. This man has been out in the cold so long his brains froze, and now they're thawing out too fast. I learned in school that when your fingers freeze, you should warm them up slowly. That's probably what's happening to his head. Here by the stove, he's thawed out too quick and is going crazy.

As I was thinking this over, I had to admit that in some things he was right. There was a reasonableness in his ideas and there was an unreasonableness. But unreasonableness was winning. He talked against the rich and the poor. He talked against God and the president, against the farm and against the town. Against work and against no work. And all the while he was waving that corncob around in the air. He talked my shirt off. He talked himself in and out, and all the while his rags and lice were buried in the barnyard. But that warm stove had hatched all his louse eggs and out crawled one lousy idea after the other.

Mostly he talked against God and all that is holy. Especially against the resurrection of the body and life everlasting. He had long since given up on the Bible. He had gone through the Bible the way he had gone through his shoe soles. "Keep away from me with all that stuff," is what he said. "I'm too smart for the likes of that and I've been around the world too many times. I only believe what I can see and reason."

I said to myself, You'll have to push harder with him. Start with a parable. I looked at him friendlylike. "Dear sir, when I listen to all you've said, it reminds me of my oxen. They only believe what they can see and reason. That doesn't amount to much. And your exit won't be much more than that. But when my oxen exit, at least they leave behind a few pounds of meat for the pleasure of us human beings, zum Wohlgefallen für die Menschen. If you stick with what you say, when you're put in the grave the worms will have a feast. However, you'll get neither praise nor thanks from 'em."

"You should have studied to be a priest," he answered and waved his corncob in my face. "Don't come at me with them conversion stories. I'm too smart for that." "I don't want to convert you. I only want to tell you a parable. In the summertime my cows are on the pasture and eating grass. Do you believe that?" "Naturally, why shouldn't I believe that?" "Good enough. Alongside of them are some sheep they also eat grass. Do you believe that?" "Why not? What are you trying to prove?" "That'll come out at the end. Next to the sheep there are some pigs. They also eat grass. Do you believe that?" "Just tell me now, where are you headed with your parable?" "Just answer me yes or no! Do you believe that pigs eat grass?" "Ja." "Good enough. I'm about finished. Next to the pigs there are a few geese. They also eat grass. Do you believe that?" "Yes, I believe that.

But — " "Now you tell me, how can this be? The animals are all on the pasture and eating the same grass. But the pigs get bristles, the sheep get wool, the cows get a hairy side, and the geese get feathers. Can you reason that out? So then tell me how you do it."

He was quiet and didn't say a thing but "nein, no I can't reason that out. But I can tell you that it's a dumb parable that makes no sense. You should let the priests tell conversion parables — it's their business. Just don't bother me with that stuff." Then he started off again and brought down the blue out of the sky. I said to myself, You'll have to push harder with him. You're getting nowhere with your parables. So I said, "Now listen to me for one more minute. Otherwise your windmill will run so fast it'll start to burn. I'm going to talk to you without parables. I really know who you are. You're the Frenchman doctor that I crossed the pond with in Anno '68. You were hanging around with a girl from Silesia. She was the one with all the education and all the lice. When they were searching for you after we docked, it was because of wrongdoing. But that's a long time ago and it's all past. Let's talk about what's going on now."

That I knew him from way back when really hit him hard. At first he was confused and didn't say a word. He was silent. Only his pipe still smoked. Then he wanted to start up again, but I said, "Just give your mouth a rest. You said that for me this was only for the time being. That's also what the fox said when the hunter began to skin him. You said, 'I have a good head on my shoulders.' That has to be true because it sits on your neck like a pumpkin, only a pumpkin doesn't think. It doesn't have to. You say you only believe what you can reason. Ja, that's what you said. It's what the angleworm said to the rooster when the rooster had him by the collar. But he had to believe it. You said, 'I don't care what the Bible says. Nowadays the Bible won't help me get where I want to go.' Do you think, though, that you're going to make it with your rags and your lice?

"No, no, no, just rest your hands and your mouth. You've talked enough for one day, and I'll soon be finished. I only want to deal with you the way you are today. You are a nothing. You have nothing, you know nothing, you can do nothing, you believe nothing. That's why you fell under the wheels. Anybody who wants to get ahead here has to work hard. In any case it's good to have a support in life and in death. It's how you feel safe. Ja well. And for you I only wish that you wake up before it's too late. Now it's bedtime. Here are two wool blankets. Take 'em and lay yourself down in the straw. Have a good sleep. But leave your pipe here, so we don't have a catastrophe with the straw."

When Wieschen and I crawled into bed, she said, "Jürnjakob, you were too sharp with him. He's a sick man." I said, "Wieschen, I knew a man in Ludwigslust. Old Doctor Steinfatt mistakenly gave him a whisky bottle full of Rizinusöl, castor oil. Two weeks later he was as sick as he was to begin with. Then he wanted to sue the doctor. But the doctor said to him, 'Just be satisfied and be done with it. Look at how much is left of you.' So he went home and it all turned out for the best."

The Frenchman doctor coughed all night long. In the morning, the snow was knee deep. "Do you still want to go to New York?" He looked at me first, then he looked at the weather. He said, "I think I've got a chill, and to walk in weather like this is impossible. Also, I don't have money for a train. If you don't mind, I'll stay here today and see what the weather does. I'll help shelling corn, but you'll have to let up. You were pretty hard on me last night." I answered, "I wasn't hard on you, I was only after the old Adam in you. You forgot to take him off when you got rid of your old clothes." He said, "You have an old Adam too. It's your pride. Only you won't admit it." Ja, so sagte er. That's what he said. I was ashamed. I said to myself, This man is good-for-nothing, but he has looked into your heart, Jürnjakob. You also have an old Adam: your pride. He sits comfortably in your heart, with his head up and he dangles his legs. We are all sinners, and the dear Lord has sent this man into your house to reveal your sins. I opened my heart to this and resolved that I would not despise him. I said, "We can't let you go on with the weather like this. We're both Germans. You've got a bad cough too that needs to get better. Wieschen will make you a tea."

His cough let up, and he stayed on. My dear friend, I can tell you this, he never got to New York. He just got stuck by us. He helped out with the chores, and I paid him for it. It went on for about two years. At first the old Adam still showed his horns. When it got real bad, I would say, "I'm going to check and see when your train leaves." He'd improve. I tried to be fair with him, because I remembered my old Adam.

There was only so much he could do. He tried, and I praised and thanked him. A mensch appreciates it when he gets praised. He even got back with the church and came to respect the Bible. Only he didn't really ever get it right.

He learned again to pray the Lord's Prayer. At first he mixed it all up, but little by little it got better. Then he even learned some verses out of the hymnal — not much, but I guess it was enough.

Only his lung didn't want to come around. It had suffered too much while he was on the road, and now it didn't want to heal. He was only sick for a little while. Wieschen was loyal and took good care of him. At the end he couldn't talk anymore. I prayed the Lord's Prayer for him and gave him the blessing. He nodded his head to us and squeezed our hands.

After a while he opened his eyes real wide and said softly, "Mother, my mother." That surprised both of us. In the two years he was with us he never once said a word about father or mother. After that he went on his way, but not to New York. He left for another city and that one is eternal. His word proved to be true: *Es ist man bloss ein Übergang*, it's only for the time being.

During the two years he stayed with us, he became a different person. He found peace, peace on the outside and peace on the inside. In no way was he a dummkopf. Evenings and on Sundays we got into all kinds of conversations. He once asked me, "How does it happen that you know so much about the Bible and the hymnal and the catechism?" "In school." "That must have been a good teacher." "He still is," I said. I told him about you and that I am a Mecklenburger. But he didn't want to know anything about that. He said, "Mecklenburg is small and doesn't even have a constitution. It's not a free country."

"You're right," I said. "They have no constitution, but Mecklenburg is nevertheless a good land and it's peaceful. We have a grand duke there, and that's something America doesn't have. And Mecklenburg is not little either, not by a long shot. You must have had a really little atlas. Just look once at all the lakes in Mecklenburg. America only has the Salt Lake, there where the Mormons live. But in Mecklenburg there is all kinds of salt water. There's the Sült over by Konow, Sült means salt water, like Sülte, Sülten, and Sülstorf. And how does one Salt Lake compare with all of that?"

How many lakes do we have here in this country? If you start with the Ontario Lake and count the lakes on your five fingers, you won't have to start over again with the other hand. But Mecklenburg has ever so many lakes. There is the Wocker Lake, the Lake at Schwerin, the Schal-sea, the Goldberg Lake, the Krakower Lake, the Plauer, Malchiner, the Kummerower, the Müritz, and it goes on and on. And then there are the ponds and wetlands by the thousands. Of course there are acres and acres of solid ground from Boizenburg and Dömitz all the way to Rostock and then to Ribnitz. *Ne, das lass man*, you'll have to admit, Mecklenburg is a grand kingdom — it spreads out all over the place.

21

Friends and Memories
· ·

Nu geiht dat Kratzen, now my pen is ready to scratch out another letter. I wanted to get started last week, but I kept making mistakes. I kept scratching at the letters, sometimes six times in a row. I thought it was that good-for-nothing pen. But no, this time it was the ink. No ink in the bottle, no letters on the paper. Otherwise, I'm pretty good with a pen. But reading what I've written, *dat is en slim Stuck,* that's a real piece of work.

Uncle Sam is showing more mercy for his children all the time. Here lately, the mailman comes every day. For that the taxes are getting worse every year. *Nu man los,* now let's get going with this letter.

I'm going to tell you something that you never even dreamed about. Once upon a time old man Suhrbier asked Jochen Möller when we were still in school how many lice there were in Egyptland. Jochen answered, "A whole potato sack full!" He meant it seriously. He always looked pretty serious, even when he was eating. I've often wondered how he knew that. Because the Bible doesn't say that Moses swept them up with a broom and a bushel basket. This all happened before we had that big fire that burned out half the village. We were all around ten or twelve years old, just that age when you begin to think about things.

Karl Gaurke wanted to try and figure out how hot it was in hell. It was turning fall and we were tending cows. All we could say was, "How are you going to do it?" He said, "You'll see soon enough." Then he took some fir branches and some old rotten wood. It was the end of summer and things were pretty dried out. He got a really big fire going along that ditch between the Plahst and the Stör, took off his clothes, jumped right in, and sat down. We all stood there and looked. *Man bloss,* man oh man, but he jumped right out in a minute or two, started to scream, and off he took. In the Krullen ditch there was still some water — there's where he cooled himself off. For a couple of weeks he stayed in bed — his behind was nothing but blisters. He even missed all our games at the "flax-breakout." The real trouble came after he was out and around and healed. His father took over and gave him a good drubbing. His father had no patience for anybody's joking around with what is holy. After that nobody even dared ask him how hot it was in hell or he'd get pretty worked up. If you see him, ask if he still remembers this — no, maybe that's not such a good idea.

It must have been that same summer, about a half-dozen of us boys were tending cows by the Guhls. Actually the cows were tending themselves — the first cutting of hay had been made, and there was plenty of pasture. We were sitting on the wall eating blackberries and got to talking about fishing and angleworms and the Chinese. That morning in school we had read that the Chinese like to eat angleworms. And we wondered about eating German angleworms.

Krischan Kollmorgen, you must know him, he's the one who married the daughter of the tailor, Jürn-Jochen. Later on, they moved to Vielank. He's the one who said why can't you eat them on a piece of butter bread? What those goofy old Chinese can do, any Mecklenburger kid can do, any day of the week. *Man muss da bloss aufpassen*, you just have to make sure they don't crawl off. A good angleworm is just as fat as any of that pickled eel you buy at the fair. I'd give it a try, but only for a trade. I'm not going to do it for free.

We agreed, "Ja, we'll do it." We'll do a trade. Then we got out our

pocketknives and dug for angleworms. We threw 'em up to him — he was still sitting on the wall. He caught 'em, wiped 'em off, stuck 'em in his mouth, and ate 'em. For every bite of butter bread, one angleworm. For one little skinny worm, he got two cords for his cow whip. For a big fat one, four cords. He didn't have to twist any cords for that whip all summer. But he had to swallow hard and even choked on 'em. Krischan was one tough kid, but he didn't offer to do that again.

We tried just about everything that summer. Only while we were messing around, our cows strayed into the *Burmeister's Hafer*, the mayor's oats, and he came out and gave us a good thrashing. The next day we asked Krischan if that worm dinner had agreed with him. He just shook his head and said, "That all depends on the worm, said the Devil, and in the dark he mistook a frog for a pear — but you, just don't tell my Grandma."

22

Our School Needs a Teacher

• •

This winter I'm going to tell you about our school and what it was like when we first came to America. These days everything is in Ordnung, it's all right. In the beginning, it was a comedy and at the same time it was a tragedy. Our children were growing up like wild animals in the bush. I was working as a hired hand on the farm, and the farmers around here were still trying to make a life for themselves and for their families. They couldn't build a school and they also couldn't hire a teacher. Our pastor had mercy on us, got on his horse — at that time he lived several days from us by horseback.

We'd get together with everybody who lived within six to eight miles. Pastor would preach and then have school for the older children, the ones who were going to be confirmed. The little ones would cluster around and listen. Quite a few of them fell asleep. If there was time, he'd work with them: learning the alphabet and starting to read. After a couple of days the Word of God would climb on his horse and go to another farm and start over. That's how it was to begin with.

When I rented my first farm, quite a few Mecklenburgers lived in the neighborhood. We wanted to have a teacher. We talked to the salesmen that came through, and we put ads in two newspapers. Nobody heard from anybody. We tried again, and this time we had one reply. He wanted us to send the money for the trip. We weren't ready for that. So we tried again. We heard from another one. He came to visit. From the backside and the frontside he was pretty ragged. His shirt was hanging out of the seat of his pants. Das war man soso, we weren't real sure about him. He hadn't been at the shoemakers for quite a while. Na, that can all be repaired. The real trouble was he smelled like schnapps from before and from behind. Probably from the inside too. We asked where he was from.

He said, "I'm just off a big immigrant ship from Hamburg." "What did you do?" "I was the chief steward." "Why didn't you stay with it?" "The Captain hated me." "*Wieso konnte er dich nicht leiden*, why do you say he couldn't stand you?" "He was always messing around with my pots and pans, and I can't stand to have somebody looking over my shoulder. Besides, he was always telling me how to cook. One day I threw a cup of coffee at him and hit him on the head. He didn't like it at all. We had it out right then and there, in the kitchen. He got the worst end of it. That's when I left." *Na, sage ich*, well, I said, "I can see that you'll manage to get your due respect in the school. But throwing coffee cups, especially if they're full of coffee is not the way we do things." He agreed that he could get along without doing that again.

He got a pipe of tobacco from me and after he lighted, I said "Let's make an examination now, because we have to test and see what you know." That's what I said — the other ones had voted me to head it up. One had said, "When I write, the letters always get in my way." The other one said, "I don't even know one times one anymore." The third one, "When I read the old stumps always get in the way." So they sat at the table or behind the stove, fired up their pipes, and listened with devotion. It was a Sunday afternoon.

"I want to test you," I said. "You go right ahead," he answered and spit. He understood what was coming. "First comes the Bible." "That's going to be bad, the Captain kept mine." "That makes no difference. You still know what's in the Bible." "Ja, a whole pile of it. Holy stories are in the Bible about Abraham and David and the shepherds in the fields and Luther and Pharaoh and Charlemagne the Great." "Na, forget about that last one. Just tell me what you know about Pharaoh." "Oh, that was a truly noble man." "Can you prove it to us out of the Bible?" "Na," then he spit, "otherwise he wouldn't be in there." That was his opinion, but he was wrong. I asked about the Christmas story. "Sure, there are the shepherds and their sheep, and how they were on the pasture." "Go ahead, tell the story." He didn't know the beginning or the end of the Christmas story. Can you believe that? I said, "Give us the story about the storm on the sea. You know that. Just think of your time on the water." "Ach, what's there to tell about a storm. One storm is like the other one. Now one time when I was coming around the Cape of Good Hope — " "That's not in the Bible. Let's see how good you are with the Old Testament. How many sons did Jacob have?" He didn't know. "Who was Jacob's father." He didn't know anything about that either. "Then tell the story about Pharaoh and his dreams." His answer to that was, "I don't pay any attention to dreams." Believe me, that's what he said. He spit again and wiped off the sweat.

"Let's take a look at the hymnal." "Wonderful, I always got A's in singing." "Singing comes later. First do you know the hymn 'From Heaven Above to Earth I Come?'" Sure. Everybody does." "Na, then say the verses." "Say the verses? All I know is the one you just said." I asked him a whole pile of stuff. He puffed away on his pipe and knew from nothing.

Na, let's get back to the test. Next comes hymn singing. What do you know there?" "Oh, a whole lot." "That's nice. We want our children to learn how to sing until the walls shake. You sing something for us, something beautiful." He took the pipe out of his mouth. He started with "Old

Adam He Had Seven Sons." "But that's not holy music!" "But Adam was a holy man!" We got nowhere with that, but I'm telling you he was all mixed up.

"Try a song like the German kids sing in school, a folksong." "I can do that. I always got the best grades in singing. First I need time to think, that was a long time ago." He emptied his pipe. Filled it. Lighted it. He drew on it once or twice. Then he spit again. Laid the pipe on the table and said, "Now I remember one." He started to sing. He sang "*Möpschen, how soon in the day you fly up with joy, into the morning sun.*" "What is that for a song? I said, "Pug dogs can't fly." "Doesn't bother me. I got a book as a Christmas present one time. All kinds of songs like that one were in there. It was a picture book. Haifisch wrote it."

My dear friend. I can tell you that what he told us and what he sang for us was all craziness. Nothing to it. We looked at each other. Heinrich Folgmann peeked out from behind the stove and said, "My grandmother talked about a man like this one. He acted just like this one. He filled himself full of booze, fell under the table, and said. 'Don't worry about it. It happens all the time. It's natural.'"

We all looked at each other. We couldn't say anything against the book, because we hadn't read it. We were in trouble. So we went on with the exam.

"Now it's time for the catechism. Do you remember it?" "Sure, but the Captain kept mine." "How many chief articles are there in the catechism?" He didn't know. "What is the fourth commandment?" He tapped his pipe and said, "This pipe is going out." "Can you say the Apostles' Creed?" He puffed around on that pipe. He inhaled. He said, "Just start me out. How does it begin?" I said the first words, then he said the first few words. Then he stopped dead. We helped. He blew smoke. He started again. He was silent. We helped again. Finally we quit and that was long before we got to Pontius Pilate.

That was it as far as religion goes. I said, "When it comes to holy things, you're not too good. But you do know something, so we're going to test you in reading, writing, and arithmetic. I took our reader. I opened it to a story. I shoved the book over to him, tapped with my pipe on the title, and said, "Read this!" He looked at the book. He looked at us. He looked at the book a second time. He looked at us again. Then he got tricky and said, "Reading in front of people was not style in my day. If your kids have to learn to do that, you'll have to look for a different schoolmaster. This is sure one crazy place here." We all looked at each other.

Heinrich Folgmann peeked out from behind the stove and said, "My grandmother knew a man. When he was a boy a brick fell on his head. That's why he liked to look at nature. He said that the crab is the only creature that leads sensible life. This would be a better world if we all lived like crabs."

If I had my way, I would have thrown this chief steward out. But we were in trouble. That's why we went over to writing. I shoved a piece of paper over to him. "Just write your name on this, so we can see what your handwriting's like." His name was Bernhard Stöwesand. But when he finished writing STÖW he had already filled the page.

At the end, arithmetic. "What is the half-side of 23?" He thought for quite a while and used quite a few matches. At the end he said, "This problem is wrong. There's no answer. 11 is too few, 12 is too many." I gave him one more problem. "Two Arabians were sitting under a palm tree on the edge of the desert. The one said to the other one, 'What's happened to your daughter, the Rose of Schiras?' The other one answered and said, 'My daughter, your servant, is driving a herd of geese to the market in Morocco. One goose walks ahead of two, one behind two, and one between two.' Now you figure out how many geese there are." I saw this problem in last year's calendar, and I also remember you gave it to us in school, but without this Rose of Schiras.

He worked on a piece of paper 15 by 20 inches and filled it up on both sides. It was all numbers. He kept coming up with nine geese. And that ended the test.

We sent him out of the room, so we could talk it over. Heinrich Folgmann peeked out from behind the stove again. "My grandmother knew a man — " I said, "Your grandmother was a very wise lady, Heinrich, but she can't help us now. We're in trouble." We didn't talk long. Then we had him come back in, "Bernhard Stöwesand, *du hast den Examen bestanden*, you passed the test." He did have to promise us to quit drinking, because we wouldn't be able to pay his liquor bills. Then we fed him, and away he went. He took my pipe along with him.

The glory didn't last long. Two weeks later Wieschen started to talk. Now, Wieschen is no big talker. She says that it's enough when one person in the family talks. By that she means me. Her tongue is not like Joab's sword, it liked to go in and out. But when Wieschen starts to talk, you better listen. She said, "It's better for the girls to darn socks than go to school. And as far as the boys go, it's better they burn stumps and pile up roots." A week later Karl Diehn and Wilhelm Jahnke pulled their kids out of school. And Heinrich Folgmann sent me a report that his grandmother knew *einen Menschen*. . . .

That he smoked in the school was nothing I would complain about, even if it was my pipe. It was the drinking that was the difficulty. One time he was full of brandy up to his teeth. Die Jungs, the boys sneaked his bottle out of his pocket and filled it with kerosene, but they got it behind the ears. I thought about giving him a few myself, even though I was the one who examined him. I didn't have to do it though, he ran off. I've never seen him again. I've never seen my pipe again either.

The next teacher we hired was a fatty, about two hundred and fifty pounds. He carried one impressive belly around with him. We all had the same thought: Wonder what that cost him! You don't get fat like that off of pennies and nickels. We were mistaken. He got that way eating at our tables. But there was more to it than eating. He was also quite the story-teller. He knew everything and he understood everything. He knew it all from the cedars of Lebanon to the hyssop that grows out of the wall. Anything he didn't know, that's what he talked about with the most con-viction. He lied us all a hole, crosswise in the belly.

At first we believed him because he lied with such conviction. It finally got to us. We were all at a meeting of the congregation. He got going there until Schröder cut him off. Schröder told him his chalkbox dream. It fit in real good. Schröder said to Mr. Fatty, "How good that you're here. I dreamed about you last night." He said, "That's good luck."

"Just wait a minute," said Schröder, "I can't dream like the Joseph in the Bible. What I dreamed was that you had died. You were at Heaven's door, and Peter wouldn't let you in. He said, 'First you have to make as many x's on the wall as lies you have told. It's required up here.' You went ahead and got some chalk. You got started right away, to get it done right away. Then I dreamed that I died one year after you did. Peter gave me the same command. So what do I do in a case like that — I get a piece of chalk. On my way I met you. You had a big crate on your back. I said, 'Where are you coming from and where are you headed? And, what's in your box?' 'Ach,' you said, 'that's the eighth crate of chalk I've ordered from Chicago.' Ja, then I woke up and the dream was over."

Not too long after that he packed up his things. We didn't have to send him away. At that time we couldn't pay much of a salary, so we had all kinds of teachers: thin ones, fat ones, righteous ones, and unrigh-teous ones.

One of them, though, we'll never forget. He had real narrow shoulders, but he was made out of wire. He wasn't very tall, but he was tall in our eyes and in our hearts. He never used a stick on any of his pupils. He never scolded. He did it all with his eyes. To some God gives a strong arm, to others a quick tongue. God gave power to him through his eyes. His eyes revealed to him what was in a mensch. He could look through those kids the way we look through window glass. He tamed the wildest of them.

When he came to us conditions in the school were bad. The first time he came in, the children were jumping on and off the benches and running in the aisles. The only place they left alone was his chair. He sat down up there, watched them, and didn't say word number one. The second morning he did the same thing, and by the third morning he had his victory. He won it with his eyes. *Der alte Fritz*, Friedrich the Great governed his soldiers with a cane, our teacher governed his with his eyes. His storytelling helped. That's how he won them over. At no other time did our children miss so little school as during his time. No bad weather could keep them home. When he visited in our homes we were honored. These days he's a superintendent some place out East.

After him the pastor taught school for quite a while. Now we have young women as teachers. Some of them are about as smart as a goose and waste everybody's time. Others are really good and have improved our school.

We have built us a beautiful new schoolhouse. In the next letter I'm going to send you a picture. The benches are made so that each bench is for two, and the seats can be lifted up. It was about time.

That old schoolhouse was close to falling down. It had been our old log church. We had taken out the organ and put it in the new church. That made the north wall start to lean. It said, "I've stood long enough. I'm

tired. I want to lie down and rest me." The other walls had the same thought. The floor was shaky. The boys knew the places where it *quiekt* and *knarrt*. That's where they stepped. Boys are like that all over the world. The floorboards even had holes in them. The children would get their feet stuck in them and then the teachers had to help them get out. He used his knife for that, and a couple times he even used an ax. That didn't make the holes any smaller.

The stove also talked, "*Mir wird heiss*, I'm getting hot. I'm going to take off my jacket." He started to unbutton it. Now the jacket was made of bricks. They were ten inches thick, but the cracks between them were really getting big. And the fire had gotten curious. The fire looked into the schoolroom and wondered what those children were up to. And the smoke said, "It's too crowded in this stove. I have to stretch out." So he moved out into the room. The air in the schoolhouse turned blue. It wasn't the teacher's fault. The firewood was wet, and it smoked. It threw a real fit as it popped and crackled. It said, "How can I be a happy fire when I've got water in my belly?" By the middle of the morning the school was full of smoke and fumes. You had to take two breaths in order to get one.

The teacher had to get the fire going already at five o'clock. Some children live five and even six miles away. In wet weather there was no way you could get through. The roads here are worse than yours, especially there by Schröder's corner, there by Lasen where the road goes down toward the Püttberg.

Most of the school kids wore rubber boots. *Man bloss*, only really, they still got stuck in the mud. Once in a while we drove them to school. Six years ago, we had a real winter. For a few weeks I pulled the girls to school on a sled. When I was a boy, I never dreamed that in my old days I would play horsy in America. But the kids thought it was great fun. If I didn't have the time, Wieschen would take the harness. If we couldn't get through, they just stayed home. They thought that was also great fun. But little by little everything has changed and gotten better. Now we also have good roads.

23

Company from Back Home

• •

Now I want to tell you the best story of all. I haven't been this happy for a long time. Who was at the door? And who was at my table? See, it was your granddaughter Magdalene. *Wat seggst nu?* What do you say to that? Now, fill your pipe, sit down in your most comfortable chair, and read on.

Our pastor left us and is now at a different church. The new one who speaks the Word of God comes from that pastoral family in Serrahn. That's where your oldest son fetched his wife. How things work out!

Children are like young birds. When they have their wings, they leave the nest. Your granddaughter left Bremen and made her way to America.

Over here, her uncle got her a job in his school. That was so I could have some joy. Only she doesn't look at all like you. According to her, she looks like her picture, and she looks like her grandfather in Serrahn. There is no damage for her in that, as far as I'm concerned. She's been over to see us several times. We have talked about home and about you. She is tall and looks good. She is healthy on the inside and on the outside. I could see that in her eyes. In the school, she soon had the situation in hand. Unbeknownst to her, I gave her some help.

Anywhere within five miles, when I met any girls I gave them the word, "God be gracious to you, if you don't love her." But the best that happened is her own doing. That Christmas Eve I was really proud of her. Up till then, I only liked her and enjoyed her. This letter tells about that Christmas Eve because you are her grandfather, and because outdoors the snow is piled high.

We all drove to church. On the way I was rummaging around in my head about the Christmases you always planned and did for us children in the village. All the families were there, and the school was crammed full. Some even had to stand outside in the garden. But inside the candles on the Christmas tree were lighted and there was a hush.

While that was going through my head, I said to myself, See, now here in the bush his grandchild is making Christmas for the farmers' children. No place on earth do stranger things happen than here in this America. But she is in a strange land and sometimes young women are fearful. I said to myself, You have to speak to her heart an encouraging word, *ein wenig Trost in ihr Herz hineinsprechen.*

With that in mind I gave the horses a giddyap and got to church before the rest of them. Yes, truly, there was some fear in her eyes. So I said to her, "*Wesen sie man nicht bange,* Fräulein Magdalene, don't have a worry. All of us are Mecklenburgers — you can count on us. And when I stand here and see you and talk to you, just imagine that I am your grandfather back home, who loves you and cares about you. He did so much good for all of us, and we all will do good for you. So now let your eyes sparkle. This Christmas will be as beautiful as Christmas was when we were all back home."

At that she put her hand in mine and said, "That's the word I needed to hear, and I'm not going to be fearful anymore. But oh gracious, that's not easy to do when you're a beginner." At that I put my hand in her hand and said, "*So mag ick di lieden, lütt Dirn,* that's the way I like you to be, little lady. And, now just turn around and look who's here. They are all from Mecklenburg. I was baptized in the Eldena church, and you were baptized at Serrahn. Did you ever dream then that we both would stand next to each other on Christmas Eve in America?" She looked at me seriously, then she laughed and said, "No, I guess I certainly didn't dream about that at my baptism. I'm sorry, I was just a baby." That was good for another laugh, and we both were encouraged.

The church was packed full. A lot of people from town were there. In the city schools there's not much Christmas. Instead of Christmas, they have moving pictures with Bengal lights, mixed up with all kinds of silly stuff, plus some hocus-pocus. It's more like the county fair and the Hanswurst shows. That is why so many townsfolk come to us to see our Christmas. We have a real Christmas. The children sang "Glory to God in the Highest," "Lo, How a Rose E'er Blooming," "O Thou Joyful Day," "From Heaven Above," and all the other songs we learned in your class-room. In between, prophecies were read out of the Bible, and the Christmas story was read. There were also questions out of the Scripture and out of human experience. Then, at the end there was congregational singing and a few words from the pastor. But the childrens' service was the main thing, and they all sang loud and clear — the place just rang.

My dear friend, I say your granddaughter harvested all kinds of praise and thanks from the parents. Which is good, because here in America the Christmas program is the real test for the teacher. It's just how things work here. If the Christmas program isn't any good, the teacher isn't any good. But in this case the response was all praise and thanks. And when she came home, the pastor was there to open the door and make a deep, deep bow. It was as if Teddy Roosevelt's daughter was coming through the front door. The pastor himself said to us, "I didn't think it could be so wonderful!"

After that, we drove home in the moonlight. We were proud, and we were happy. A person really likes that feeling in his heart, to be happy and contented way down deep, especially on Christmas Eve, *erst recht am Heiligabend*.

Now, I need to continue the story. Now, she's gone. She went on to visit another uncle. He's a pastor in Wisconsin.

She thought about staying here until Easter. That was what I wanted to hear. It's different to talk with a tall, beautiful woman — instead of discussing things with your horses and cows.

Between New Year's and Easter, she was in and out by us a whole lot. When it got to be evening, I would take her home in the wagon or on the sleigh. I only dumped her over once. The sleigh tipped over because the road was so bad. She got up and she laughed. Then she threw a few snowballs at me. An old man enjoys that.

Evenings we often sat together and told stories of yesterday and of today. Me? I liked best to talk of yesterday. She? She liked best to talk of today. I liked best to talk about my village back home. She liked best to talk about life in America. So, we got along well with each other. So, we also began to say *du* to each other and not *sie*. [*Sie* is the polite way for Germans to say "you." *Du* is what Germans say when they are good friends.] She even started to call me *Onkel*. She laughed and said, "Now I have a full half-dozen uncles." She said that as if they were worth a thousand dollars each in the saving's bank. "Which half-dozen do you mean?" "The half-dozen here in America." At that both of us had a good laugh. She is a commonsense girl, and there aren't too many like that here. "You can include your daughter Berti in that," said Wieschen when I read this out loud to her. "Wieschen," I said, "that's surely the case. And I'll write that to Magdalene's grandfather back home in Mecklenburg."

There are a lot of nice girls around, but some have bugs in their heads and are only waiting for a man-child to run onto their path. And, as they say, that can only be good if there's love. But who can do anything about that? Na, unser Herrgott, the Lord God must really like all the breeds, because look how he made the world of so many different colors.

We often talked about America and the people. I scolded here, and I scolded there. She looked straight at me and give me her opinion, "Why did you come here then? You've got it so good on your farm, and really, you've got nothing to complain about." Saying that, she laughed me right in the face. So I answered, "I want you to understand something, Magdalene. Every and any German has to have something to complain about, otherwise their skin doesn't fit. Their inside mensch — their person — is made that way. And, you wonder why I left home. I will tell you this. I wanted to be a free man, and I wanted to farm my own land, stand on my own ground. Not just a few ruten of rented ground, but land my children would inherit. Isn't it born into a person that you want to have your own place, your own hüsung, and isn't that good and proper as a birthright?"

Magdalene didn't laugh at this. She said, "Onkel, that's a big idea what you say about being free. I like it." I said, "If that's an idea, I don't understand it. Idea is a foreign word to me. I don't know what it means. There's no idea that will buy me a farm. The way to a farm goes through the valley of sweat and work. But it's the little man, the day laborer, who can make his way here in America better than in the old country. Because the Germans work hard and because they value the land, they are respected here in the States. We could have even more respect here, but some of us despise where we've come from and want nothing to do with it. There will have to come a time of grief and anger for the German Americans. Then they will close ranks. Then they will count for more in the States and in the White House.

"Some folks get along better in life when they pitch their memories overboard and hang their German jacket on a nail. Not so by me. And, many are like me. Our boots carry dirt from the homeland all through life, until at the end we finally pull 'em off. One has sand on his, the other one has clay. It doesn't make life easier, but I wouldn't have it any other way. I wouldn't want to miss that."

That's how I said it to her. She listened close, and she nodded agreement, "Onkel, you said it right. And that's why you've done so well in this new country." "Ne, Kind, my child, it's not only why, it's wherefore, and it's therefore. Nowadays I walk broad on the soil, but in the beginning I walked a narrow path. All my life I've went through sand up to my ankles and heavy clay. A man walks a heavy gait and thinks slow thoughts when he's come through all that. But when your life is farming, your thoughts are different from the kind who skips along on the roadway. Here, in this new country, grain is for trade in the market. But because of where I come from, I know how much sweat and work it takes to bake a loaf of bread from that grain. You start with the plow, then there's the seed, then the scythe, then the threshing flail, and finally there's Father Köhn's oven. That's how I know it in my heart, and I have to thank the old country for that.

"The old country is still with the best things in life. It was hard over there, and I was poor. But the memory of that is like rest after a day's work. All day long I'm busy and have no time to recollect, but in the evening is when it comes, and it's good to recollect. In the evening you see better into your soul than in the daylight." My good friend, that's what I told her those weeks and now I'm telling it to you.

She said, "Then, Onkel, you're probably going to go back to your village in your old days, and there's where you'll find your rest." "Ne, I sure won't do that. The village and the people are no longer what they were back then. And I want to hold in my heart that picture of what they were. I also don't want to move to town when I quit farming. I surely won't move to Chicago. People run around there like chickens with the heads cut off. I don't want to live there. I've got too much mud on my boots — I'm not for the city. People there move from one street to another every few months or every couple years. The houses, the faces, the neighbors, the workmen, everything changes there the way you change clothes. Their kids cannot *fest werden*, get sure about themselves.

"That's another reason why I hold onto my old village the way it used to be. There where young Diehn mows the meadow where his grandfather used the scythe. The children of that young Sass kid play in the same house with the straw roof where their great-grandfather was diapered and laid in the cradle. Friel's kids shake apples off the trees their grandfather planted. And the storks that *klappern*, rattle their beaks on Brüning's house are the descendants of the storks who built their nests there when that old man was a little kid, around 1800 or so. I can barely remember him. And you, my dear friend, today you are teaching children in the same village where your father and your grandfather worked as teachers. The job has been in your family over a hundred years.

"I can't really explain how I feel about this in my heart. You know what I mean. In this country, if you've been here ten years, it's a long time. No stories and no memories of old times grow here and connect us with our fathers and with the ground under our feet. Nothing like that grows in the cities here for sure.

"It's possible that too many memories are from evil, *vom Übel*. It's like too much ballast. That's probably also true for a nation's people. *Der mensch*, the ones who wants to go forward need sharp eyes. They can't look behind them too much; they've got to rub old dust out of their eyes. That's probably also true for nations. *Der mensch*, the ones who wants to get ahead and be a winner has to be young and has to have faith. When you're old, it's hard to be a winner. Instead you sit with your memories and try to catch your breath. To me, memories are something beautiful and holy.

"See what I mean. These are some of the thoughts that creep out of the corners of the room and out of your heart in the evening. Nobody around here will lend me a penny on them. Usually you just don't talk about this, and when you do talk about it, it comes out the wrong way. Using a pen to bring it out doesn't always help either. *Ja so sünd de Mekelbörger*, that's the Mecklenburgers for you. Usually they don't talk about what has been good and the best. When they do say it, it's either too late or they get it all confused. I told this to my mother in those days when she was going downhill. She looked at me with big eyes — she was surprised. Today when I think about it, those were hungry eyes. But then my throat went dry, and all I could do was pat her on the cheek and hold her hand. You know, she understood me, she was my mother. It's like this: the North German doesn't talk about the inside things."

I had to unload all of this. Your granddaughter brought it all to life, and now I'm her Onkel. There's frost on the ground here and I'm busy telling this stuff. Usually you don't get these things out of your dresser drawers, and now I'm going to get something out of the lowest drawer. That's the old holy songs we learned when we were your pupils. Look, they went along with us when we crossed the big water. They rode along with us on the ox cart when we drove into the bush. They lived alongside us in the log house. They got covered over with sweat and work. Then they woke up again. When we moved into the new house, there they were. And now our children play them on the organ, and in the evening we sing them for devotions: "O Lord, Send Us Dear Angels" — you know that it starts way high. "Lord My Shepherd, Wellspring of Joy," "Write My Name," "Let Me Find This Night," "Shall This Night Be My Ending." And all the others. Our children pray the same old verses we prayed by you in the school.

My dear friend, I can tell you that when we sing those songs and pray those prayers I am taken by the strangest feeling. I close my eyes, and I'm not an old farmer in America, with tired bones. I'm a little boy and I'm with you. I'm in school, on the long benches, and we're singing at four o'clock in the afternoon. The winter school term is over. I can see the whole schoolroom. It's getting dark — the windows are steamed over, so that drops of water are running down. The walls are damp and on the left hand side, in the corner, stands the brown tile stove. Behind your table hangs the blackboard, and you are standing in front of it. You are looking at us, and we are looking at you. There are pictures on the walls and all the Christmas garlands and wreaths are still up. All of that I see clearly. I could touch it with my hands. This picture comes alive when we sing those old songs, and just think how many years ago that is. Remarkable, isn't it?

Wieschen agrees. She says it also happens to her. When she worked for you in your household, you sang those verses for devotions in the evening. So now when we sing them, she can see your whole sitting room. Over on the right side, up high, on the bookshelf is the devotion book. She always got it down. Next to the sofa hangs the wall clock with roses on the face. On the left side there is the cupboard with the green curtain in front. Your desk stands by the window. While we're singing, the verses paint her a picture of your sitting room, along with you and your children. It could be that nowadays the verses don't mean as much to young people — that's how it goes. We will not forget them. We also have been careful not to let our children forget them. We want our children to love them and honor them. *Und nu will ick*, and now I'm going to shove in that dresser drawer, close it, and stick the key in my pocket.

24

Old Stories in the New Land

· ·

Now again it's a long winter with little to do. I'll start my winter letter again because summer is no time for writing. That's why my letters are *Winterbriefe*, winter letters.

My dear friend, in your school we always thought: if we could only be done with school and be free. Now our children are wishing that same thing. They do take after their parents.

When the children are together, they usually talk English. Which is why we have to be sure that they learn German. We do that, and the German songs help. In the evening when the work day is over, I like to sit by the stove, and Wieschen spreads out in the rocking chair. Behind the stove you see a beautiful winter scene. The children are in the sitting room or they're outside singing the songs we learned by you in the school: "*Ich hatt einen Kameraden*, I Had One Faithful Comrade," "The Lorelei," "All The Birdies Have Arrived," "Now May Has Come." And believe me, the songs sound as good and as German here on the farm as they did in the old country. You can surely believe me about that.

The children learn these songs in the German school. We have two kinds of schools: the congregation's and the state's. When I write about the congregation's school, I mean the German school. The state's school also has some German, but we started the congregation's school, so that our children would learn German and become good Christian people and Americans.

This winter I have been looking into the children's reading books. They are growing up and laying those books aside. Look at us, we're growing old, and we're taking up those books again. Don't think though that we don't have enough to read. At this house, we have lots of paper, and it all has black print on it. But you don't have to believe everything printed there.

There's the *Germania*. That's the big newspaper. Then there's the little newspaper for this Springfield area. You'll never believe what's all in these papers. It's quite a bit different from your newspapers.

Here's a sample of what you find in our little papers: "Fred Miller bought a seventy dollar watch for his son Charley in Mrs. Wilson's shop. In our village the boy's name would have been Karl Möller. Henry Schmidt tore up his hand on a nail; given the circumstances, it's healing well. Mr. Acreman has visitors from Virginia. They last saw each other ten years ago. Mr. A. has given a party with plenty wine for all." *Wat seggst nu?* What do you say to all that? Ja, that's what's in our newspaper. The newspaperman puts it in because Fred Miller and the others subscribe to it and want to read about themselves. Well it's about the same as when you read in the *Ludwigsluster Anzeiger* that a barn burned down over by Grabow.

We also get the *Abendschule*, the Evening School. It's a big, thick magazine with pictures and stories and reports from America and Germany. It comes every two weeks.

But me, I'm forever going back to the old readers. They smell like home. Many of the old stories from back there are in those readers. One thing I have to ask you about. It's been on my heart — you'll have to explain it to me. When I sit in the house here most of the winter, I get to thinking about what I'm reading. When I was young I didn't do that. Now I sit there and wonder about what I'm reading. I start to shake my head and think about it: what's printed there is nonsense. You need to explain that to me. Wieschen agrees. She said, "Jürnjakob, too much of that thinking isn't healthy. It's about time for things to warm up outside so that you can get busy with your work. Jürnjakob, you're getting bees in your bonnet." Ja, that's what she said.

There are really good stories in those old readers. I still remember them from my school days: Doctor Know It All, the Bremer City Musicians, the Wolf and the Seven Little Goats, Red Riding Hood, Frau Holle, Jack and the Beanstalk, and the funny story about the Trolls of Cologne. I also like to read Luther's version of Aesop's fables. There is meaning in those stories and they're still worth thinking about today. You can talk about them with the children too — those stories always fit. There are also some pretty good poems in the reader.

Other stuff is in that book that doesn't really need much in the way of explanation. My boy was reading about cats: "The cat has a round head, a long tail, and four legs." And it says about the earth: "The earth is not evenly level. There are many high mountains." I offered my opinion. "Get your nose out of that book. Look out the window and you'll see hills. The earth wasn't even level at home. We had the *Buchenberg*, the Buchen Hill, the Schnellenberg, the Püttberg and still more. The boy read more: "Water freezes in the winter." I said, "It's good that that's in the book. How else would we know what happens when it's fifteen degrees above zero." He read more: "*Der Mist*, manure is important for success in growing crops." I said to that, "Ja, that's comforting to know that manure is mentioned." The boy read on: "A sheep is smaller than an ox." I asked, "Where did you read that?" "Page one hundred eighty-four." "You need to remember that page. When you go into the barn all you have to do is turn to that page. Then you'll know right away if you've got a sheep or an ox."

Next it was lions. He read on further. "When a lion is hungry, his mane stands on end and his tail goes up and thumps on his back. That's when he goes after everything in his way. But, if he doesn't wag his tail, you don't have a thing to worry about." "Read that again." He did it, and I said, "So, if you're out doors and come against a lion, just turn right to that page in the reader, and look at the lion's tail. If he lets it hang down like a cow's tail, you can run up to him and chase him off. But if he's got his tail up and over his back, like the cows do when they're being foxy, then it's time to get out of there. Otherwise he'll knock you down, and he'll dump over mother's milk cans and bucket and anything else that gets in his way." To that he replied, "I know one better than that, Father. I'll singe his fur with a shotgun."

Then he read *den Herringbrief*, the Herring Letter. Toward the end it says, "When I eat another herring, I'll surely remember everything the teacher told us about this valuable fish. And the next time you eat a herring, think about my letter and imagine the life cycle of this remarkable citizen from the northern ice sea. And, continue to be loving to your friend Paul." I said, "That's an impossible story. *Pass du man lieber auf*. Just please pay attention to this when you eat your next herring, and don't get any bones in your throat. That's better than thinking about this remarkable citizen of the northern ice sea." He said, "Ja, Vater, but then why is it in the reader?"

My dear friend, why are things like this in the reader? Anyway, I suppose it's not too difficult to understand. Once the kids open their eyes, they see how things work. In the winter the water freezes. The sheep is smaller than the ox. They don't need a book to figure that one out. They know that long before they can tell one letter from another. Them who don't know, they are the *Schlafmützen*, sleepy heads, they won't learn it out of a book either. In a way, they can use it in life.

How can you respect authors like this? You go back and forth: this one is good, that one is no good. Just like our famous Fritz Reuter says, "*Hier geiht hei hen*, first he comes here, then he goes there." That's why you need to explain this reader to me, what do you say to these ideas of mine?

There's still one more thing I want to write about. I need to tell you about two boys. [Translator's note: This is undoubtedly the Katzenjammer Kids of comic strip fame, Hans and Fritz.] Their names are usually Jakob and Fritz, but sometimes they're different. It's the same boys, it's just that their names are different. They don't live in this country. They live in the children's Sunday papers and in the readers. They are bad boys and don't behave. They don't go to school, and they never study. On Sunday they steal the neighbor's best apples. But when they bite into them the apples are rotten. And then comes an honorable old man with a long beard. He pastors around with them and says a long verse:

In the beginning destroy all that evil is
Otherwise all that is evil will destroy you
Today you can destroy it while it's small
'Cause tomorrow it will be bigger than you all.

Then they get converted, but only for this one story. The next day they steal their mother's money, jam, and candy. After that they get into the mouse poison, and then have to be in bed for quite a while.

Or they plan to get a sausage out of the neighbor's pantry. But somebody surprises them. They jump out of the window and break a leg. Then here comes the honorable old man again with the long beard and the sermon, and they get converted. On another day they tease a big old dog on a chain. The dog breaks loose and bites them on the leg. In another story, on a Sunday they're out in a boat fishing. A storm comes up and lightning strikes close by. But the honorable old man shows up. He saves them again and recites his long sermon verses. He knows a whole pile of them. Again, he converts them and dries them off.

Just look. That's how it goes with those kids in the Sunday paper. I've been there: stolen apples, fell out of a boat, teased dogs. In the end it came out different with me: the stolen apples weren't rotten, the dog didn't get loose, and we boys didn't eat any mouse poison. If anybody really gets in trouble, it's the boy with the good conscience, who doesn't run. The roughnecks all get away in good time. I was even there when they set fire to a house. Just as I was there when a poor kid got it from a rich kid. But the honorable old man with the long beard and the sermons never showed up.

It's not all bad that stories like these show up in the papers and books, 'cause some Unband good-for-nothing learns his lesson. Life, though, is sometimes different than the stories. The stories are invented. But can you tell me, does life match up to what's in the stories or do the stories match up to what's in life? You need to explain that for me, so I finally get smart.

There are conversion stories for the big people too. Once upon a time back in Mecklenburg, there was an old man who earned his daily bread tying brooms. His name was Mellinger. He won five hundred marks in the lottery. The story is three pages long and ends up telling that he had begged the money for the lottery ticket, boozed away his winnings, and died in the poorhouse. The story doesn't tell where he came from, but we know he wasn't in America. In America the lottery is illegal. But don't think there isn't a lot of betting going on. Even Wieschen won a few dollars making wagers. But that's a while back. She doesn't do it anymore. Wieschen says, "Betting is all right — the only trouble is the people making the wagers disappear when they lose, and then what do you have?"

The way I see it, money is better than no money. The way I'm sitting here on my farm, I say, "I've made my way by working, not by playing the lottery or making bets. It's just too uncertain. But I admit that it's neither unrighteous nor is it in any way sinful if the old broommaker drinks up his five hundred marks ten times over. It would be difficult for the man writing stories for the Sunday paper to meet everybody's standards. Especially when a person gets stiff bones sitting around all winter and gets thick-headed with bees in his bonnet reading that stuff.

I wrote you about Luther's translation of Aesop's fables and how they make you think deep thoughts. My dear friend, reading the fables is not easy in America. The children ask questions that kein Mensch, nobody can answer. Even Wieschen does that — asks questions you can't answer. I read: "A dog swam the stream with a piece of meat in his mouth." Wieschen said, "That woman should have kept the door closed so that dog didn't get into the kitchen." I kept on reading but only with my mouth. In my heart I said, "There is sense in the fables, but what my wife says also makes sense." After that, I read: "A rooster scratched in the Misthaufen, manure pile, and found a costly pearl." Wieschen says to that: "The dog snatches meat out of the kitchen, and pearls lie around in the manure pile. That's a real operation. The woman in Jesus' story who looks for her coin until she finds it makes more sense to me, even if it was only a dollar. That was really a woman."

In my heart I was grumbling because she made fun of Luther's fables. So I said, "Wieschen, I cannot respect that woman as an example. When she found that dollar she went ahead and invited all the neighbor ladies over, as if to say, "wonder of wonders, look at what I've found. Naturally then, she cooked coffee, served up cake and candy, and there went that dollar together with the other nine. And who knows, maybe it even cost more than that." After saying this, I said to myself, that's a mistake. But it was too late. They all jumped on me and said, "Father, that's not even Christian, what you're talking. That woman is in the Bible, and besides it's a parable." I couldn't defend myself.

On another day, I read: "A mouse wanted to cross a river and couldn't. The mouse asked a frog for some advice and help." Right away, the children asked these pesky questions, "Father, why didn't the mouse just stay on its side of the river? Father, did the mouse have some string or did the mouse use its tail to tie itself to the frog? Father, if the knot was tied really tight, the frog wouldn't have been able to swim." I interpreted the fable for them: "Who digs a hole for others to fall in, falls in himself." They weren't satisfied with that either and said, "The mouse was totally innocent and yet got eaten along with the frog. Where's the justice in that?" Their questions wore me out, and I finally said, "One fool can ask more questions than seven wise men can answer." Then I got myself out of there. Once I had escaped, I said to myself, when a man is a father in America, he sometimes gets into a sweat trying to explain Luther's fables.

Darum habe ich lange Zeit, so for a long time I didn't read any more of Luther's fables. I turned to Solomon's proverbs in the Bible. That's another debate. It's wisdom for everyday life, but again the children got to me with their questions.

As an example, I said to the children, "A fool can ask more questions than seven wise men can answer." But no fool can hold out when seven wise men stand around him and pepper him with questions. In all the books, wise people are forever talking and asking questions.

"Salt and bread, make your cheeks red." I say, "Ham and bread is a good combination." "Don't buy a cat in a bag." Nobody does that anyway. Besides, people usually give away kittens. "Don't look a gift horse in the mouth." Nobody does that either, because nobody gets a horse as a gift. "Who lies once is never believed." Plenty people lie and deceive all their lives. For them it's a way of doing business — they make good money at it. "You can get many patient sheep in a small stall." Impatient sheep and the rams that use their horns in the stories, on the train, and at the hotel are served like the president. "Flies can be caught with patience and spit." That only works for people who have nothing else to do. It sure doesn't work here on the farm. In the summer when there are plenty flies, I have no time. In the winter, I have plenty time but then there are no flies. If a wise man comes and advises me with a good proverb like that, should I drop everything to spit and catch flies? If Wieschen or the neighbors catch me doing that they'll stick my body in bed and put cold cloths on my forehead. And even if I do that for a whole day and catch ten or fifteen flies, what's in it for me?

Ja, so ist das mit den Sprichwörtern, that's the way it is with proverbs. But when you look at them with other eyes, they are stupid, and you can't live your life by them. But you know what? Wieschen says, "Jürnjakob, it's lucky for us that you want to start plowing tomorrow." "Wieschen, what do you mean by that?" "Because you'll get rid of that look in your eyes. Working with the pen is not as healthy as working with the plow. And as for the wise man, put him to work with the manure spreader. He will do more good there than with all that preaching. As it is, he always comes too late with his proverbs and his sermons.

That made me think, and I said to myself, "What that woman has just said could well be in a wisdom book. It could be shouted out on the streets because it has meaning. She has eyes of her own. She looks at the proverbs and fables with her eye on the home and the farm. She looks from there at everything and every person. That's why her eye is so sure and healthy. Her confidence comes from the inside and not from the outside. I've walked at her side all these years, and I have never seen that. You have to respect a person like her. She's a whole different nation that has its confidence from the inside and never veers away from that center, neither to the right nor to the left.

25

Jürnjakob, You're Homesick

· ·

My dear friend! All my letters have been winter letters. This is a summer letter — it has a skinny body. When you see it you'll be surprised and say, "Hopefully the old man isn't sick. A skinny letter is against his nature. He just doesn't do it." Well, it's not the kind of sickness that you call a doctor for. It's something in me that has made me feel uneasy, and it won't go away. It just sits there in me. I have to write you about it.

Last Sunday afternoon Wieschen and I were sitting at the table, talking about this and that. You know how it goes. It wasn't long before our conversation led us back to our old village. You know how it goes. Then it happened that I finally said, "*Wat ist das*, Wieschen, what is it and how does it happen that when we get to talking we always find ourselves back in our old village. Wieschen stopped darning socks, looked at me quietly, and said, "Jürnjakob, you're homesick." "What did you say?" "You're homesick," she said. She looked at me quietly. "You're homesick for our old village." "You tell me that's being homesick? We've never had that before. Where does that come from *mit einmal*, all of a sudden, now that we've gotten old? How can we be homesick? We only talk about the old country now and again." "Jürnjakob," she said and looked at me again quietly, "you've had it all these years and so have I, and you've denied it." She said that as matter-of-factly as someone would say, "Now the sun is soon going down."

I was so taken and shocked that I couldn't speak another word. I took up my cap and my Dad's old oak walking stick and for two or three hours I stalked the fields. I said to myself, Jürnjakob Swehn, you're homesick? That's a sickness for old people who can't make it in this country. You'll soon be here forty-eight years. How can you be homesick after all that time and after you're as old as you are? [Translator's note: It's 1906, Jürnjakob Swehn time, and he's sixty-six years old. He's been married forty-six years.] I had to stand still and catch my breath. Then I went on. "You've had it all these years and so have I" is what she said. I stopped again. How can I be homesick when Wieschen is at my side, and the children have been born here and are all grown up. You've got your own place. You've sowed the seed and harvested *auf eigen Grund und Boden*, on your own ground and your own land. I lifted my up eyes and walked further on. How can you be homesick? Here is where you've made your living and not in Mecklenburg. Here you're surrounded by *Landsleute*, your own country-men. God's sun shines here as well as over there. What are you homesick for? Surely not for that old, broken-down cottage or for the new young faces of people over there you don't even know.

That's how I questioned myself, and that's how I discovered that she was right. It has nothing to do with making your own way. And it has nothing to do with growing up poor and living in an old, broken-down cottage. I have fought it, but it's stronger than I am. It can't be changed into dollars — it has to do with what's inside you.

I stood still again. You're still back there, under that old straw roof with all your soul. The people you knew are there, the ones you played with as a boy, on the pasture, on the Plahst, and down in the Dannenkamp. When you started growing up you herded the cows with them on the Guhls and in the Strickel. Now they're back there in the village, sitting behind the stove and having a pipe. If they could see you here, they'd say in Platt-deutsch, "*Nu löppt hei as unklauk*, now like a dumbbell he's running around in his fields, trampling down his beautiful clover. He'd do better to come over here, and we could sit together a while, *beten bi uns sitten güng*. Then we could talk over the old times." And those straw roofs of the farmers' cottages, they stand there broad and solid and gemütlich — there're no houses like that in the States. They can tell stories. And the kids going in and out, do they take after the old-timers? And what about our old teacher?

Those straw roofs and the people under them have grown old, and, Jürnjakob, you've grown old. But you can't forget that village. Every year the memory grows stronger, and you've rested yourself in those memories of the old country. Sometimes it's made you feel young again, in your old days and in your tired hours. There's something there you just can't get your fingers on, but it's still there. America has its goodnesses, but there's also something missing here: time to think and time to remember. That's why on the inside you're still a stranger in this land.

Then I stood still again. If that's what it means to be homesick, it's not a sickness. Then being homesick is the best thing that home can do for you. Then your homeland is the best of all memories. And if you take the wings of the dawn and travel over half the earth, work nigh onto fifty years as a farmer in Iowa, and you'll not get past those memories. They'll tie you up like thick ropes, because no power on earth holds on to you like your homeland.

I headed back to the house. Looking at my farm the questions all rose up again. The sun by now had gone down, and I was tired. Wieschen was waiting for me by the fence. She said, "It's good that you're back. It's evening now, and it's high time that you're home." "Ja, I said and took her hand, "it's evening and *da macht man dass man nach hause kommt*, and a person needs to be headed home. But where is home? I thought it was here on the farm with you at my side. But now I'm not sure and I've lost my way." She said, "Hans will bring the hay in by himself in the next day or so. There're only one or two loads left on the lower pasture. You stay home and write our old teacher. All this thinking doesn't help anything."

"Ja, I'll do that. That's a good idea. But first I want to look in the Bible and see if there's something about being homesick." My dear friend, I found nothing. You'll have to be the teacher once again and we will be your kids in school. You have to explain to us what it means to be homesick and show us the right way. As a person gets closer to the end, he discovers that life has been arranged real good. So when you get old you need a kick in the behind, so to speak. Makes you want to sit down and catch your breath. Anyway, you have more time to think about things on the inside. Wieschen and I have done quite a bit of that lately, and these last few years we've gently, gently fallen asleep during our talks. But this time there is hurt on the inside, big hurt, and our eyes have grown old. We're walking in the dark. You have to show us the way.

26

Mark This Page in Your Bible

• •

My dear friend! Wieschen says, *"Dat is en schönen Breiw,* that's a beautiful letter from you, from Mecklenburg. Now, Jürnjakob sit right down and answer him and tell him 'thank you.'" Which is what I'm doing here, and I'm liking doing it. You wrote us a good and great word. "Blessed are those who are homesick for they will return." It's almost as good as if one of those old prophets walking though the mountains in the evening, called it out to his people. I got busy right away and looked it up the Bible. It could be in the Beatitudes, Matthew 5 — that's where it belongs. Wieschen says, "Jürnjakob, there is something in the Bible about a different homeland. 'Like the evening star, it shimmers through the clouds.'"

I thought about this for quite a while. Then I said, "Wieschen, again you are right. You can read it however you will: *Es gibt immer einen Trost,* there is real comfort in it, something in that Word brings peace to a man's heart. And your parable about the evening star fits in real good for two old people who can't find their way anymore. But now we're out of the dark. Now this Word is a light to our path. Now we know where we're headed. No longer is our heart so hard-pressed and so full of fear. It's not a word from the *Krammarkt,* the dimestore, but it's a word about the secret hidden in the human heart. It's a real little word, but in it you have given us something big. Therefore I want to thank you with my whole heart.

Now everything will fall into place. You wrote, "You need to take your own counsel, and you'll do it when your time comes." That is most certainly true. Then you wrote, "With my whole heart I will stand by the two of you in everything that you want to do — and that you decide to do." That cheered us up. You said, "If I would counsel you to come back home to Mecklenburg, what would your children say?" My dear friend, I can tell you that my second son already understands farming much better than I. He's going to take over the farm. My oldest boy, the doctor, will stay with his patients. Berti, our daughter will come along for the visit, unless somebody fit for marrying gets in the way.

You also wrote, "I can't imagine what your president will say. Won't he think that your old teacher is taking away one of his best Iowa farmers. He's never taken vacation before, why should he do it now." My dear friend, I can tell you this. It makes no difference to me what the president thinks. It's none of his business. I have farmed enough in my life. Now I want my rest and I'll find that with all of you back there in the old village, better than here.

You wrote about *Wiedersehen*, about happy reunions and the joy of looking back over a long life. Then there are the kids I went to school with. You said we were united with each other in sorrow and joy, in time and eternity. But you also wrote about laying down my wander staff and that the time for that is not far off. That saddened us and made our hearts heavy. I said to Wieschen, "Let's go home."

When that will be, we can't say. But now we know *wo unser Zuhause ist*, where our true home is. Our old teacher has once more shown us the way. He also is homesick and wants to go home. And like us, he's headed for that other home, the one that shimmers through the clouds. The one he means when he talks about the evening star. The word that he wrote us about that home, he wrote out of the fullness of his heart. If we could just see his *Angesicht in Ehrfurcht*, his countenance in awesome fear, that would be a gift of God's grace. We would be thankful to the Lord. And now we'll put that letter in the Bible, Matthew, chapter five. It should be close at hand, always. We greet you with our soul.

Afterword Hartmut Brun

. . . .

Johannes Gillhoff, the author of Jürnjakob Swehn, was born in 1861 in Glaisin, Germany, a rural village in Mecklenburg-Vorpommern. His father, grandfather, and great-grandfather had been the teachers in the local school. It was a tenure of about one hundred years.

During the years 1854–1908 approximately three hundred and fifty people from the area immigrated to the United States. Many of them settled in Iowa. A town in Illinois named Eldena may indicate that some settled there; Eldena was the market town for the Glaisin area.

Johannes Gillhoff's father corresponded with some two hundred and fifty of these immigrants. So letters from America arrived regularly in the household. In 1898 the teacher-father gave his collection of those letters to his son, Johannes, who decided to shape them into a book.

Johannes Gillhoff was not an especially gifted author or editor. He needed time to complete the task. He rewrote the manuscript several times before he considered the content, form, and style of the book acceptable. The process went on for eighteen years. In the end, he did write the book. And he destroyed the letters, which means there is no proof for the book's plausibility.

In 1916 *Die Tägliche Rundschau*, a Berlin newspaper, printed Gillhoff's work in serial form. The author was fifty-five years old. The readers' positive response persuaded the editors to publish the series as a book. The first run in 1917 was a conservative thousand copies. Thus began the book's victory march, which continues until today. More than a million copies are in circulation. It's been translated into Danish, Norwegian, and Dutch, and now into English. Currently the book is available in German from several different publishers. Portions have been reprinted in newspapers and magazines. The book qualifies as a bestseller.

Jürnjakob is the archetype of the upright, staunch, honest mensch. By means of the letters his father collected, Johannes Gillhoff created a literary figure who personifies the nineteenth-century German immigrant on the way to a better life by means of resolute ambition and hard work.

Jürnjakob is an immigrant. When someone leaves the country of birth, it's always a sign of unhappiness and dissatisfaction. Gillhoff's book is a critical book; immigration is, implicitly, a critical act.

The German public's fascination with the book has not so much been with its plot and action as with its style and language. Gillhoff used the letters to create a hero (or antihero), the clumsy and awkward but also clever and successful farmer who writes to his teacher back home.

Jürnjakob is the Mecklenburger original who thinks and speaks Low German but doesn't write it. His letters are a mixture of Low and High German, which contemporary Germans call *Missingsch*. Actually, the book is the first example of *Missingsch* in print. In his English translation Trost imitates Jürnjakob's style and language by including both Low German and High German words and phrases. The translation is also a mixture, a *Missingsch*.

Enjoying his success, the author retired from his career in public education in 1924 and founded a magazine: *Mecklenburgische Monatshefte* (Mecklenburger Monthly Magazine). He was sixty-three years old. Articles focused on local art, culture, literature, history, and nature. It was a successful venture and soon took a leading place among North German regional periodicals.

Johannes Gillhoff died on January 16, 1930. He was sixty-eight years old. A Gillhoff society commemorates his life and work annually in Glaisin. They award a prize, sponsor papers, and maintain a museum in what formerly was the Glaisin schoolhouse. In 1976 Gillhoff's grave in the cemetery at nearby Ludwigslust was declared a national landmark of German cultural history.

INDEX OF FAMILY NAMES

Other Bur Oak Books of Interest